THE CIRCLE OF STONE

DARKEST AGE BOOK THREE

THE CIRCLE OF STONE

A. J. LAKE

SPECIAL THANKS TO LINDA CAREY

BLOOMSBURY

First published in Great Britain by Bloomsbury Publishing Plc
Published in the United States by Bloomsbury U.S.A. Children's Books
175 Fifth Avenue, New York, New York 10010
Distributed to the trade by Macmillan

Library of Congress Cataloging-in-Publication Data
available upon request
ISBN-13: 978-1-59990-079-7 • ISBN-10: 1-59990-079-3

First U.S. Edition 2008
Typeset by RefineCatch Ltd
Printed in the U.S.A. by Quebecor World Fairfield
1 3 5 7 9 10 8 6 4 2

For Mike: first, last and always

PROLOGUE

In a cave underground, the dragon Torment brooded.

He had no lair now. He had lived all his long life in the mountain that had birthed him, the rocks groaning in agony as he burst from them. He had rested in the high caves, preyed on the creatures that lived on the mountain's slopes, and flown through the flaming crevasse at its heart, to do the bidding of the one who had summoned him. Now master and mountain were gone. The caves of his home were red-hot slag and grey ash, and Torment, damaged and half blinded, had fled from the dreadful heat to this low, cramped place. It had held some of the little ice creatures once, and Torment made them his prey . . .

He roared, and the sound brought snow thumping down outside the cave entrance. His lair was gone, the prey had all disappeared, and everywhere the rock was hot and painful even for him to touch. But that was not the worst. The voices were still with him. They were silent now, but he could feel them curled up in his head, waiting to call on him again.

In another place, the ice dragon slept, enfolding a hill like a white cloak. Her great shoulders twitched, scattering rocks down the slopes, as she dreamed of flight – the winds rolling around her; the white fields stretching away below.

She was dreaming about the last time she had tasted the snow-wind and felt the air swell beneath her wings. There had been another dragon: she had swatted it down. There had been fire, coming suddenly out of the air as she tried to rest, and nearly engulfing her – but her wings had been powerful enough to take her far away, to a place where the snow lay undisturbed. Where was the voice in her head now, the tiny call that had woken her? It had spoken to her: pricked her out of sleep, goaded her into the air. And then it had vanished, leaving her to return to her sleep. Deep in her dreams, she wondered if she would ever hear the voice again.

Under the heavy pall of smoke, in the fiery heart of *Eigg Loki*, another dragon howled.

He was all made of fire. He had been a long time forming: countless years of close-banked rage had twisted his shape out of the heat of the earth. For a century or more his maker had been imprisoned in the caves above, and in all that time the dragon had writhed in the fires below the surface, gaining form and breath until he dreamed the burning dreams of his master. And today the dragon had awakened.

His master was free of these cramped walls of rock. He'd broken out into the world beyond, the infinite space outside of these walls, and had already begun to split himself, spread himself, and to devour. The dragon gathered itself to follow. Nothing would exist but the glory of fire.

He was held back. A new thought came into his mind and stuck there, like a rock that could not be burned: *Not yet. Later.* He thrashed and spat, straining upwards as his master shot into the air, away from him, and disappeared.

Alone and thwarted, the fire dragon screamed, pouring his flames from the mountain until the sky above him turned black. It was not enough to burn clouds. He would burn everything, everywhere . . . when he was free.

CHAPTER ONE

Eigg Loki still burned. Its red light was visible through the trees, and its low thunder sounded all around them. *They must be more than five leagues away by now,* Edmund thought, but he could still feel the rumbling beneath his feet.

He stopped for a moment to look back. He could no longer see the snow fields through the black trunks, but the sight of the mountain was still imprinted on his mind's eye: the waves of molten rock pouring from it; the snow giving way before the tide of fire and clouds of ash sweeping over the land. Edmund wondered how fast those tides were moving. He and his six companions had walked across the snow for most of a day before the fire erupted, reaching the shelter of the forest not long before sunset. But there would be no more rest now. The fire was creeping towards them across the ice: the trees could not shelter them against this. Already, the lake where they had fished not three days before would have turned to steam, and then to a pit of blackened rock. He thought unhappily of *Jokul-dreki,* the glacier dragon who had carried him and his friends down the mountain: he had jolted her out of her sleep by picturing the destruction of her home, and now it had happened. At least he had seen the great dragon flying away. She would be safe – for now.

'Come on, Edmund!' Cathbar had come back for him, and laid a heavy hand on his shoulder. The captain's voice was urgent. 'No standing about: those fires are moving!'

Edmund hurried after him. They abandoned their recently gathered firewood, and loaded the water bottles on one of the two horses. The young girl from the Snowlands, Fritha, went ahead of the party, finding paths between the scaly trunks. Cluaran the minstrel and his quiet friend Ari followed her with the horses, who flattened their ears nervously. On Cluaran's horse, his mother, Eolande, sat with her head bowed, the only member of the party seemingly unaffected by the general haste.

Edmund walked behind, with Elspeth. She was walking as fast as the rest of them, even though her face was still pale beneath the smoke-grime, and she unconsciously nursed her wounded right hand. When he touched her arm she turned to him with a wan smile.

'I was trying to hear Ioneth,' she said. 'I can feel her voice in my head, if I concentrate – but it's so weak.'

Edmund looked down at her hand, its palm marked with a livid red slash. 'Do you think . . . Will she be able to fight, now?'

'She has to.' Elspeth's voice was filled with determination. 'She gave her life to make the sword! It's the only reason we're here. It'll come back, and we'll find Loki and kill him.'

Edmund did not answer. He had been there when the crystal sword was destroyed, only a day ago, in Loki's underground cavern. Elspeth had gone in to kill him. Instead, the demon-god had tricked her into freeing him, and the sword that should have saved them all was gone. Maybe Ioneth's spirit still lived – he had too much faith in his friend's good sense to think she was deceiving herself – but he had *seen* the blade shattering. He trudged on beside Elspeth without speaking.

The sun had long since set, but the bloody light of the fires still followed them through the trees, and the air felt unnaturally warm. Edmund was beginning to sweat inside his thick furs. The patches of snow underfoot were giving way to damp, slippery pine needles, and melting drips from the branches above fell on to their heads.

'Slow down!' Cathbar called, ahead of them. 'Something's wrong.'

Fritha came running back, her face pale – and Edmund saw what they had seen. The red light that surrounded them came from ahead now, as well as behind. At the same moment they heard the crackle of flames. Both horses whickered in panic.

'We must get upwind of it,' Cathbar said urgently, turning back the way they had come, but Fritha shook her head.

'We go to the river,' she said, and started off at an angle, beckoning them to follow.

She led them at a run through the dark trees, while the air grew hotter and the red light ahead began to flicker. The smell of smoke stung Edmund's nose, and he heard Elspeth breathing raggedly. Ahead of them both horses were trying to break into a canter, giving little whinnies of fear, while Cluaran and Ari ran beside them, each talking to his charge in a low voice. Only Eolande, effortlessly keeping her seat on the leading horse, seemed not to have noticed the danger they were in.

'It's here,' Fritha called over her shoulder.

It was a stream rather than a river, not wide but deep, with stony banks sloping down on each side. The fire was visible on the far side: a yellow bank of flame in the near distance, veiled in smoke.

'It's moving away from us,' Cathbar said. 'Look at the trees.'

Edmund peered into the smoky gloom, wrinkling his nose. The trees on the far side of the stream seemed oddly small and slender – and he realised they were stumps, stripped of their branches. Many seemed to have fallen, and lay in strange diagonals against the others. There were no leaves or branches to cut off their view of the fire; only bare trunks.

'They've already burned,' said Cathbar.

The horses were standing still, wild-eyed and sweating, and Edmund found himself moving close to their steaming flanks, though he did not feel cold. The whole party huddled together, as if for reassurance.

'This is Loki's doing,' Cluaran said, with certainty.

Ari nodded. 'Not even lightning could make a fire like this in winter,' he said. 'We're lucky he started it where he did. But for that stream, it would be burning here.'

'You think it was luck?' Cluaran retorted. 'Even weakened as he is, Loki could find us and burn us with a thought.' He gazed bleakly at the distant flames. 'No – he likes to play games with his enemies.'

They stared at each other; a circle of pale faces in the red-lit gloom.

'He's somewhere in the forest, isn't he?' Elspeth said.

Edmund's throat felt tight. 'What should we do?'

'I say we let him wait for us,' Cathbar said. 'Stay where we are till daybreak so we can get a proper sight of him when we meet him. Besides,' he added with a pointed glance at Eolande, 'didn't my lady here tell us he was strongest by night?'

Cluaran looked thoughtful. 'You have a point,' he agreed. 'His illusions may have less power by daylight, though if he chooses to use force . . .' He let the words tail away. 'If we are to meet him, I would rather we saw him clearly.' He looked around the group. Ari was nodding, and Elspeth, rubbing at her hand again, made no objection. Edmund's legs felt like water at the thought of walking through the dark towards the fire-demon, and he nodded too as Cluaran asked, 'Are we agreed?'

'No,' Fritha said.

She reddened a little as they all turned to look at her. 'I mean,' she said hesitantly, '*you* will stay here; that is good. But I will go on now.'

Edmund saw his own consternation reflected on the faces of the others.

'My home is on the other side of this river,' Fritha said quietly. 'I must go there and find my father.'

She was already turning from them when Elspeth started forward, taking her by the arm. Edmund thought he saw a glint like tears in his friend's eyes.

'I'm going with you,' she said.

Edmund expected Cathbar to argue, but the captain nodded. 'You're right, girl,' he said. 'We owe him that much.'

It was true, Edmund knew. Grufweld had given them hospitality he could ill afford, and allowed Fritha, his only child, to guide them on their dangerous journey. 'I'll come too,' he said, though his voice sounded thin and strained.

Cluaran exchanged a look with Ari, and sighed. 'Come on, then,' he said. 'The way should be easy to find, at least.'

The river was barely wide enough to wet their feet, but once on the other side Edmund felt as if their last refuge had gone. Smoke curled around him, stinging his nose and eyes. The flames came no closer, but their heat and the smell of the burning hit him like a solid force. And all around them were scorched trunks, hot to the touch; some of them were crowned with dull red embers that showered sparks on the travellers as they moved through them. Cluaran and Ari led the horses at the back of the party, and the animals stepped cautiously on the hot ground, the whites of their eyes showing.

Fritha led them swiftly, and Edmund wondered how she could find her way in this charred wilderness. Her haste infected him, and he quickened his pace, fearing every moment to come upon Grufweld's hut and find it in flames.

He became aware that the reddish glow around them had grown brighter, and the heat more intense. Then, from ahead, he heard the crackle of burning, louder than before – and Fritha gasped and stopped.

She was standing at the edge of a clearing that was ringed with the blazing skeletons of wood, and charred stumps. Ash and smoke hung in the air in a thick pall, pouring from the trees whose trunks still burned. Inside the clearing the ground was black and featureless, bare of everything but ash.

Fritha had turned, white-faced. 'We must go on, quickly,' she said, her voice tight. 'Look!'

At the far end of the clearing, maybe a hundred paces away, was a wide gap in the forest. The trees were not as badly burned here but they had fallen to right and left, leaving a broad channel like the wake of a man walking through tall grass. In his mind's eye Edmund saw Loki, grown to giant size as he had been when they last saw the demon, standing in the midst of this devastation and laughing before setting off to leave a trail that his enemies would follow. He ran to Fritha's side, and her horrified face told him that the trail led towards her home.

It was agreed between them without words that they could not go through the dreadful clearing: the horses shied back if they approached it, and not one of them wanted to set foot on that blackened ground. Fritha led them in a wide circle around it, squeezing the horses between the trunks that still stood; skirting the ones that still blazed. She moved at a run, barely looking back to check that the others could follow. Both Edmund and Elspeth were breathless by the time they reached the beginning of Loki's trail. The smell of burning was less here, and the light of the flames was behind them. But the ground was ripped and broken, and lined on both sides with twisted roots as thick as a man's leg where the trees had been torn up and thrown aside.

Fritha took a deep breath, before stepping on to the unnatural path. '*Komm!*' she called, and began to run down the wide track.

The slash in the forest canopy above their heads revealed a sky that was beginning to lighten.

'It's near morning,' Cathbar said. 'Or as much morning as we're going to get. If his power is less by daylight, maybe we've come in good time.'

'I wouldn't rely on that,' said Cluaran.

Fritha had stopped ahead of them and held up a hand. She waited until they came up to her before speaking. 'My home is near here. We must *lymskast* . . . go soft.'

The swathe of torn trees ended only a hundred paces further on. The trunks closed in ahead of them again – but through them, Edmund could see weak grey light. They were at the edge of Grufweld's clearing. His heart started to thump.

'Stay close,' Cathbar hissed – but Fritha was already rushing forward, out of the trees. Edmund and Elspeth followed close behind.

Fritha's home was just as he had seen it last. Edmund let out a breath he had not realised he was holding as relief washed over him.

The snugly built hut with its wolf-hides nailed over the door, the drying-shed behind and the neatly stacked woodpile all spoke of peace and order. Even the fiery glow from the kiln where Grufweld burned his charcoal looked warm and reassuring. Edmund felt Elspeth's grip on his arm relaxing. As the other three came out of the trees behind them, Fritha gave a cry of joy and started forward.

The hides over the hut's door swung abruptly aside, and Grufweld appeared in the opening. The huge, bearded man's face looked tired and worn, but he held out his arms in welcome to Fritha.

'Come inside, quickly!' he called. 'There's danger out here!'

Edmund and Elspeth followed Fritha towards the hut, and the welcoming glow of firelight within.

A roar of fury interrupted him. From behind the charcoal-kiln a figure rose, black and shapeless, waving a fiery rod. It lumbered towards them, howling unintelligible words. Cathbar yelled and ran at it, drawing his sword.

'Stop!'

Fritha, a dozen paces from the door of her home, had stopped dead, turning to face the apparition.

'*Fethr?*' she stammered.

The black figure put its hand to its head. He had been draped in thick furs, Edmund saw now – and he gasped as the man threw back his hood.

Facing Fritha across the clearing, brandishing a charred stick like a weapon, was another Grufweld, the mirror of the man in the doorway – and with the self-same horror in his face.

'It's a trick!' cried the first man. But Fritha was standing still, midway between the two, looking from one to the other in bewilderment.

Cold horror took hold of Edmund. *I was looking for a burning giant*, he thought, *and all the time he was here – Loki, in the form of Fritha's father. But which one?*

Elspeth's face was white and she was staring at her right hand, as if willing the sword to appear. Cluaran, Cathbar and Ari had all drawn their weapons and were looking vainly between the two Grufwelds. One of these men was their mortal enemy – but which?

From behind him he heard Cluaran's voice, low and choked: 'Your skill, Edmund – use it, for pity's sake!'

Edmund forced his eyes shut. Even that tiny movement seemed an effort. In the welcome darkness, he felt outwards . . . and touched something huge: a wall of thick black smoke, pushing back at him. Waves of dizziness washed over him; he swayed, and felt Elspeth gripping his shoulders. 'Try again!' she whispered. 'Please.'

Swiftly, he sent his mind the other way. The poisonous smoke was all around him, filling his sight . . . but he found a chink in it. There was Fritha's face, pale with terror. And there, behind the sight, was an answering terror in the man whose eyes Edmund had borrowed: the fear that he would lose his daughter, as he had lost her mother.

Edmund realised he had fallen to his knees. His body would not let him rise, but he opened his eyes and brought his hand up to point. The man in the doorway spread his arms, calling pleadingly to Fritha. The fur-clad man only stared.

'Him!' Edmund shouted, pointing at the man in the black furs. 'Fritha – that one is your father!'

Fritha was already running away from the hut, towards the man by the kiln. He dropped his stick and ran to embrace her. At that moment, Edmund found he could move again. He scrambled up and pelted across the snow to Fritha and her father. Elspeth followed with Cluaran, Ari and Cathbar.

'Stay behind us!' Cathbar ordered. He barged into Edmund, pushing him and Elspeth towards the scant shelter of the kiln, and wheeled to face their enemy.

But Loki had gone.

There was no Grufweld standing in the doorway. There was no door. The hut was a charred heap on the ground; the snow beneath their feet was not snow but feathery grey ash. Even the kiln was a smoking ruin.

Above their heads, a shape of fire was gathering, like a great bird with a trailing tail, impossibly huge against the featureless grey sky. The tail hung down, a single tendril of flame, caressing the ashes of Grufweld's home. Then it whipped into the air. For an instant the thing turned its head to look at them – and it was gone, faster than an arrow-flight. A single clap of thunder shook the ruined trees around the clearing.

There was nothing left of it but a smoke-trail, like a scar across the sky . . . and the echo of mocking laughter.

CHAPTER TWO

Elspeth dreamed.

She was a small child, running fearlessly through the darkness of the caves and out on to the ice fields. Her sisters kept ahead of her, their black hair streaming in the summer wind. Try as she might, she could not keep up with them. They pounced on her from behind a rock, and the three of them rolled, laughing, in the snow.

She saw another time: her mother telling her to gather cloudberries. There was a feeling of dread in her – she did not know why: she had done this many times before – but the coldness grew as she wandered further and further, in search of the best patches. She filled her basket with the red-gold berries and walked home – but home was not there any more. It was all black; the air was hot, and her mother and sisters had vanished. Bewildered, not yet crying, she ran to the cave-mouth, now full of bitter-smelling smoke. A wave of heat pushed her back, and she recoiled, coughing in the suddenly thick air.

A tall man was standing there as she ran back across the ice. He was very pale, with white hair and eyes the colour of water, not like anyone she had ever seen, but she stopped when he called to her. His accent was unfamiliar, hard to understand.

– You had better come with me, he said. What is your name?

– Ioneth, she replied.

Elspeth woke with a start. She was lying wrapped in rough, scratchy fur, with bodies pressed close to her on each side, and the ground hard and uneven underneath her. They had slept close together for warmth, she remembered. Grufweld had made a small fire from the remains of his charcoal – Elspeth could feel its embers warming her feet – but none of them had had the heart to gather branches for a larger blaze. The bitter smell of smoke was still in her nostrils, and the sky that she could see between the trees was as grey as ash. But the pines themselves were straight and unburned: Loki had not walked here.

The smoke-smell brought back images from her dream – Ioneth's dream. *Were those your first family, the ones that Loki killed? And who was the man who rescued you?* He had looked a little like Ari, she thought. The voice inside her head did not reply, but Elspeth thought she could feel a faint stirring of memory and regret.

She put the dream aside: they must take up Loki's trail as soon as they could, and Cluaran and Ari were already up and feeding the horses. She sat up, waking Edmund and Fritha on each side of her.

'Still no sun,' Edmund muttered as he opened his eyes. The lowering sky lay like a weight on all of them, and there was little talk as they packed up their furs and skewered the cold remains of last night's roasted rabbit for their breakfast. They were heading south, following the direction in which Loki had vanished the morning before. They trudged all day through the trees, pursued by the greyness and the ashen smell, but without finding any other sign of Loki. Ari was their guide now: the caves where the Ice people made their home were to the south. He moved with an urgency that Elspeth could well understand, having seen what had happened to Grufweld's home, though the pale man was as quiet as ever.

Fritha and Grufweld came with them; the hut had been burned so completely that there was nothing left for them in the forest. Grufweld told how he had returned from his trading trip to the smell of burning, and the sight of his home in flames. The next moment the flames had vanished, and all had seemed as it was when he left it, but Grufweld knew what he had seen – and knew, too, the stories of Loki and what the demon-god could do. He had spent the night in the trees at the far side of the clearing, sheltered by his cart and the one wolf-pelt he had not sold, hoping that his daughter and her companions would return to him. He and Fritha stayed close together now, and Elspeth could not look at them without a stab of guilt: *They've lost everything because of me!* She was the one who had unleashed Loki. She found herself walking faster. But Fritha and her father had not lost *everything*, she reminded herself: they still had each other. For a moment Elspeth remembered her father, drowned such a short time ago, and the greyness of the air seemed to thicken around her till she could see nothing else.

'Don't go so fast!'

Edmund came puffing up beside her. 'You can't keep up this pace!' His voice was half-admiring, half-accusing, but his face was bright with relief, and Elspeth realised that he had been worried about her.

'Cathbar says you should be watching your strength for a while, after . . .' His words trailed away, and Elspeth avoided his gaze. Neither of them wanted to remember the fight in Loki's cave. Her failure. 'You could ride,' Edmund suggested instead, pointing ahead to where Cluaran was leading one of the horses, with Eolande sitting impassively on its back. The other horse was behind them, harnessed to Grufweld's hand-cart, which held their scant supplies.

Elspeth shook her head. Edmund was right: even the short burst of speed had tired her, and her breath was coming faster. But she was no horsewoman, and she was not going to add to the load on the cart. 'I'm well,' she told him. 'I just wish we could get out of these trees.'

'Ari said it shouldn't be long now. We should reach the Ice people by midday.' Edmund looked up at the sky between the dark branches. 'Not that we'll be able to tell.'

But the trees began to thin soon after, and gave way to a plain of snow edged with white-capped hills. Ari quickened his pace still more, veering east towards the hills with the confident tread of a man going home. The snow was crusted over with ice, and he, Fritha and Grufweld moved over the plain as smoothly as if it were grass. Elspeth had learned from her last journey over the ice fields to walk softly, sliding her fur boots so that they did not break the surface, but she and Edmund still stumbled from time to time, sinking calf-deep in powdery snow. The horses and the high-wheeled cart left deep tracks, and soon all Elspeth's attention was taken up with staying on her feet and avoiding the ruts. The tiredness was becoming an ache in her bones, but she would not give in to it.

They had crossed maybe half the distance to the hills when Ari's steps faltered. A faint smudge of darker grey had appeared in the air ahead, insubstantial at first but slowly growing clearer against the snowcaps.

Smoke.

Elspeth saw Ari's shoulders jerk. 'Cluaran,' he said, his voice harsh, and muttered something that Elspeth could not hear.

Cluaran was at the pale man's side in a moment. By the time Elspeth and the others ran up, the minstrel had turned back to unhitch the horse from Grufweld's cart.

'Ari will ride ahead,' he announced. 'Go,' he said to Ari, leading the horse over to him. 'We'll follow as quickly as we can.'

The voices came first. Elspeth had expected to hear screams, or keening, but there was just a man's voice calling something inaudible, and a couple of quiet replies. As they reached the foothills, low outcrops of rock pushing through the snow, there was a child's thin wail, swiftly hushed. The sounds would have been reassuringly ordinary but for the thickening haze in the air, and the horribly familiar stink of ash.

They were approaching the hill in a drawn-out straggle. Eolande would not walk, so Cluaran had hitched her horse to the cart, and the beast now plodded at the back of the group, led by Cathbar. Cluaran strode out in front, as if anxious to make what speed he could. But the minstrel stopped when he rounded the final outcrop. He was standing quite still as Elspeth and Edmund joined him and saw the blackened ground.

The plume of smoke had been hidden by the side of the hill, but now it loomed taller than the hill itself, dark-grey and choking. It rose from a pit in the rock whose sides looked like black glass – and all around, feathery ash lay like drifted snow. Behind the pit, the side of the hill seemed to have cracked open: there was a rubble of charred boulders, some twice the height of a man, and beyond them, a black and empty space.

'What has he done?' Cluaran whispered, and rushed forward into the darkness. Elspeth followed him, with Edmund close behind.

The ground underfoot was level, like a passageway. Elspeth groped for the wall as the rock closed in around them, and felt the smoothness of masonry under her fingers. After a moment, her eyes grew accustomed to the dimness. 'Oh no,' Edmund muttered beside her, but Elspeth could only gaze in awe and dismay.

Before them was a giant chamber, filled with tiers of seats that sloped down to a central space. To one side, faint light came in through a great rent in the wall, rubble-edged and showing a sliver of pale sky. It lit the circular floor, smooth and flat but now charred black – and the wreckage of a carved stone chair, charred like the ground and the seats around it; split into two halves.

'The judgement hall,' Cluaran muttered. 'I never thought to see it like this.'

'Nor I,' said a cracked voice from the shadows. Elspeth spun to see a tall old man, white-haired and even paler than Ari, with brows like two crags. When he spoke again his voice was flat with exhaustion. 'You failed, then, story-teller; or failed us. I see you have found your children, but what is that to us? Now *our* children are dead.'

'Not all of them, I think,' Cluaran said quietly. 'Erlingr . . . I grieve for this . . . for you. It's as you say: we were betrayed, and we failed. Now, if you wish, I'll go – but I would help you, if you'll allow it. I have medicines and supplies, and there are willing hands among my companions to help you rebuild.'

'Do as you will,' the old man said. He walked heavily over to one of the stone benches and sank down on it, dropping his head into his hands. 'I was wrong, it seems, and I have paid for it – I, and all my people. The monster has taken his revenge on us, as you said he would.' He raised his head, his pale eyes almost lost under the overhanging brows. 'The survivors – most of them – will be in the water-caves. Go to them if you will. I have no help to give them now, no comfort.'

'But it's now that they need you most!' Cluaran cried. 'Come with me – let them see that you are still alive and strong. That will be the best help they can have: to know that Erlingr still leads them!'

But the old man bowed his head and would not move or speak again. After a while Cluaran turned and left the chamber, gesturing to Elspeth and Edmund to follow him. Erlingr did not look up to see them go.

'Who is he?' Edmund asked in a low voice, as they came out again into the grey daylight.

'Their leader – once,' Cluaran said shortly. He sighed. 'I fear that Ari must take that responsibility now.'

The rest of the party had reached the hill. Grufweld and Fritha were leaning exhaustedly on the cart, gazing in horror at the destruction before them, while Cathbar tried to calm the horse, whose nostrils flared at the new smell of burning. Only Eolande, on its back, showed no trace of emotion or tiredness.

'We'll leave the cart here,' Cluaran told them. 'But bring any medicines or salves.' He looked up at Eolande. 'Will you lend us your skill, Mother?' But she stared at him blankly until he turned from her, shaking his head.

Fritha ran to collect her pack, and Cluaran led them around the foot of the hill, skirting the black pit as widely as they could. The hillside was scarred and blackened in both directions as far as they could see, with the same glassy, black surfaces where the rock had melted. They passed another fall of boulders, and Fritha gave a muffled exclamation, pointing down at one of the rocks. She bent to look more closely – and recoiled, her face white. Following her gaze, Elspeth saw a man's bare foot.

'Leave him!' Cluaran ordered. 'He's dead. There will be others we can help.'

Elspeth followed him, feeling suddenly cold. She had not heard any more voices, she realised: not so much as a whisper. What had happened to Ari's people? Were there really any left? And where was Ari?

Further along the ridge the stink of smoke lessened and the rocks became only soot-blackened. Elspeth found to her relief that they were no longer walking on ash, though the snow had vanished.

Cluaran stopped, listened and whistled. 'The stream is still flowing,' he said. 'Come on.'

Soon Elspeth could hear the faint splash of water – and then, the stamping of hooves on rock. Around the next outcrop, a thin trickle ran into a shallow basin in the stone, and beside it, Ari's horse was tethered to a bush.

Cathbar tied up their own horse and helped Eolande to dismount. 'Is there anyone alive here, apart from us?' he asked, grim-faced.

'Oh, yes,' said Cluaran.

The sound of water grew louder as he led them to what seemed at first to be a shallow cleft in the rock. A darker area at the back revealed itself as a tunnel – but before they could enter it, two men appeared, brandishing spears. One of them was Ari.

He relaxed when he saw them, though his face was drawn with grief and shock. 'These are my friends,' he told the other man, who went back into the tunnel, shouting something. Ari turned without another word and led them inside.

The tunnel opened into a series of caves. Water dripped from the walls of two of them and pooled on the floor of the third – and every dry spot was crowded with pale-eyed, white-haired people. *There must be a hundred of them*, Elspeth thought: men, women and children; some standing, blank-eyed; others weeping softly, or crying out in pain. *It's my fault*, she thought wildly. *I unleashed him!* She wanted to turn and run.

'Some of these are *brent* – hurt with the fire,' Fritha said, behind her. 'I have medicine for that.' She fumbled with her pack to produce a sealed pot, and hesitated, looking wide-eyed at the Ice people. 'Do you think it will work for them,' she whispered, 'as it does for us?'

Edmund came forward. 'I'm sure of it,' he said to Fritha. 'Elspeth and I will help you.'

Elspeth was glad to have work to occupy her. She tried not to look around the crowded caves, but busied herself with practical tasks along with Edmund: fetching clean water, improvising bandages and splints, and setting up beds for the younger children in the driest areas.

Fritha also seemed overwhelmed at first: Elspeth guessed that she had never been among so many people before. But as the fair-haired girl tended a child with a badly burned arm, hearing his cries subside and listening to the thanks of his mother, she seemed to forget her nervousness. She moved around the caves, speaking to the Ice people to find those whose burns and cuts were the worst, and making her small pots of salve last longer than Elspeth could have believed.

They stayed among Ari's people for the rest of the day. There was always more to do: as the worst injured were tended and given beds, Grufweld and Cathbar fetched more of their supplies from the cart and scouted with some of the men for other safe caves. Elspeth, moving in a haze of weariness, heard Cluaran talking urgently to his mother, who had stayed at the edge of the outer cave.

'You could help! I know your skill in these things. At least help me to find the right herbs.'

Eolande went slowly outside, followed by her son and Ari. The pale man stopped in the cave door, and turned to speak to Elspeth and Fritha.

'We'll make more burn-salve for you. Thank you for all you're doing.'

Fritha gave him a nod of acknowledgement, but Elspeth could accept no gratitude, not when she knew this was all her fault. When one of the women smiled at her in thanks for a cup of water, she felt her eyes filling with tears and had to turn away.

Many of the children they tended were orphaned. When Loki had dropped from the sky the day before, the Ice people told her, he had torn open the hill that housed the judgement hall and sent fires raging through the caves on each side, destroying whole families in their homes, and burying countless others in the rubble. When the men ran out to fight him, the wooden spears had burned in their hands, and the men had followed, their bodies turning to ash. Out of a community of three hundred, maybe one third was left.

My fault. The words rang in her ears, and she thought she could feel Ioneth stirring in pain.

'Please tell me,' she asked one of the women, 'when Loki . . . when the monster left you, how did he go? And which way?'

The woman looked at her incredulously. 'It just went! It turned into a big ball of fire and went back to *hel-viti* – to hell. Where else would it go?'

'It flew to the south,' put in a soft-voiced girl. Her eyes were very large in her thin face and she cradled her bandaged arm as she spoke. 'To the sea.' There was a small chorus of agreement. Some of the children had watched from the mouth of the water caves as the demon became a fireball and soared away. They had watched it out of sight, hoping it would never return.

'And in the sea, the fire will go out!' piped up a small boy with a bandage over one eye.

'It surely will,' Fritha told the child, hugging him. Over his head, she looked anxiously at Elspeth.

'He won't come back here, that's for certain,' Elspeth said, trying to fill her voice with confidence. *I'm sure he won't*, she thought. *He means to go much further than this.*

But wherever he goes, I will follow.

CHAPTER THREE

It was a party of five who set off southwards the following morning. Edmund could see that Elspeth was desperate to follow Loki, and Cluaran and Cathbar seemed to share her sense of urgency.

'I've no notion how we'll fight him now,' Cathbar said. 'But if a way comes up – well, I'd rather be on the spot and able to take it. It's that, or stand by while he goes on burning.' He had gone out with a rescue party the day before, finding one or two survivors, but many more of the dead.

Ari said he would stay with his people: as Cluaran had predicted, many of them had already started to look to him as their leader, and they left him deep in discussion with the elders about ways to open up new caves for those made homeless and replenish the supplies that had been destroyed.

He shook hands with Cluaran before they left. The pale man looked somehow older, Edmund thought, his face marked with the horror of yesterday's loss, and maybe with his new responsibilities. 'I'll not see you again,' he said. 'My place is here now.'

Cluaran nodded. 'Did we do wrong, Ari?' he asked. 'If we had not meddled with Loki, this would not have happened.'

Ari shook his head. 'We both know he would have broken free, in our children's lifetimes if not in ours. And the sword . . . Ioneth . . . came to us now.' His face twisted. 'Find her again, Cluaran. For all our sakes.' He turned to Elspeth and Edmund. 'If the sword returns, strike well,' he said to them. 'Wherever you go, and however you fare, our people's friendship goes with you.'

Fritha and her father, to Edmund's surprise, chose to stay with the Ice people too, at least over the winter. Fritha's skill as a nurse had made her valuable to the community already, and she could not bear to leave the motherless children. Grufweld's trade, charcoal-burning, was less useful to them – the Ice people had little use for fire, except sometimes for cooking – but his strength, and his skills at building and hunting, would be much needed in the days to come.

Fritha hugged Edmund and Elspeth fiercely before they left.

'You are *vin-fastr* . . . true friends,' she told them. 'You will kill this monster, and then you will come back to see us. But if you cannot come . . . I will remember you always.'

'I'll come back some day,' Edmund promised, mortified to find that his eyes were pricking. Before he could turn away Fritha leant forward and kissed him. Edmund felt his face glowing, and the place where her cool lips had touched his cheek burned for a long time afterwards.

Grufweld waved away their apologies for the trouble they had brought on him. Cluaran offered the charcoal-burner a gold coin, given to him by the king for his journey, but Grufweld courteously refused: the nearest villagers had little use for coins, and besides, hospitality was a matter of honour and need, not a thing to be bartered. Cathbar, however, was not to be put off: after pumping Grufweld's hand repeatedly, he insisted on making him a present of his hunting knife.

'Least I could do,' he said gruffly, as they walked away. 'He lost a good axe back in that fire, as well as his knife – and those Ice folk know nothing about metal.'

And now they made their way across the snow plain towards the coast. They had left all their supplies with the Ice people, taking only the two horses, Cluaran's gold coin and his remaining bag of silver. The horses were much needed: Elspeth, for all her eagerness to be gone, was not yet fully healed, as Cathbar had feared, and yesterday's walk had worn her out. Well before noon (though it was hard to judge with the sunless sky), she had begun to stumble almost at every step, and Cluaran had made her ride. The other horse was ridden by Eolande, who sat straight-backed and still, her face empty.

The snow grew thinner as they went, and the trees grew closer on both sides. Around noon they were walking through pines again, mixed with leafless birch and aspen. Where the pines were thickest there was no snow at all, and Edmund was glad to feel the carpet of needles beneath his feet again. He thought that Cluaran walked with a new spring in his step too, even while leading his silent, blank-eyed mother.

Elspeth was very silent as she rode. Edmund walked close by, stealing anxious glances at her. He knew she preferred to walk, but she rode well enough, and she did not seem to be in pain. Her wounded hand was healing well, with only a dark-red mark across the palm. But her gaze was often turned inwards, and he often saw her face crease with distress. He spoke little to her: he feared he already knew what troubled her, and he could think of nothing to say that would give any comfort.

The trees thinned, and suddenly there was the distant roar of the sea. Edmund looked up at his friend – surely that sound would cheer her! But to his horror, her eyes were full of tears. Almost soundlessly, she muttered, 'No! Not again . . .'

And at that moment Edmund caught it too, and his heart sank. With the far-off sound came a scent – not the sea, but the acrid smell of smoke.

Elspeth was white and shaking by the time they reached the harbour village. A pall of thick, greasy smoke rose from ruins so charred it was impossible to tell what they had once been. Edmund found himself dragging his feet as they approached, and realised that the others were doing the same: as if to put off the inevitable story of terror and misery. Cluaran, Edmund saw with a jolt, was almost as pale as Elspeth.

'This is the place where I landed,' the minstrel said quietly. 'Did I bring this on them?'

'That's foolish talk,' Cathbar insisted. 'He was always going to attack somewhere!' But Cluaran seemed not to hear him.

There was a row of huts that had escaped the fire, and a few people in front of them: two women, looking out to sea, and a middle-aged man standing in a doorway. Cathbar hailed the man, introducing themselves as travellers.

'Looks like you've had trouble here,' he said. 'We'll be glad to help, if we can.'

The man wiped his hands on his long apron and looked at them without replying. Edmund wondered if he were simple, or if he had been struck dumb by shock, but after a while he found his voice. It was hoarse, as if he had trouble speaking, but Edmund could understand enough of the Dansk tongue by now to make him out.

'I thank you, but there's nothing you need to do. We are all well here.'

Simple-minded, Edmund thought; and Cathbar clearly thought the same. 'That's a bad fire you've had,' he tried again. 'Was nobody hurt? No one's house burned?'

'No,' said the man, and started to laugh. While they gaped at him, the women came up.

'It's true,' one of them said. 'We thought we were dead for sure – but every one of us escaped.' She smiled at them, her eyes shining. 'We were saved.'

The village had scant hospitality to offer, but the prospect of telling strangers about their miraculous escape brought most of them out of their homes with small gifts of food. The travellers were seated around the fire in the chief's hut and given mugs of sour beer, while the chief's wife told them the tale and a dozen other villagers crowded in the doorway to add their own details.

The burned buildings, the woman told them, were their boathouse and drying-sheds. Two nights before, one of the sheds was struck by lightning out of a clear sky: they heard a thunderclap, saw a bolt of white light and ran out of their houses to see the blaze already taking hold. They fought it as best they could with buckets of sea-water, but to no avail: long before dawn the fire was raging through both sheds ('fiercer than a storm,' said the chief's wife, with gloomy relish), and had caught the boathouse where they kept one of the two passenger boats that the men used to ferry travellers to the mainland.

'Everyone was crying!' put in a young boy. They knew that the dried fish that was to feed the village for the rest of the winter must have gone up in smoke, and with it all the fishing nets, their livelihood. The boat, their finest, gave them all their contact with the outside world, as well as extra income in the summer months; now it, too, would be gone. And then the wind had changed, and a corner-post from the shed had crashed down on the other side, carrying the fire towards their homes.

'Such screaming and running there was!' cried one of the listeners.

'I thought us all dead and buried for sure.'

'But then . . . *he* came.'

There was a man, a stranger, appearing out of nowhere. One moment they had been running for their homes, desperate to save young children and treasured possessions. Then there was a voice behind them, loud and commanding, and the man was there, fire burning all around him, with a sack of fish over his shoulder and his arms full of nets.

'Beautiful as an angel he was,' a young woman sighed.

Some said he walked through the fire without being burned; others, that he moved too quickly for the fire to touch him. It was certain that he had saved their livelihood. He led them in extinguishing the burning beam that had threatened their homes, stamping out the straying flames himself. ('And those fires, they vanished as if they were scared of him,' said a man.) Then he helped them to rescue their boat from the burning boathouse, taking one rope himself with the strength of a dozen men. He did not rest until the fire was contained; their homes and possessions safe. Then he joined them in their celebrations while it burned itself out behind them.

He would give no name, the chief's wife said, and would take no reward. He said he was a traveller, come here to find passage south to the mainland. They did not often make the journey in winter, but this time . . . The chief himself, her husband, had gone as boat-master, and young men had fought to be allowed to row. They had left this morning on the very boat that the hero had saved from the flames.

There was silence after the woman finished her story. Edmund did not dare to catch Elspeth's eye. The image was all too clear in his mind: the fire ball crashing down, straight from the devastation of the ice caves; and Loki, the deceiver, taking on the form of a handsome hero, striding forth to resolve a disaster of his own making. What mortal man could have so much power over fire? For an instant he saw the same realisation on the faces of Cathbar and Cluaran – then Cluaran shot him a warning glance, fractionally shaking his head.

Edmund wanted to shout these credulous people out of their delusion. *It was Loki! Loki – the monster who started your fire, who has murdered hundreds like you. How could you be so blind?* But he knew exactly how. Looking at the bright faces around him, he knew that the villagers had been given their own miracle: nothing he could say would persuade them to give it up.

'Truly a tale of wonders,' said Cluaran at last, and there was just the right tone of awe in his voice. 'Mistress,' he went on, 'we too are travellers, though no heroes; hoping to take passage for the south. It's a poor time of year for a voyage, I know . . . but your story has fired me with a wish to see this man for myself. I can see from my companions' faces that they feel the same. To which port did your men take him?'

The woman's face glowed. 'You're right: not many people can say they have looked on a true hero! He went to Alebu, in the Danish kingdom.'

'And,' Cluaran went on smoothly, 'you said you had a second boat?'

The other boat was much older than the one saved from the fire: unwieldy and somewhat battered; but even so, the villagers were not entirely happy to let it go out in winter before the first had returned. But Cathbar pronounced the boat sound, and when Cluaran presented the village with the two horses as well as the hire of the boat in silver, the remaining boat-masters agreed to find another crew but explained that they would not be able to leave until the next morning. Cluaran passed himself and Cathbar off as enterprising cloth merchants looking for a new market in the far northern towns, and Eolande, Edmund and Elspeth as a widow with her children, now under his protection and returning to her family after her husband's death. Eolande's silence and abstraction made the tale easier to believe, and no one commented on how little Edmund looked as if he could be her son, or Elspeth's brother. Edmund suspected the villagers were too absorbed in their own story to pay much heed to anyone else's.

They had little difficulty in finding a crew: the remaining young men of the village were eager for the chance to see their hero again, and the old boat was soon fitted. They set sail that same day, heading south on grey, choppy waters. The town of Alebu was a little way down the western coast of Daneland, the sailors said as they took up their oars. The journey should not take much longer than two days.

In fact, it took three, in fierce winds which blew them off course for the first day. Edmund was disturbed to find how uncomfortable the motion made him at first. Every pitch of the boat reminded him of his first sea journey only a few weeks ago on the *Spearwa*, and the deadly storm that had ended that voyage. The shipwreck, and the attack of the dragon Torment, had set him on a path he still found hard to believe; given him a skill he had never wanted, which set him apart from his own people; and sent him on this endless round of travelling, from which it seemed he might never be free.

But it had also given him Elspeth. He looked at his friend's face as she stood in the boat's prow. Elspeth was happier than he had seen her since their descent to Loki's cave. She was still weak, and fretted that she could not be more than a passenger on the ship, but the colour had come back to her face, and the same motion that unsettled him seemed to calm her. She spent much of the voyage gazing over the waves, her hair whipping about her face; cradling her right hand with her left. She seemed glad of Edmund's company when he came to stand beside her, but neither of them spoke aloud of Loki, or of what might lie ahead.

The squally wind proved a friend to them in one way. For the first time in days the sky cleared, and the sight of the sun raised everyone's spirits, though it did little to counter the cold. Cathbar and Cluaran took their share of the rowing, and even Eolande, sitting near the bow of the boat, seemed a little more alert. As he grew more used to the swing of the waves and the close living on board, Edmund began to feel a sense of escape – as if they were leaving the nightmare behind, rather than following it.

On the morning of the third day the helmsman sighted land, and as the sun reached its height they came at last to the port of Alebu.

Far to the south of them, in the kingdom of Wessex, the king's advisor, Aagard, stepped back from his fire, shaken by the images he had seen there. He was too old, he thought despairingly: wise enough to see the threat and know it for what it was, but without the strength of vision to follow it – or to challenge it.

'Loki goes south; that's certain,' he muttered. 'And our friends pursue him but are blind to the truth. The demon-god has split himself into more than one and walks in many guises and travels faster than a mist through the land.'

The destroyer was still fettered in some way, Aagard was sure of that. Years ago, he had caught a glimpse of that mind, and seen the fires there. Nothing but total annihilation would satisfy Loki if he were free.

His aim now must be to free himself completely, then. And he would work through trickery, or by bending others to his will . . . as he had done before, here in Wessex. The mad sorcerer Orgrim still lived, confined in the king's strong-house, blind and barely able to speak, now that his master had abandoned him. But when he had served Loki, he had controlled the kingdom.

'Trickery; deceit; working through others,' the old man said aloud. 'But which others?'

His divination was over: there would be no more visions tonight. But as he stared, unseeing, into his small fireplace, he thought he saw fire like a red cloud, spreading to engulf the world, and black smoke that quenched the sun.

CHAPTER FOUR

The port of Alebu was more familiar to Elspeth than any place she had seen in the Snowlands: a harbour town, busy even on the winter evening when they arrived: its docks scattered with sailors, merchants rich and poor, and the drifters who came to find a day's work or to fleece unwary travellers. The people spoke Dansk, as Fritha and her father had done, but their accent was closer to the one that Elspeth had heard when she first learned the language aboard the *Spearwa*. She felt she should be at ease in a town like this, with one foot in the sea; but she could find none of it reassuring. The three days aboard the boat, even with a foolish crew who would not recognise her as a fellow sailor, had felt like a return to her old life with her father, when there had been no sword, no demons to fight, and no constant, nagging sense of failure and guilt. With her first step on land, all that heaviness returned, and with it her sense of urgency. Loki was here somewhere. She had no idea how to find him; still less how to stop him – but she *must*! She looked down at her right hand, healed now but for the wedge-shaped band of red across the palm, and thought she felt an answering throb there. Her head swam suddenly, and she stumbled, throwing out her arms for balance.

'Elspeth!' Edmund was beside her in a moment, his face filled with concern. Cluaran came up on the other side to take her arm.

'I'm fine,' she told them. 'Just not used to being on land.' The cobbles under her feet did feel strange to her, as they left the harbour and made their way past the first houses.

'We'll find an inn,' Cathbar said. 'You need to get your strength back.'

They left the sailors who brought them standing on the quay, arguing. The men had been alarmed to find their own boat – the newly made and newly rescued pride of their village, which had carried the hero here – abandoned at the quayside, with no sign of its master or crew. Their enquiries brought little result: the boat had arrived more than three days ago with eight men aboard; all eight had walked into the town the same day, and had not returned. *That means they sailed here in only a day!* Elspeth thought. It was too fast to be natural.

It seemed there were a number of visitors to the town just now: the only inn of any size was crowded, with barely space for the five of them. The hostess told them that a healer had just arrived in Alebu: he had cured the town's richest merchant of an ague, and word had spread. She had not seen nor heard of any party of boatmen who arrived three days ago, but assured Cluaran that there was nowhere else in the town where so large a group could have stayed together. 'They could have gone for work inland, with one of the farmers, maybe,' she said doubtfully. 'Though there's not much work to be had this time of year.'

Elspeth suddenly realised that the woman's voice was becoming fainter, as if the speaker had moved away from them. Her head felt heavy and her legs weak; she reached out to Edmund for support.

'Your young one looks all in!' the woman cried. 'Let her lie down – you can search for your friends later.'

They found her a pallet by the fire in the smaller of the inn's two rooms, and she slept almost at once. She woke only once before the next day: it was dark, lit by nothing more than the fire's embers, and other guests were sleeping around her. On the pallet next to her lay Eolande, but the Fay woman was not asleep: she had pulled herself up on her elbow, and Elspeth caught the dark glitter of her eyes, as if the woman were watching her. She must have stirred, for Eolande turned away at once, and Elspeth was quickly asleep again.

Next morning, her head was still heavy, and Edmund gave her an anxious look as they sat round the hostess's table eating her barley bread.

'You're still not well,' he said. 'We could rest here today, perhaps, before moving on.'

'There's nothing wrong with me,' Elspeth insisted, alarmed at the thought of any delay.

'You should take her to the *grethari*,' the hostess said, ladling water into cups. 'The healer. They say he has great skill: he goes from place to place, and cures all that he touches.'

'Let's seek him out!' Edmund said eagerly.

Cathbar looked at Elspeth. 'Maybe we should, at that,' he said.

'I'm fine!' Elspeth said, trying to keep the irritation out of her voice. She *could not* be ill; couldn't they see that? 'We need to get moving!'

But for now, there was no trail for them to follow. Speaking to the inn's other guests, they learned that today was market day, and the usual influx of traders to the town had been swelled by people hoping to see the *grethari*. But there was no word of a party of strangers from the north; nor even of one man, handsome and commanding, with the bearing of a hero. It seemed that both Loki and his fellow travellers had vanished into the air.

'We need supplies,' Cathbar said. 'Maybe we'll learn something in the market.'

The market was small even by the standards of Elspeth's home town of Dubris. They bought bread, dried fish and blankets for the journey, and Cathbar spent a long time in discussion with a smith, and came away with a narrow package. Then, passing by a Frankish pedlar's stall with Edmund, Elspeth heard the news she needed.

'No word of a lie, mistress,' the man was saying to a customer, as he carefully detached a tin brooch and two needles from his hoard. 'A forest fire, not ten leagues from here, and in weather as cold as it is today! I saw it with my own eyes.'

He repeated his story to Edmund and Elspeth after the woman had gone, and asking around the other traders confirmed it. It had happened only the day before yesterday, they said, in the great forest to the south: lightning must have struck a tree, as sometimes happens in the winter storms, but there had been no storm, and the fire had spread till the smoke could be seen for leagues. Several traders had seen it, or smelt the smoke, as they made their way to Alebu for the market, but no one could guess what had made it spread so disastrously, particularly in winter.

'It's still burning, as far as I know,' said a farmer. 'I heard that lightning had nothing to do with it and that bandits may be to blame.'

'I have never heard of bandits in these parts.' The pedlar looked concerned.

The farmer came over. 'That may have been true once but I have heard strange tales this week, there is something in the wind. Some of us are travelling south together tomorrow, when the market ends – the townspeople of Eikstofn and the farms round there. Come with us if you want: the more the better, I'd say.'

'I'll do that,' the pedlar said. 'I've no wish to go back that way alone if there really are bandits out there.'

The news seemed to banish Elspeth's weakness. She and Edmund had exchanged glances as soon as they heard of the fire, and she was sure they had both thought the same thing: *Loki is laying a trail for us.* She wanted to set out at once, but Cluaran said they would wait until the next day, so they could travel alongside the returning traders and find out where the fire had started.

Cathbar agreed. 'They know this region,' he pointed out, stowing the long parcel in his pack. 'And in these parts, there's safety in numbers, even without Loki.'

They started before dawn the next day, rising with the other travellers who stayed at their inn and making their way through the grey light to the forest road. The Frankish pedlar hailed them on their approach, and fell in with them as they set off. His name was Menobert, he told them, and he was heading all the way south to Francia. He asked where they were bound.

'South, as well,' was all Cluaran said, and Menobert nodded amicably, not at all put out by the evasive answer.

Menobert was a stocky, black-moustached man; cheerful and chatty. He told them of the drought and poor harvest last year, which had led to such hardship this winter, and that he wouldn't be surprised if some folk had left their farms and turned to banditry. Elspeth saw Cathbar nodding grimly as he heard that, and checking the hilt of his sword.

They took the main road to the south: it was wide enough to allow a cart, though few came down it. The road was rutted and icy as they set off, but as the sun rose the snow and ice underfoot began to melt. The muddy road beneath her feet felt wonderful to Elspeth after so long making her way across snow. They made good progress, and even Eolande, who had refused to walk across the ice fields, seemed to have no objection to going afoot here. At first there was little sign of the banditry that the farmer had seemed to fear, but before noon they met a couple of farm-women, sisters, who were very happy to travel in their company, for fear of being robbed. They had been to visit the *grethari*, they told Elspeth, the travelling healer, who was now staying in a tiny settlement just to the west of the road, and there had been an outbreak of looting and pillaging in the village that looked like it could spread. Elspeth realised that the healer must have left Alebu before she and Edmund even arrived there, and all the pilgrims who had filled the inns hoping to see him had had a wasted journey. But their innkeeper had said the man had not been there long.

'He travels fast, doesn't he?' she said.

'Truly, I couldn't tell you,' the younger woman said. 'We only heard of him yesterday, from a traveller. But his name is already well known in this land. It has spread like fire.'

'And with reason,' her sister enthused. 'He took the pain right out of my sore shoulder, just by laying his hands on it.'

'And what does he charge for such a service?' asked Cluaran wryly.

'Oh, no money!' The woman sounded shocked. 'He says that his gift belongs to everyone; he cannot profit by it. He'll take a meal with you, that's all.'

'Though he could have eaten twenty times over, if he'd had a mind to,' her sister put in. 'So many people were in line to see him.'

'One of these travelling holy men, eh?' said Menobert dismissively. 'There are too many peddling miracles these days. Sweet-talkers who pull in idle men and make them forget how to do a day's work. Then *they* take to the road and live off charity, and find still more wastrels to convert.'

'He's not like that!' The woman was indignant. 'You haven't seen him.'

'I've seen many of them, though,' maintained the trader. 'I could find three new religions to follow in a day's walk.'

The first woman threw up her hands in mock-defeat. 'Well, there are always some who won't take a gift when it's offered. For me, I'm glad there is such a man as the *grethari*, in these hard times.'

They walked all day, stopping only briefly for a meal by the roadside at noon. Other travellers had joined them as they walked: another trader, and a young man who had also been to see the *grethari*, and shared the two sisters' zeal for his healing powers.

They made camp at sunset, in a field that seemed to be a regular stopping-place. A small copse of oak trees, though leafless, offered protection from the teeth of the wind, and kept off the light snow that fell during the night. For other protection, Cathbar and Cluaran took turns with the rest of the men to keep watch: however little there might be to tempt bandits here, it seemed that no one was prepared to take any chances.

They moved off quickly when dawn broke and after some distance met an old man driving three goats, heading in the opposite direction. He warned the travellers of the dangers they might expect on the road ahead.

'In all my years on this road, I've never seen so many ruffians together,' he complained. 'Swordsmen, brigands . . . They seem to have sprung out of nowhere. I hear there was even a bunch of pagans on the highway, kicking over a shrine.'

'And so you are heading north for your safety,' commented Cluaran, who had been listening. The goatherd nodded.

'Keep your head down and your purse hidden,' Menobert assured them all, as the goatherd took his leave. 'That is the only way to stay out of the way of rogues. But these fires, now . . . you can't sidestep those. Remember the one I told you of? There's some here that say it's still burning! Perhaps we could seek it out,' he added drily, peering through the flurries of snow. 'We could do with the warmth.'

'Another forest fire?' exclaimed a market-man, overhearing. Menobert obligingly retold the story of the tree struck by lightning, even when there had been no storm.

'Oh, I heard about that,' the man said dismissively. 'That was days ago. There've been others since then! One only yesterday, much further south, in the woods down near Varde. They say,' he lowered his voice conspiratorially, 'they say bandits are definitely laying them.'

'Why would they do that?' asked one of the farm-women. 'And why this sudden unrest?'

A thought struck Elspeth. Could these new bands of bandits in the south have anything to do with Loki? The demon-god had headed in this direction and was expert in bending men to his will. Fire was a language he was fluent in.

'I've heard that they wait at the edges of the fires, to rob people as they flee,' the man said. 'There are some folk who never care what they destroy.'

The squall stopped as they walked, but the fields to each side of the path were still snow-covered, with only one or two distant, isolated houses to show that this was a place where people lived. As the day drew on the fields were increasingly dotted with trees, which grew nearer and closer together until the road was skirting the edge of a forest. A brisk wind started up, and suddenly there was the unmistakable smell of smoke. The travellers halted, avoiding each other's eyes; no one wanting to be the first to speak.

At last, the man who had been blaming bandits gave a short bark of a laugh. 'There, now,' he said. 'I wager the charcoal-burners will be finding it too hot for them tonight.'

Elspeth exchanged furious glances with Edmund, thinking of Grufweld, their generous host, and the destruction of his home. She was about to say something sharp, but Cluaran nudged her.

'These children are tired,' he announced to the travellers in general. 'We need to stop here for the night. I thank you all for your company.'

Their recent companions were horrified at the idea, and begged him to reconsider – especially Menobert. It was so close to the forest, and bandits could be in there. There was only another league to go to Eikstofn, the next village, one of the farm-women said, and if there was no lodging there, they could give the poor children a bed at their farm, half a league further on. But Cluaran was adamant.

'Thank you for your kindness,' he said. 'It's generosity to strangers that gives all of us hope, in these strange times. Maybe we will meet again on the road – but we must stay here tonight.'

He put his hand on Elspeth's shoulder, and she tried to look as if she was too exhausted to walk another step. The other travellers set off again, with many waves and backward glances from Menobert and the two women. Cluaran watched them out of sight, then briskly shouldered his pack again.

'We passed a track into the trees, not a hundred paces back,' he said. 'There will be charcoal-burners, not a doubt of it; and they'll be able to tell us more about these fires and whether they were started by bandits or lightning. Loki could still be behind either. Come on!'

He was already striding back along the road, and Elspeth made haste to follow him.

'Wait!' Edmund called. 'What if the fire's still burning?'

'All the more reason to help anyone we find in its path!' Cluaran replied without turning his head.

'We'll more likely find those it's left behind,' Cathbar growled, but he and Edmund followed, leading Eolande between them.

It was not yet evening, but the sky had been grey all day, and once among the trees it seemed almost twilight. These were not the conifers of Fritha's forest home in the Snowlands: Elspeth recognised oaks, elms and lindens, although all the branches were still in bud; the old leaves reduced to mulch underfoot. The path that Cluaran had found was no more than a winding track through the trees where the leaf mould was slightly flat-tened. But he moved confidently, and once when he turned to check that they were all behind him, Elspeth was sure the minstrel had a look of contentment on his face, as if he were happier in these dreary surroundings. Eolande too, she saw, was showing more animation than she had done for days, not speaking but looking about her with something like interest. Cathbar was still leading her by the arm, but she walked with a firmer step now, and after a while he allowed her to follow on her own.

Cluaran led them on and on through the featureless trunks. Elspeth thought the ever-present smell of smoke was growing stronger, but there was no haze in the air, and no sight or sound of burning. There were no sounds at all, in fact. Menobert had assured her that the forest was full of bears and wild boars, but she could not even hear birdsong.

'Can you find any animals?' she asked Edmund quietly. He had been walking for some time with the abstracted look that told her he was casting his mind around, feeling for other living things whose eyes he might borrow.

'None near us,' he said. 'Some further off that aren't threatening – deer, I think. But they're scared, Elspeth. Wherever the fire is, it's frightened them badly.'

'It's not animals I fear.' Cathbar had caught them up, and Elspeth saw he was holding out the long package he had bought at the market in Alebu. 'It's very likely there are bandits in these woods and it is no coincidence that these bands of marauders have sprung up like weeds with Loki abound once again.' Elspeth's heart began to thump as she guessed what was coming. 'I know you've no weapon now, girl, but you're a fair fighter – I saw you with that shining blade. There's no way to know whether these bandits are in the thrall of Loki but there's fighting ahead of us, I'm sure of that. So, here.' A little red in the face, he thrust the package at her.

Inside the heavy oiled cloth was a sword, sheathed in leather. 'It's not fancy,' Cathbar said. 'But the blade is good, and it's light. I told the smith it was for a boy,' he added, his tone apologetic.

Is that what I must do now – walk about like a soldier, with metal at my belt? Ioneth – where are you? But there was no answering voice. Wordlessly, Elspeth took up the sword, trying not to wince as the unfamiliar hilt met her still raw palm.

Cathbar nodded. 'Good. And when we stop tonight, you can practise with it.' He showed her how to fix the sheath to her belt, and then strode ahead to talk to Cluaran as if he had no more to say to her. But Elspeth saw him glancing back at her as he went.

The light around them was fading when they reached the first signs of the fire. There had still been no sight or sound of flames. But suddenly Edmund coughed, and at the same instant Elspeth felt the familiar, acrid tang in her throat. An opening in the trees ahead showed the grey sky, yellow-tinged with sunset. Curls of smoke rose against the yellow – and there was enough light to see the first blackened trees on the far side of the clearing.

Cluaran was bending over something, and when Elspeth saw what he was looking at her throat tightened painfully. What had seemed like a large stump or a mound in the earth was a building: the remains of a hut, part-burned.

'This was a woodcutter's hut,' said Cluaran quietly. 'There's an axe blade on the floor. The clearing must have stopped the flames: there would have been snow on the ground here yesterday.' He straightened. 'We're at the edge of the fire.'

'Any sign of the man?' Cathbar asked, his voice flat.

Cluaran shook his head. He had broken off a piece of the charred wood and was sniffing it. 'We can hope he escaped – but there's no way of telling. The fire has been out for many hours, perhaps more than a day.'

'We should go on, then!' Elspeth said. The thought of walking into the blackness beyond the charred hut made her feel sick – but she had come this way to find Loki. 'We need to find the source of the fire, don't we?'

'It is the best lead we have,' Cluaran agreed. 'But not at once – tomorrow, when we can see where we're going. We might as well spend the night here.'

Edmund and Cluaran laid out their bedding and supplies under the trees on the unburned side of the clearing. Cathbar insisted that Elspeth should practise with the new sword while the dim light lasted, and she could find no reason to refuse. To begin with it was hateful to hold the thing, it felt so alien to her, and she was slow and clumsy, giving way before the captain's feints and failing to get any blows in herself. After a mere dozen exchanges, Cathbar knocked the sword from her hand entirely.

'No, no!' he cried in exasperation. 'You're fighting like a . . . like a beginner! Try again.'

'You might try switching hands,' put in Edmund, who had been watching. 'Your right hand must still be sore.'

Elspeth took up the suggestion gratefully. The new blade still felt strange and unwieldy in her left hand, but the sense of wrongness had gone. She began to make progress, and by the time darkness fell, Cathbar pronounced that she would do fairly. Cluaran extinguished their tiny cooking fire before they slept; without the massed bodies of yesterday's travelling companions around them, it would be a cold night, but Elspeth hardly cared. At least there was no snow here. She felt exhausted, and gladly dropped on to her blanket beneath the trees, lying close to the others for warmth.

61

They were woken in the night by shouts. Elspeth opened her eyes, shivering, to see the leafless branches above her swaying in the wind, and a thin moon in the black sky over the clearing. Cathbar was already on his feet, and Edmund was sitting up, his face pale, eyes closed, searching.

'There are several of them,' he said quietly. 'Men with knives, attacking something . . . or someone.' He pointed through the burned trees, and added, 'Very close.'

They crept across the clearing and among the charred trunks, with Edmund leading the way. It was only twenty paces before he stopped, pointing – but Elspeth could see the men herself.

There were seven of them, all big, all in heavy furs and armed with knives. They were in a small clearing made by toppled trees; charred, stripped trunks surrounded them. A rickety handcart lay overturned nearby, its contents spilled over the ashy ground, but the men were paying it no attention. They were bending over something small and moving. One of them spoke, his voice jeering.

'Cut his head off; that'll free it!'

The other men laughed. From the ground between them, Elspeth caught a flash of bright hair in the moonlight as the small figure twisted away from them. A voice rose, thin and pleading – a child's voice.

Elspeth had the new sword in her hand and was rushing forward even as Edmund lunged to hold her back.

CHAPTER FIVE

Elspeth! No!

Edmund choked back the words, letting out only a stran-gled gasp as Elspeth dashed forward. She was on the men almost before they could turn, aiming a vicious blow at the knife-arm of the nearest. The man reeled away, clutching his arm and yelling, but two of his fellows had turned on Elspeth in an instant, lunging at her with their hunting knives. Even in the darkness they could see their assailant was smaller than them, and they laughed as she swiped furiously at them, and darted back out of range into the trees. Edmund could see that the sword's greater length would be no advantage here: the trunks might be charred and dead, but they were still solid. He drew his own small knife, but before he could run to Elspeth's aid he was grabbed roughly by both shoulders.

'Idiot!' Cathbar growled in his ear. 'You want to get yourself killed too? Use your bow!'

Already, Cluaran had loosed a shot at one of Elspeth's assailants. The man fell among the dark trees with an arrow in his back – but in another moment all the remaining bandits had surrounded Elspeth, lunging forward to slash at her with their knives. As she whirled and swung at them, the men closest to her danced back among the dead trunks, jeering, while the others closed in.

It had taken Edmund a moment to ready his bow. He shot at the same time as Cluaran – but one arrow glanced off a tree and went wide, while the other hit a man's shoulder, leaving him still on his feet. The bandits were an indistinct mass of darting, shouting figures among the black trunks, with Elspeth hidden in their midst – they would have to go in close to rescue her.

'Stay where you are and keep shooting!' Cathbar hissed at both of them – and leapt forward, roaring.

'This way, men! One silver for every head you take!'

He had felled one bandit before he finished speaking. The other men froze, looking wildly around them for more attackers – and at that moment Edmund fired his next arrow. He caught one of them full in the chest, hearing at the same time the whirr of Cluaran's bow by his ear.

He could not tell what became of the final arrow. In the dark, it seemed the robbers had not seen the fall of their first comrade; had still thought themselves attacked only by a girl. Now, faced as they thought with a band of armed men, they turned and fled. Three were left dead on the ground, and more were wounded, judging by the sounds as the others crashed away through the trees.

Elspeth was on her feet, breathing hard. There was blood on her sword and a long rip in her fur jerkin, but she seemed to be unhurt.

Cathbar strode to her and took her by the shoulder, but when he spoke his voice was cold. 'That was a stupid thing you did, girl. Stupid and dangerous: it put us all at risk. I gave you that sword to protect yourself: not to run into fights you can't win. If there are more battles ahead you follow my orders, do you hear?'

Elspeth's flushed face had turned white, but she nodded.

'Good,' Cathbar said. 'Now, we can't ask these dead men whether they are in league with Loki but we can see what you've rescued.'

He was lying curled on the ground where the robbers had abandoned him: a young boy, dressed only in overshirt and leggings, with rags tied around his feet instead of boots. He curled himself up tighter as they approached, shaking with muffled sobs. Elspeth knelt down beside him.

'Don't fear,' she said in Dansk. 'The men have gone, and we won't hurt you.'

Slowly the boy raised his head. He was about seven or eight years old, Edmund guessed; thin and wiry-looking. His face was streaked with dirt under a mop of light, unruly hair. His eyes, still wide with fear, looked very dark against his pale skin.

'We want to help you,' Elspeth told him. 'Do you have any people we can take you to? Your family?'

The boy shook his head, moving his lips as if feeling for the right words. When he spoke it was in a terrified whisper.

'No one . . . they're all gone. Lost in the fire.'

Elspeth had instinctively put out her hand to him. At his words she drew it back as if the touch had burned her, and her eyes filled with tears. Edmund saw her lips move: *Ioneth!*

'This is *his* doing,' she said fiercely, turning to Edmund. 'He's killed them – burned everything – just as he did to . . .' She turned back to the boy, who was still watching her with huge, frightened eyes.

'Come with us,' she told him, her voice gentle again. 'We'll find a safe place for you.'

'With us!' exclaimed Cluaran, behind them. 'For how long?'

'Until we find someone to take him in,' Elspeth replied hotly. 'We can't leave him!'

'We can't take him far, either,' Cluaran said. 'Back to the road, perhaps. His people, if he has any, live close by: he can't have walked any distance with those rags on his feet. And we have very far to go, Elspeth. A child will slow us down.'

'Then leave me here with him!' Elspeth retorted.

The child's face was starting to crumple. Edmund felt a rush of compassion for the little waif. 'I agree with Elspeth,' he said. 'We can't leave him alone: he's too young, and the bandits could come back.'

'Just until we find someone to take him, then,' said Cathbar. After a moment, Cluaran nodded.

It was close to morning – already the sky was lighter, though the faint moon was masked by scudding clouds. They had taken the boy back to their campsite, but none of them felt able to sleep again, so Edmund and Cluaran took their bows and went hunting, leaving Elspeth and Eolande to care for the child, while Cathbar kept guard.

'Do you think the boy lives here, in the forest?' Edmund asked, as he and Cluaran made their way through the ash-dusted trees on the unburned side of the clearing.

'If he did, he could be useful to us: show us where he's come from, and perhaps where the fire started.'

Edmund was shocked. 'Is that all you can think of – how he can help us? He needs the most help himself!'

'And we'll give it.' Cluaran's tone was serious. 'We'll find his parents, if they're to be found – and if not, there will be those who'll take him in. But he'll not be the last orphan we meet, Edmund. If we can't find Loki – if we can't stop him – the world will be full of orphans soon enough.' He walked in silence for a while, then turned back to Edmund. 'And our first step is not to die of hunger ourselves. So get busy, lad, and find us a deer.'

It was only rabbits that they found, but they came back in the pale light before sunrise with three of them, enough for a good-sized breakfast. Elspeth and Cathbar had a fire going in the centre of the clearing, with a trench scratched around it in the dirt to keep it from spreading. No more snow had fallen, and sitting around the small blaze, toasting his meat on two sticks, Edmund felt some of the chill leave him.

The boy was fast asleep, curled up as close to the fire as he could safely get. He had told Elspeth a little about himself before he slept: his name was Wulfstan – Wulf – and he did not live in the forest. His parents were traders, Elspeth said.

'He said they travelled and sold things, and they came through the forest some days ago. I think they visited settlements among the trees. It was hard to understand him; he was very scared – but I think he may not even be from around here. He doesn't seem to know the language well.'

They had brought the broken pieces of Wulf's handcart with them. It had contained nothing but a blanket, a water flask and some food supplies; most of them ruined by their spill in the dirt. 'He said he took the cart and ran when the fire started,' Elspeth explained.

'We'll find his people,' Cathbar said gruffly. 'Or find what happened to them.'

The boy woke while they were scattering the fire, and ate his share of the rabbit with a speed that suggested he had not eaten for days. His terror seemed to have lessened: he looked warily at Edmund and the two men, but spoke to them readily enough.

'You killed the bad men,' he said to Cathbar, through a mouthful of meat. 'I stay with you now.'

Edmund saw what Elspeth had meant about Wulf's speech: he spoke Dansk with an odd, lilting accent, as though the language were strange to him, and sometimes looked blank when he was asked questions. But he had clearly taken to Elspeth, and when she rose to fetch her blanket from the tree where it had been airing, he jumped to his feet, still chewing, to help her roll it up.

'I can help,' he insisted. 'Let me, Elsbet!'

Elspeth, smiling, moved aside. To Edmund's surprise, the child rolled the bulky cloth quite neatly. Wulf was clearly used to life on the road; perhaps he might not slow them so very much. But he was thinly dressed for winter. His overshirt was ragged and far too large for him: it slipped over his shoulder as he worked, showing a thin metal chain around his neck. The thing looked poorly made, but Wulf pulled his shirt protectively over it, and Edmund remembered with a shudder that the bandits had been preparing to kill the child to get it.

Elspeth had seen where he was looking. 'He told me that little chain came from his father,' she whispered to him. 'It's all he has left.' And her eyes darkened with pain.

They moved off not long after sunrise, heading into the path of burned trees. Some still had branches attached at crazy angles; others had been stripped bare by the fire and stood like the spears of a ghostly army. Many others had fallen. The ground was covered in ash, rising in clouds around their feet at every step, and a haze hung in the air above them, blotting out the sky: there was no colour but grey. Elspeth kept close to the little boy, and Cathbar and Cluaran were talking in low voices. For the first time in days, Edmund found himself walking beside Eolande. The Fay woman paid him no attention, but to his astonishment he saw that her normally expressionless face was full of sorrow. From time to time she held out a hand to one of the trees, touching its bark with the light caress of a mother afraid to wake a sleeping child.

'Are they . . . will any of them grow back?' he asked her, but Eolande just looked at him vaguely, as if his voice were no more than a bird-call.

The damage to the trees grew worse as they walked on. Soon, the stripped trunks became stubs no more than man-high; then low stumps, their tops smeared with white ash. Around their feet the ash was now ankle-deep. At the front of the party, Cluaran and Cathbar stopped.

'This was no fire set by bandits, although they may have taken advantage of those that managed to escape,' Cluaran said, pointing.

It was a hundred paces ahead of them, but clearly visible through the stumps: a great circle of blackness. The ash had piled like snow around its edges, drifting downwards into the pit with each breath of wind. It was wider than the black hole they had seen in Grufweld's forest, and there were no stumps around it: the place had been a clearing when the fire hit it. The sad heaps of ashes within the circle gave way to charred wooden beams at the edge: this had once been a settlement.

Elspeth had come up beside him and stopped, her eyes wide with horror. Beside her, Wulf scuffed with his feet in the ash as if it were snow. Elspeth reached down to touch something among the blackened debris at the circle's edge – then recoiled and turned away, grabbing at the child as she did so.

'Come away, Wulf,' she said, and her voice shook.

Edmund fought back sickness as he looked down. The thing Elspeth had seen was a charred human bone.

'It's still hot,' Cathbar muttered. From the drifting ash around the pit, wisps of smoke rose into the cold air. '*He* did this; no question of it.'

Elspeth was standing at the edge of the clearing with her back to them, her shoulders shaking as she gripped the boy's hand. Eolande stood beside them, rigid and stony-faced.

'How many . . . ?' Edmund could not get the words out. 'How many people would have been here?'

'Twenty, maybe,' Cluaran said softly. 'There's space for a dozen huts, I'd say.' He turned away. 'It would have been quick,' he muttered.

'He must have come down as a fireball, and then . . .' Cathbar looked around. 'Where did he go then?'

No path had been smashed through the trees. The black, levelled stumps stretched around them in all directions, giving way to taller trunks in the far distance.

'Edmund?' Cluaran called – but Edmund was already searching: casting his mind around for any sign; any flicker of life. Nothing. Apart from themselves, it seemed that the whole forest was dead. He cast further, finding only a few small creatures hiding in deep burrows or fled into water. 'I'm sorry,' he said. 'There's nobody.'

Elspeth had come over to him again, the child trailing behind her. 'We should look for Wulf's parents,' she said. She bent down to the boy. 'Wulf,' she said, 'can you remember anything about where your family was when the fire started?'

The boy thought. 'There was a river,' he said.

Edmund cast his eyes back to the creatures that had been looking at the water: a small bird, perching nervously on a clump of reeds; a vole or water rat, submerged to the nose, watching the bubbles and flecks of white ash as they floated past its whiskers. He opened his eyes.

'It's this way,' he said.

They found a stream-bed first, dried to a channel of cracked mud. Further along the mud became sticky, interspersed with a few damp pebbles, but they had not yet reached water when they came to the remains.

There were two heaps of ash, at the stream's edge, one of them covering a blackened end of wood that had recognisably been a plank. Edmund froze, as he spotted several teeth littering the ash piles. He also noticed that the ground was speckled with streaks and blobs of dull colour.

'Metal,' said Cluaran, kneeling to look at the blobs closely. 'This might have been a brooch or ring: brass, with a blue stone. That long one could have been a knife: cheap ware, to have melted so easily.' He stepped back. 'They must have been here to trade with the forest dwellers,' he said, 'and the fire caught them before they could reach the river.'

Wulf was staring at the little heaps in silence. These must have been his father's wares, Edmund thought, and wondered at the child's calmness. Elspeth moved close to Wulf as if trying to comfort him, but the boy did not move or cry: he seemed not to understand.

The trees at the stream's edge were burned stubs as far as they could see. As they made their way along the channel again, every fallen trunk in the distance filled Edmund with dread – but they made no more sickening discoveries.

The mud in the stream-bed became sluggish liquid, then a trickle of water. The endless ash beneath their feet began to mix itself with brown earth . . . and then Cluaran stopped with an audible breath of relief, and Edmund followed his gaze upwards to see undamaged branches, already in bud, at the top of a blackened trunk. At the same moment, he heard the distant noise of water flowing over stone.

He found himself almost running as they followed the sound. And then it was ahead of them: a real river, not wide but deep; the trees on the far bank untouched by the fire.

It was Eolande who reached the water first. She had been walking at the back, so silently that Edmund had forgotten her, but at the sight of the river she gave a cry – the first sound they had heard from her in days – and rushed to kneel at the bank. She dipped her hands in the water and threw a shower of gleaming drops over her head and face. Edmund saw now that she was covered with a white film of ash – all of them were. Cluaran put a dusty hand on his mother's shoulder.

'Let's follow it till we're clear of this damnable ash; then we can all wash.' The river-water made trails like tears down Eolande's cheeks, but she looked up at him almost with a smile.

Edmund walked with Elspeth and Wulf along the river, under trees still in bud. Everyone's spirits had lifted with the return of life around them.

They reached a bend where the river widened with a shallow beach on the outside bank, and gratefully stopped to wash. Wulf showed an unexpected modesty, wriggling away and blushing when Elspeth tried to help him take off his overshirt.

'You're a girl!' he protested.

In the end, Elspeth and Eolande moved a little upriver to wash, and Edmund stayed with Wulf, along with Cluaran and Cathbar. The boy undressed readily enough once Elspeth had gone, but he wanted no help, and still seemed to avoid the others' gaze. Glancing at him as they knelt at the water's edge, Edmund was shocked to see a livid slash across the boy's chest – a recently healed scar, dark red against his pale skin.

'How did you do that?' he blurted out. The boy ducked his head and covered his chest with his thin arms, and Edmund fell silent, rather abashed at having pried. But he could not help looking at Wulf with a new curiosity. Tough and self-possessed as he seemed to be, the child had clearly not had an easy life. Had an animal gored him?

They scrubbed the ash from their hair and skin, shivering in the cold, and jumped up and down on the bank to warm themselves, banging their dusty clothes on tree trunks before putting them back on. With the grime removed, the boy looked less of a waif: still painfully thin, but strong and wiry, with a pale, freckled face and sharp blue eyes. His hair was drying out to a light red-gold, though it was still wild, and his clothes were beggarly. The rags around Wulf's feet had been holding together the remains of shoes so thin that the leather was ripped under both soles. His overshirt, though wool, was so coarsely woven that the wind could blow through it: Edmund draped his own fur cloak over the boy's shoulders, ashamed that he had not thought to do it before. Even the necklet that the boy so treasured was a cheap thing, made of iron, probably, and so short that it was more like a collar. But when Edmund touched the chain as he was fastening his cloak about Wulf's neck, the boy squirmed away.

Wulf came back to let Edmund finish fixing the cloak; his pleasure in the well-made garment was obvious. When Elspeth and Eolande rejoined them, he was showing it off to Cathbar, lifting his feet carefully to keep its hem clear of the ground.

Elspeth looked at Edmund with shining eyes, putting a protective arm round the little boy.

'That was good of you,' she said.

They agreed to spend the night by the river, and head back to the road at daybreak and travel south again, towards Varde, where the other forest fire had been reported. It wasn't much of a lead but it was all they had and they desperately needed to pick up Loki's trail again. 'The goatherd on the road spoke of unrest and fighting in the south, too,' Cluaran said, 'and I'll wager that's a sign of Loki. It was always his way to set men against one another.'

The air was clear, and the low sun dazzled Edmund. The budding branches, and the blue sky above, put all of them in good spirits: even Eolande spoke a little.

Just before they reached the road, a change in the wind brought them a familiar, choking smell, and all conversation died.

Some freak gust had brought the forest fire to the very edge of the road. Suddenly they were walking through bare, blackened trunks again, and when they emerged on to the trodden dirt of the track, a gust of ash came out with them.

At the road's edge, someone had set up a marker, carved out of wood so blackened that at first sight Edmund mistook it for a burned stump. It was large, almost Wulf's height, and following the child as he ran to inspect it, Edmund saw that a design had been crudely carved into it and rubbed with something white – ash maybe – to make it stand out.

'It's a shrine, I think,' Elspeth said. 'Can you tell who it shows?'

'Can't you?' Edmund asked, surprised. 'It's Christians who set up roadside shrines, isn't it?' His mother's people marked sacred sites: springs, or ancient trees. He could not imagine any place less holy than the desolation they had just left.

'We wouldn't use burned wood!' Elspeth's tone was shocked. 'And this is no saint's picture.'

Edmund peered closer. 'It must be a local god,' he said. It was horribly appropriate here, he thought. The crude image showed a man's head, narrow-eyed and grinning. Lines shot out all around the head, like a stylised image of the sun's rays. And the hair and beard were shown as rows of sharp points, like teeth, or horns.

Or like flames.

CHAPTER SIX

Aagard shifted uncomfortably in his seat, watching the woman's face across the carved wooden table.

'They're pursuing an enemy they cannot see, and with no certainty that they can fight him,' he finished. 'I'm sorry to bring such ill news.'

Branwen, Queen of Sussex, shook her head.

'Not so ill,' she said. 'You tell me my son is alive and unhurt, when I'd feared he was dead.' She gave him a wan smile. 'I know my debt to you, Master Aagard. Beotrich told me it was you who saved Edmund when his ship was wrecked. Now you've restored him to me again.'

Aagard marvelled at the queen's composure. He had written to her before, to give her the terrible news that her son had been taken by the dragon, but this was the first time he had seen her. With her brown hair and eyes she looked very little like her pale son; only in her quiet manner, and a certain cast of her head, was there a resemblance.

'But you've not come here just to give me news of Edmund, have you?' she said. 'Welcome though it is.'

'No,' Aagard admitted. 'King Beotrich is sending emissaries to all the kingdoms on this island.' He drew a deep breath. 'To warn you to prepare for war.'

Branwen listened as he told her the news they had received several days ago: tales of armed men rampaging through Daneland and Saxony, burning all in their path.

'Beotrich sent scouts to Saxony to check the truth of the rumours. They met a stream of vagrants, many of them women and children, all driven from their homes. These people told the same story: bands of men had fallen on their villages without warning, destroying all that they found. They would arrive in a troop, the villagers said, and attack without any order given. Some said they sang as they marched towards them, and laughed as they killed.'

The queen's eyes were wide with horror. 'Armies of madmen . . .' she whispered.

'Armies driven by Loki,' Aagard said. 'In the time he has been free of his prison, he has spread his poison far and wide by being in many places at once. He draws men to him, and binds them with their own desires, to do his will. That was how he nearly escaped, a hundred years ago.'

'And how he enslaved my brother,' Branwen said softly. 'Beotrich told me of that, as well.' She blinked away tears. 'And you think he's sending an army here?'

'I'm sure of it,' he told her. 'We know that some of these

men have reached the port towns and taken their ships. Already, we hear of attacks on the northern coast.'

'But why here, when Loki was bound in the Snowlands?'

'I cannot see into his mind,' Aagard said. 'But I can guess the shape of his thoughts. He knows that these kingdoms joined forces against him a hundred years ago, and that we still oppose him. He seeks revenge on us all.'

Branwen rose to her feet. 'Then we must band together again to defeat him,' she declared. 'My husband, Heored, is in the north with most of his men, aiding his cousin of Northumbria against marauders from Gwynedd, a long-held enemy. I'll send word to him of the growing threat. I know he'll return as soon as he hears from me, and join our strength to yours.'

She saw him to the door herself, dismissing her guards, and stood with her hand raised in farewell as he rode away. Aagard hoped that her messenger to Heored would make haste – and that the other kings would be as prompt to respond to the danger. With enough men along the coast, they might hold off the armies that Loki sent against them.

But what of the demon himself? For days now, Aagard had not been able to glimpse the fiery presence in his visions.

'He is everywhere and nowhere,' he muttered as he rode. 'And when he does choose to show himself – what can Elspeth do?'

Elspeth's hand had been throbbing all day. But there was still no sign of the glowing light that heralded the crystal sword's appearance, and Ioneth's voice had fallen silent again: try as she might, she could catch not a whisper of it inside her head. After all the days of travelling and searching, they were no closer to finding Loki. The ugly shrine by the roadside had seemed to taunt her, bringing the demon's burning face before her eyes again, but Edmund was right: it could only be some local god. Loki *had* walked in the forest, she was sure of it – but there was no way of telling where he was now.

Elspeth's frustration was tinged with relief. What could she do even if they found him, if Ioneth had not returned?

Once she had thought she heard the low voice again. After she had rescued the boy, Wulf, she had held out her hand to him and heard that his family were gone – and for a moment, Ioneth had cried out in her head and burned in the hand that touched him. She knew why. The child had lost his parents just as Ioneth had lost hers, taken by the same monster. Elspeth had vowed at that moment to protect the boy until they found a place of safety for him. It was some comfort, if their mad quest was foundering, to have this small, manageable responsibility.

Wulf had been holding her hand as they walked, but she had loosed it when the throbbing became too uncomfortable. Edmund, walking alongside, took the boy's other hand instead, and Elspeth smiled at him. He had not had to come with her: he had a wealthy home to return to in Sussex – a kingdom, in fact. She still had to stifle a laugh at the thought of Edmund, her quiet, thoughtful friend, commanding armies as his father must do. And here he was, cold and tired in an impossible search, without even a cloak to his back. Wulf was still wearing his thick fur, swathed in it almost to his feet, while Edmund was wrapped like a beggar in his sleeping blanket.

'I'm heated with all this walking,' she told him impulsively. 'Would you take my cloak for a while?'

'You won't stay hot for long,' Edmund warned her – but he allowed himself to be convinced, and took the heavy fur cloak. Feeling the cold wind cutting through her woollen sleeves, Elspeth realised how much he must have needed it. The sun was already high in a clear sky: it would get no warmer today.

The trees began to grow closer until they were walking down a narrow passage between brown trunks. Elspeth found the gloom under the trees oppressive, and could not forget the choking dust and charred stumps of their last venture into the forest. She stayed close to Edmund, whose spirits never seemed to waver, while Wulf held on to her arm. The throbbing pain in her right hand seemed a permanent part of her now, always there on the edge of her awareness; every now and then becoming fiercer, like lightning streaking up her arm. She wondered for the hundredth time whether it was a sign that Ioneth was growing stronger, and listened in vain for the voice inside her head.

'Edmund,' she said at last, giving up the attempt, 'do you think we'll ever find him?'

Edmund did not ask who she meant. He was silent a long time before answering. 'I don't know,' he admitted. 'It seems impossible sometimes. We can't track him, not as you'd track a brigand – we're just following stories and rumours. But I *feel* that we're close to him here, and I know Cluaran does too.'

The trees grew thicker and darker. Twice they found wooden shrines at the edge of the forest path, one showing another version of the bearded man with the sun's rays behind him, and one with a crude image of a hand surrounded by the same rays.

'Do you think these are new?' Edmund wondered, inspecting the second shrine. It did have a recently cut look, Elspeth thought.

'Menobert said there were new religions springing up everywhere.'

'It's a sign of the times, like Menobert said,' Cathbar put in. 'When there's trouble and danger, everyone looks for something new to believe in. It doesn't matter what.'

'No one seems to be visiting the shrines, though,' Elspeth pointed out. They had been heading south on the road for half a day or more, without meeting a living soul.

Cluaran led the way, with Eolande beside him. He seemed resigned to Wulf's continued presence, and Elspeth made sure that the child stayed close to her, determined that he should not be thought of as a burden. She was reassured to find that Wulf had no trouble matching their pace and never complained of tiredness, though his rag-bound shoes slid about on the leaf-mulch underfoot. When they stopped for the night, it was clear that he was determined to be useful. He ran deep into the trees to collect firewood, and returned dragging a branch longer than himself and so thick that Elspeth was amazed he could lift it at all. While they struggled to break his prize into sections, the boy ran off again.

'Don't go too far, Wulf!' Elspeth called. 'It's getting dark.'

'Leave the boy,' Cluaran told her. 'You can see he's at home in the woods; he won't come to harm.' The confidence in his voice cheered Elspeth: Wulf was becoming accepted as a member of their group.

Wulf returned at sunset, very muddy and holding out the front of his overshirt filled with mushrooms. Cluaran inspected them and pronounced them edible, his voice filled with surprise. 'Who taught you to know mushrooms, boy?' he demanded. Wulf laughed delightedly, but did not answer.

They cooked the mushrooms with wild onions in Cluaran's cooking pan, and shared out the stew with the last of their bread, sitting around the fire. The bitter wind had died down, or was stopped by the trees, and looking around at the flame-lit faces of her friends, Elspeth felt an unexpected peace. Tonight there was no ravening wildfire, destroying all it touched; their fire was a kindly thing, casting a small circle of warmth and light against the darkness.

'This is good food,' said Eolande, and Elspeth was startled by the sound of the Fay woman's voice. Cluaran offered his mother more of the stew, while Wulf beamed with pride.

Edmund, wrapped in his own cloak once again, raised his water flask to the boy like a cup, in friendly salute. The ring of firelight was a haven, Elspeth thought, if only for one night. While the circle lasted, nothing would harm them.

Cluaran banked the fire at last, and they lay down to sleep in its mild glow. Wulf lay between Elspeth and Edmund, wrapped in the blanket from Eikstofn, and smiled as he slept.

Elspeth woke suddenly in the night. For a moment she remembered other midnight alarms and her skin prickled, but there was no sound or movement. The fire's embers still warmed her feet, and all around her was soft breathing. She relaxed, trying to recover the fragments of her dream. She had been Ioneth again, the child of the ice caves; not running or frightened this time but sitting at home with her mother and sisters, singing and learning to weave a mat, the melody winding in and out with the to-and-fro of the shuttle. A good dream – though Elspeth had never known her own mother, nor learned to weave. *Were you skilled at it, Ioneth?* she asked inside her head, and wondered if there had been a whispered reply, too faint to catch. The song continued to wind around her thoughts, and she hummed a snatch of it, thinking she would sing it to Wulf in the morning.

Wulf! With a shock, Elspeth felt the empty ground beside her. Edmund was a gently snoring mound a little further away, but between them was only a crumpled blanket. The boy had gone.

Elspeth pulled herself up, looking about in panic. A bright quarter-moon showed the empty road stretching away to both sides. She caught a glimpse of bright hair.

'Wulf!' she hissed, angry and weak with relief at the same time. 'Come back here!' But the boy had already skipped back behind one of the trees.

'Wulf!' she called, louder now. The only answer was a distant rustling as Wulf made his way deeper into the forest. With a sigh, she wrapped her cloak more closely around her and followed him, still calling.

There was no clear track through the trees, and the moonlight that filtered through the branches turned the undergrowth into a mesh of shifting gleams and shadows. Elspeth pushed on in the direction Wulf had taken, blundering into thickets and cursing under her breath as she barked her shin on a hidden stump. There was no sign of the boy up ahead, and after a few more paces she stopped and listened for him. There it was, a soft footfall over to her right. She turned to follow the sound, hoping that she would be able to find her way back. At the same moment she heard something else behind her.

There were bears in the forest, the pedlar Menobert had told them, and great hoofed beasts, elk and aurochs, that could outrun a man and trample him to death. She had not even thought to pick up the new sword. 'Wulf!' she cried desperately. Prickly branches pulled at her as she forced her way on.

A bush just ahead of her shook with laughter. A small hand pulled aside the branches and Wulf's face poked out, pale with moonlight and glowing with mischief.

'I found something, Elsbet!' he crowed. 'I'll show you – come.'

'No, Wulf!' Elspeth tried to sound stern. 'We must go back right now!' She wondered if she could tell what direction to take. She tugged at Wulf's hand, and the boy scrambled out of the bushes.

'Let me show you, Elsbet!' he pleaded, pulling at her hand. 'It's so funny!'

There was a sudden movement in the trees behind them. Elspeth wheeled to find Cluaran striding towards her, his face thunderous.

'Back now – both of you!' was all he said.

Wulf seemed to know when he was beaten. He shrugged and turned back at once, running past Cluaran as if he knew the way perfectly, slipping through the prickly branches with ease.

'I expected more sense from you, Elspeth,' Cluaran told her. 'Wulf is a child – but what were *you* thinking of, losing yourself in the forest at night?'

'Wulf ran off,' Elspeth said defensively. 'I went after him to bring him back.'

'And never thought to wake anyone?' Cluaran demanded. 'Your fondness for the boy is addling your brain! What use is this journey – is all that we're doing here – if you get yourself lost or killed?'

87

That was the reason for his anger, Elspeth realised suddenly. When Wulf had run off into the trees earlier that evening Cluaran had been unworried: it was the danger to *her* that had scared him.

Or not so much her, as the fear of losing Ioneth again.

Half abashed and half angry, she said no more while they made their way back to the camp. Cluaran had shown friendship to her before – of course he had, she told herself – but never this much concern. This must be because she was his last link with his beloved. She had told Cluaran that Ioneth was still inside her head – and it was true, even if the voice no longer spoke to her. Those dreams she had been having, of the small girl in the ice caves, they must come from Ioneth. A scene from tonight's dream came vividly back to her: sitting at the loom, helping to push the heavy shuttle back and forth. The melody from her dream filled her head.

Cluaran gave an exclamation, and she realised that he was staring at her. 'What are you singing?' he asked.

'Oh, just a tune,' she said, embarrassed. 'I heard it somewhere.'

He shot an odd, intense look at her, but said no more.

Wulf was waiting for them when they reached the camp, unabashed and unharmed by the adventure. It was almost daybreak, so Cluaran busied himself scattering the remains of the fire and Elspeth helped the boy to roll up his bedding while the others roused themselves. The morning dawned grey and cold, and they moved on as soon as there was light to see by.

Wulf was the only one of the party in high spirits. The boy ran on ahead to inspect another wayside shrine and look for squirrels, and chattered about them to Elspeth and Edmund. Cluaran stayed close to Eolande; both of them seemed to have lost the pleasure they had taken in the forest the day before. Elspeth was still out of humour with Wulf for last night's escapade, and even Edmund was tense, answering Wulf in very few words. It seemed that a cloud hung over all of them.

'Have you noticed how quiet it is?' Edmund asked Elspeth after a while. 'No birds.'

He was right. When they moved off at dawn the trees above them had been full of birdsong. Now there was none at all.

The path widened, and abruptly emerged from the trees to join a larger road, running towards the south-east. They stood at the roadside, staring.

The mud of the road, and some of the field beside it, had been churned up by men's feet; many of them. There were dropped hunks of bread in the ditch along the road's near side, and a torn piece of grey cloth lay in the mud, stained with what looked like blood. Further along, at a spot where the travellers seemed to have made camp, the roadside trees were scarred and blackened, their lower branches ripped off. A young sapling had been torn up by the roots and partly burned, and the rubbish included smashed barrels and animal carcasses, some of them half-eaten.

Cathbar bent to look at the footprints. 'I reckon they stopped here yesterday; maybe last night,' he said. 'They won't be close enough to hear us now, but they'll be camped somewhere ahead of us. Several dozen of them, I'd say: look how they've covered the road.'

'Who do you think they are?' Edmund asked. 'Would bandits walk in such a big group?

'Not normally, but these are not normal times and I'll wager these bandits are certainly more than they seem.' He frowned at the pile of debris, and the slaughtered animals. 'I think we should go carefully,' he said.

They kept to the ditched side of the road, walking in single file; accompanied all the way by the massed footprints and the scraps that the men had dropped. Then Cathbar, in the lead, stopped with a muffled curse. In the ditch ahead of him, a man lay face down.

Elspeth ran forward, hearing the others close behind her. But Cathbar was shaking his head as they came up.

'He must have got careless, for all his talk of caution,' he said heavily. 'I'm sorry we weren't with him.'

The dead man was the pedlar, Menobert. Cathbar had turned him over, and he lay now with his eyes open, a surprised expression on his face and a great wound in his chest.

The pedlar's murderers had not even robbed him. The purse of coins still hung from his belt. And beside his body his pack lay split open, slashed by sword-strokes, its cloth packages and tin bracelets spilling into the mud.

CHAPTER SEVEN

The snow had melted, but the ground was too hard to dig a grave for Menobert, even if they had had the tools. They collected stones from the pasture walls that the bandits had destroyed in their passing, and Edmund helped Cathbar and Cluaran to raise a cairn over the pedlar's body by the roadside.

'It's the least we could do for him,' the captain said, as they finished the work. 'The first friend we met in this land, he was – and a good companion on the road.'

They stood for a moment by the makeshift grave. Elspeth had thrown back her fur hood, gazing intently down on the stones, and Edmund heard her murmur something under her breath. She covered her head again as they moved on. 'The prayer for the dead,' she told Edmund shortly. 'He was a Frankish man – a Christian, like my father.'

She lapsed into silence. There had been neither prayers nor a burial marker for Elspeth's father, Edmund remembered.

They followed the road for most of the next two days. Edmund found its emptiness oppressive: there were no other travellers, only the muddy track, churned with the feet of the men who had gone before them, strewn with their leavings and lined on each side with the damage they had done.

Once, on the second day, he did find some human eyes to look through, over to the east, deep in the forest. There were women and children among them, Edmund reported, and no sense of immediate threat. Cluaran wanted to keep going but Cathbar insisted that they needed supplies, and asked Edmund to lead the way into the forest.

It was a tiny community: not more than half a dozen houses, a flock of goats and a barley patch in a clearing. The people were frightened and suspicious: bands of brigands had been passing that way for several days or more, they said, tearing down trees and shooting arrows at anything that moved. The men had crashed through the forest only ten feet away from them, hunting some poor animal, but had not found their homes. A day or two later, hearing a great uproar in the distance, two of their young men had ventured out of the forest and met fleeing people on the road: families who spoke of a whole village destroyed, and bandits who killed for the sake of killing. The next time armed bands tramped into the forest the settlers had abandoned their homes and hidden in the trees, not daring to move or speak until the men had passed.

'Keep to the forest paths, if you must travel!' one of the women begged them, looking fearfully at Wulf, who sat cross-legged at their feet, shredding the leaves from a twig. 'There's nothing but murder on the roads. You can't take the poor child into such danger!' She put out a hand to stroke the child's red-gold hair; he endured her touch indifferently, not looking up from his task.

Cluaran gave the woman an appraising look. 'Mistress,' he said, 'we must go on, but the child need not. We found him abandoned, and have been searching for a safe haven for him. Perhaps you . . . ?'

'No!' Wulf was on his feet, the stick cast aside. 'No! No! I must stay with Elsbet!'

The forest woman smiled and shook her head, while Elspeth soothed Wulf.

Cluaran shrugged in defeat. 'If he must come with us, he must,' he grumbled.

The forest dwellers offered the travellers the hospitality of their branch-built huts for the night, saying that it was too dangerous to travel by dark. Edmund was glad to sleep under a roof again, though on a hard floor next to two snoring boys. But he could tell his hosts were uncomfortable at the presence of strangers. He didn't blame them. It sounded as if Loki was doing a fine job of encouraging men to murder and plunder. They had exchanged their smoked meat and bread for a silver coin, and allowed the guests to fill their water bottles at the stream beneath their shrine – but they looked askance at the two men, and spoke little even to Edmund. When the party left at first light the next day, the forest dwellers were clearly relieved to see them go: even the woman who had taken an interest in Wulf stood in her doorway only a moment to bid them farewell. Edmund, walking at the back of the party, looked back once: the little circle of huts had already merged into the forest, as still and silent as the trees themselves.

He sent out his sight more and more often as they returned to the road, but for all the massed footprints and debris around them, there was no more sign of human life.

Cathbar was leading them now. The road had veered westwards, and the hills which might hide an army were clearly visible ahead of them. The track began to climb and dip, making their progress slower. As they toiled up a particularly steep slope in the dull morning light, the captain halted them.

'Something ahead, on the other side,' he said tersely.

Edmund checked the road ahead, finding nothing but a flock of crows. He borrowed the eyes of one as it scanned the rutted ground for carrion, then hopped forward and pecked . . .

'Oh,' he said.

It had been a ferocious battle. The road, and the field alongside it, were churned to indistinguishable mud, and strewn with men's bodies.

'They're all dead!' he gasped. 'We have to go some other way . . .'

'There is no other way,' Cathbar said, grim-faced.

The sight and the smell hit them together as they reached the top of the hill. Edmund gagged. Elspeth, suddenly white-faced, pulled Wulf to her side and covered his eyes, while he wriggled to get away.

'An uneven fight, I'd say.' Cathbar's voice was sombre as he swept the ghastly scene with a professional eye. 'Those in leather armour, look, there, and there – they have shields, and better swords. They're the foreign army, no doubt: some lord's men, by the look of them. Few of them dead, and many of the others; they'll be the victors here.'

'Then why haven't they buried their dead?' Edmund asked hoarsely.

Cathbar gave him a kindly look. 'It hits you like this, the first few times,' he said, 'but you get used to it. Come on – we must keep moving.'

He strode down the hill and began to pick his way through the bodies. Edmund looked at Elspeth, who was pale and wide-eyed. She moved closer to him, still clasping Wulf by the hand, and together they followed the captain.

'Look there,' Cathbar said to Edmund, pointing to the forest which lay to their right, a little way back from the road. 'See all those footmarks? The losers ran – tried to hide themselves in the trees – and the foreigners ran after them. That's why they're not here now.'

He was talking to distract them from the horror at their feet, Edmund knew, and he was grateful – but something had caught his eye; something on the shield of one of the dead men. Revulsion made him faint and dizzy, but he stopped to look closer.

'When they've killed all the enemies they can reach, they'll come back to honour their fallen comrades,' Cathbar was saying. 'Unless they're barbarians, of course, with no sense of respect . . .'

'No. They'll come back.' Edmund's voice sounded far away to his own ears. He gestured at the shield beside the dead warrior. Instead of a boss, it had the image of a bird incised in the steel: a great seabird with outstretched wings. Edmund fumbled at his throat to reveal the brooch he always wore beneath his furs: the same bird, cast in silver.

'He was a thane of Sussex,' he said. 'These are my father's men.'

'What are they doing here?' Elspeth demanded.

Edmund had been asking himself the same question. He had not seen his father for two years: the thought of meeting him here was like a strange dream. 'I don't know,' he said.

They had walked over a league from the battlefield, and were resting at the foot of a steep hill that offered some protection from the evening wind. Wulf was feeding sticks to the fire: alone of all the party, the child seemed unaffected by the horrors they had seen, and Edmund wondered again what he could have gone through in his short life. Cathbar and Cluaran were arguing about the route, both sounding more angry than was warranted, Edmund thought. Eolande had been hardest hit of all. She had moved rigidly through the slaughter, led by her son, until she stumbled, at the very edge, on the body of one of the Sussex dead: an older man, barrel-chested and grey-bearded. She had stood gazing at him as if turned to stone, until Cluaran dragged her away. She had refused all his attempts at comfort, and now sat alone with her head in her hands, keening softly to herself.

Cathbar's voice rose. 'I tell you it's only sense, man! He can give us protection – help us find the creature.'

'What makes you think he'd believe us?' Cluaran demanded. 'Or that he'd let his son go haring off after demons? We've no time to spend persuading him!'

'They're talking about your father,' Elspeth said to Edmund. 'Do you want to look for him?'

'Of course!' The answer burst from Edmund before he could stop himself. 'I mean . . .' he faltered. Elspeth was avoiding his eyes, and the joy he had felt at the thought of seeing his father suddenly seemed like disloyalty.

'Only if we can, without holding up the search,' he told her. 'Finding Loki is the most important thing.'

Elspeth sat silent for a moment, then looked up, her face serious. 'You know your father better than Cathbar,' she said. '*Would* he help us?'

Edmund hesitated. How well did he know his father, in fact? He had last seen Heored leaving for battle: a stern man, taking it for granted that his wife and son would uphold their duty to his kingdom for however long he was away.

What would he say to a son who now followed a different duty?

Raised voices broke in on his thoughts. Eolande was on her feet, pulling away from Cluaran, who held her by the arm. 'I cannot!' she wailed. 'I can't see it again. Cluaran – how can you make me? Let me go!'

'Go *where*?' Cluaran shouted. 'You think you can survive on your own out there! Cathbar – hold her! Help to make her see reason!'

'He's right, lady.' Cathbar had regained his usual tone of calm authority. 'We'll be fine if we stay together. This is no country for a lone traveller. Sleep now; we'll look for a safer path in the morning.'

'You think I care for *safety*?' Eolande protested, but she was already weakening. Cathbar and her son led her back to the fire, and helped her to lie down.

While Cluaran covered his mother with the warmest of the furs and sat down to watch beside her, Cathbar began to shake out his own bedroll.

'Best if we all turn in,' he said, and Edmund felt tiredness wash over him like a wave.

He woke in the grey hour before dawn, suddenly and completely alert. Beside him, Elspeth was breathing deeply, with Wulf curled up near her. There was no birdsong, and he wondered what could have woken him. He raised himself on his elbow, and gasped. On the far side of the dying fire, Cluaran sat hunched and fast asleep – but the fur blanket next to him was empty. Eolande had gone.

There was a movement behind him, and he jumped up to see a figure darting away around the side of the hill. Edmund grabbed his cloak and started after her.

The Fay woman walked swiftly, as if she knew where she was going. Edmund broke into a run, calling her name. As he rounded the hill he saw where she must be heading: a small stand of trees, not a hundred feet away. *She's always been happier in the woods*, he remembered, and quickened his pace. 'Stop!' he panted, but Eolande gave no sign that she had heard him.

He caught up with her just as she reached the trees. When he grabbed her sleeve she turned and looked at him with a puzzled expression, as if she did not know him.

'Please,' Edmund said breathlessly, 'you must come back. It's not safe . . .'

Recognition filled Eolande's face, and she gave him a small, sad smile. 'You are kind, child,' she said. 'But it's no good. I must . . .'

Then she was staring over his shoulder, her eyes widening in fright. 'No!' she cried. 'Oh no . . . The murderers . . . Edmund, run!'

Edmund whirled. Three fur-clad men were running towards him, only a few paces away. He drew his dagger, lunging at the closest of them – and a fourth man stepped from behind the trees and pinioned his arms behind him.

Eolande had disappeared. Edmund struggled and yelled, hoping his voice might carry back to the camp, until one of his attackers stuffed a cloth into his mouth, nearly choking him. He kicked out, and saw a flash of grey, darting away behind the men's backs. It vanished around the hill as they knocked his feet from under him.

CHAPTER EIGHT

Elspeth woke with a start, shrill cries ringing in her ears. She threw out an arm for Wulf, her heart pounding. Ever since the child had refused to leave her, there had been a nagging fear at the back of her mind: how could she keep him safe, wilful as he was, among so many dangers?

But Wulf was sleeping peacefully, curled up on his blanket by her side. The cries came from outside the circle of firelight – from Eolande, running towards them.

'Edmund! Help him . . . don't let them take him!'

It was only then that Elspeth saw the empty space where Edmund had lain. Cathbar was already on his feet, his sword in his hand. Cluaran was rushing to his mother's side.

'We were under the trees . . .' she faltered, 'and bandits took him!'

Elspeth had scrambled to her feet. Cathbar was running, disappearing around the hill with a speed Elspeth had never seen in him before. Cluaran lingered only a moment longer, his arm around the weeping Eolande.

'You stay here!' he cried to Elspeth. 'Look after her, and the child. There may be more of them around.' He released Eolande. 'I'll come back,' he said, and raced away after Cathbar.

Eolande was standing as if frozen. There was a soft stirring as Wulf sat up.

'Where have they all gone?' he asked sleepily. 'Have they left us?'

He sounded merely interested, not fearful. Elspeth fought to control her voice. 'No! Edmund has been . . . has run into bandits. The others have gone to rescue him.' She turned to Eolande. 'What happened?' she demanded. 'Why were you away from the camp?'

'I was going to the forest, to walk in the trees again,' Eolande whispered. 'Edmund came after me . . . and then they were all around us.'

'How many of them? What did they do to Edmund?'

But Eolande stood in silence, avoiding Elspeth's eyes, while the tears ran unchecked down her face. Elspeth did not trust herself to speak to the woman again. 'Wulf,' she called, 'help me roll the blankets. We must be ready to leave quickly.'

They had made up the packs and were scattering the ashes of the fire when Cluaran returned.

'There are five of them,' he said, 'heading into the hills with Edmund. He's still alive – we saw him struggling. Cathbar's following them now. Elspeth, take Eolande and the boy back to the forest-dwellers. They'll give you shelter till we return. Cathbar and I will ambush the bandits as soon as they stop; then we'll find you in the forest.'

'I'll do nothing of the sort!' Elspeth flared. 'How could you think I'd turn my back on Edmund?'

'Stop throwing yourself into danger!' he flashed back. 'I can't . . . I will not let you risk your life needlessly.'

'I'll take no more risks than you,' Elspeth insisted. 'Let Eolande take Wulf back to the forest, if you think it's best.' Wulf clung to her hand, wailing, but she refused to look at him. 'I'm coming with you,' she told Cluaran. 'If you won't let me, I'll follow you.'

Cluaran sighed. 'Very well. But if we meet the bandits, you follow my orders, and Cathbar's. Understood?'

'I would like to come too,' said Eolande. Her voice was hoarse, but quite calm now. Both Elspeth and Cluaran turned to her in astonishment.

'It may be that I can help,' she said. 'It was my fault Edmund was taken.'

'And the child?' Cluaran demanded. 'We must move fast – there'll be no resting until I've found Cathbar again.'

'I can run!' Wulf piped.

Cluaran wasted no more time arguing. 'Come on, then,' he said. 'Stay with me, and keep your eyes open.'

He walked fast and silently, not looking back. Elspeth wished he would go even faster: she felt she could have run the whole way. Wulf trotted tirelessly beside her, apparently unconcerned about where they were going or why, so long as he did not have to return to the forest. Elspeth had explained to him that there was danger ahead, but not even concern for Edmund seemed to trouble the child's high spirits.

Eolande matched her son's pace easily, and was as silent as he was. Only when they reached a stand of trees, a little way into the next valley, did she speak.

'This is where it happened.'

'I know,' Cluaran said shortly. 'We found Edmund's knife on the ground. But no blood: it seems for once, these brigands didn't want to fight.'

'Why do you think they took him?' Elspeth asked. Cluaran only shook his head.

It was a question that Elspeth had not asked herself before, in her relief that Edmund was alive. But now it nagged at her. Edmund's captors could be one of the bands of bandits that roamed the country, possibly aligned with Loki. If this was the case then this could all be some kind of trap. Another one of Loki's tricks.

'So be it,' she said, half aloud. 'I will meet you head on.' Wulf looked up at her curiously, and she fell silent.

They were no longer on the road. Their path led them westwards between two hills, then curved around the base of the larger of the two. Cluaran halted them here. 'This is where I left Cathbar,' he said. 'Wait.'

Elspeth looked around while Cluaran examined the ground. They were in a valley backed by the two hills they had passed, facing a much steeper rise.

'This way,' Cluaran called. He kept his voice low, and Elspeth noticed for the first time how quiet it was. As Cluaran led them out across the valley's floor, she felt uncomfortably exposed, as if eyes might be looking down at them from every direction – but wherever she looked, nothing stirred.

At least they had clear tracks to follow: the men's booted feet had sunk deeply into the turf. One or two prints strayed outside the general ruck as if their owners had staggered – as a man might if he carried a struggling captive, Elspeth thought. But at the far side of the valley the ground grew stonier and their progress slowed. Elspeth watched Cluaran searching for prints from one patch of grass to the next, and fretted, wishing she had Edmund's skill to look for their quarry beyond her own sight.

Cluaran gave a sudden cry of triumph, and gestured to them to join him. Elspeth was the first to reach him. He was pointing down towards the rocks at his feet. 'Good man!' he exclaimed. 'Look, Elspeth – Cathbar has left us a marker.'

It was a rune roughly scratched out on a lichen-covered rock: a bird with outstretched wings and an arrowed beak. 'Edmund's white bird,' Cluaran said. 'It's pointing uphill, between those two ridges. Now we can make speed again!'

The sight of the little symbol raised Elspeth's spirits, and she let Wulf race her to the foot of the hill. The pass that Cathbar's marker had indicated gave on to another, higher ridge, where there was a track to follow. 'Keep your wits about you,' Cluaran warned. 'It's too quiet here. Something has scared the birds away.'

They discovered the reason for the silence all too soon. As they approached the ridge, the wind brought the grimly familiar taint of burning. Soon they were looking down into the next valley, and another ruined settlement.

Fire had ripped through the centre of the village, cutting a smouldering black swathe through the huts. The homes still standing at the settlement's edge had lost walls, or stood at crazy angles, roof-posts poking out of their thatch like broken bones. There was no movement – no sign of life at all.

'There's nothing we can do,' Cluaran muttered, supporting Eolande, who was white-faced and shaking.

'Do you think the men who took Edmund did this?' Elspeth asked.

'No – though they may belong to the same rabble. But it took more than five men to do this work.' He stared at the desolation below them, then turned back to the path. 'Come on – our way lies along the ridge.'

The track petered out after a while, but Cathbar had left them another bird-sign, its beak pointing towards the south-west, where a faint trail led along the hillside. The new path dipped, then climbed again among rocks. The coarse grass of the valley did not grow up here, and loose stones shifted under their feet. As the day wore on, Elspeth found her breath quickening and her legs moving more slowly, in spite of her fear for Edmund.

'We'll need to stop to find water soon,' Cluaran called. Elspeth wanted to protest, but it was true: the weather had turned warmer, making her sweat as she walked, and her water flask was nearly empty.

Halfway up the next hill Cluaran found one more marker, scratched into the dry earth. It was hastily done, but the bird's head pointed unmistakably upwards. The sight gave Elspeth fresh strength, and she ran ahead, leaving Cluaran and Eolande behind. Only the child kept pace with her: he seemed as agile as a goat, and never missed his footing, though the stones underfoot grew more treacherous as they climbed. They reached what seemed to be the top of the rise and Wulf, with a little whoop, ran ahead of her – and vanished.

Elspeth cried out in alarm, running the last few steps herself. Instead of a steep downward slope she found a shallow dip in the rock, leading to another, smaller rise. There was a little pool of water at one end of the dip: Wulf was lying by it, full-length, drinking greedily. Beside him, sitting on the ground, was Cathbar.

He raised a hand in greeting as the other two came up. 'I guessed you'd be here before too long,' he said; Elspeth heard relief in his voice.

He had tracked Edmund's kidnappers to an encampment west of here, he told them, on the other side of the hills. 'Edmund was on his feet, but closely guarded,' he said. 'Whoever they are, they're well-led. They've picked a hard position to attack, and posted sentries, so I couldn't get close. We'll have to make our move after dark.'

Cluaran looked up at the sun, not far past its zenith. 'We'll go as near as we can, then, and rest while we plan,' he said. 'It'll be no bad thing to get our strength back before we attack.'

Cathbar led them a little off the track. 'We're less likely to meet someone that way,' he told them. 'If they're the same men who burned that village we passed, I'd as soon not come across any of them unawares.'

They were heading downhill now; the ground was patched with green again, and below them a scrubby growth of hawthorn, huddled beneath an overhang in the hill, had put out its spring leaves. Approaching the bushes, Cathbar slowed and turned around, putting a finger to his lips.

'There's someone there,' he whispered.

At the same moment a figure burst out from the bushes and rushed at them. Cathbar threw himself to one side as a blade whipped past his head. Elspeth's left hand flew to her sword hilt – but the captain was already stepping back from his assailant, his arms spread wide.

'We mean no harm, mistress!' he cried.

She was a skinny young woman, pale-haired and freckled, seemingly not much older than Elspeth. She grasped a rusty strip of metal that looked as if it might have been a ploughshare. 'What do you want?' she demanded. Her voice was fierce, but she lowered the rusty blade as she looked at Elspeth, Eolande and Wulf.

'Nothing,' Elspeth told her. 'We're just travellers, looking for a safe place to rest.'

'Safe!' the young woman echoed bitterly. She ducked back into the bushes, and Elspeth heard a whispered conversation before she emerged again.

'You can share our shelter, if you've a mind to,' she said. 'Though there's not much room.'

The rocky overhang extended behind the bushes to form a shallow cave, only a few arm-spans deep and too low to stand upright. A woman, much older than the first, shifted to make space for them as they forced their way through the spiny branches. Beside her, stretched against the rock wall, lay a young man, his eyes closed, breathing raggedly. He had a bloodied bandage around his chest and his face was deathly pale.

'Come in and welcome,' the second woman said. Her face was lined with tiredness, though her brown eyes were bright. 'It's a bad time to be out on the road: there are murderers about. If you came through the hills, you'll have seen what they did to our village.'

Her name was Wyn, she told them, and the young man beside her was her son, Reinhard. 'He's sleeping, to recover his strength,' she said, but Elspeth saw Eolande, who had squatted down near the young man, catch Cluaran's eye and shake her head very slightly.

The armed men had come down the eastern road the day before, Wyn told them: a horde of them, shouting and singing.

There were rumours of a foreign army in the area, but when these men left the road, trampling on the freshly sown fields, and attacked their walls, the villagers heard them shouting to each other in Dansk.

'The men went out to stop them,' she said, her face still drawn with horror at the memory. 'There was some talk . . . the villains were shouting at our men to join them . . . and then they ran at them with their axes and swords.'

Most of the men were dead; her husband among them. The old folk, women and children had run for the hills while the murderers were setting fire to their houses, but she and her neighbour Sigrid had stayed to help some of the wounded escape.

'We saw four or five get away,' she said. 'And we brought Reinhard with us.' She turned to Cathbar. 'Did you pass by our village? Were those madmen still there? Was anyone stirring?'

'No sign of life that I could see,' Cathbar answered gravely. 'I'm sorry, mistress, that we did not stop to see if there were any there to help. We were following a companion of our own who was kidnapped – maybe by the same men.'

'Not by them,' the younger woman, Sigrid, said sharply. 'They were like wild dogs, not men. They wouldn't take prisoners.'

Wyn was sitting upright. 'We should go back,' she said. 'If the murderers are really gone, our neighbours will be returning – there'll be so much to do.'

'You're a fool.'

It was Eolande's voice. The Fay woman gazed stony-eyed at Wyn over the young man's unconscious form. 'What good can you do?' she demanded. 'Lay out the dead? They're lost to you! Your town is lost . . . your husband . . . What good is it to do anything?'

'What good would it do to stop?' the woman retorted. 'If my neighbours and friends have lost their men, they'll see them laid out decent, and at peace. And they're not all dead!' she added fiercely, reaching out to stroke her son's forehead.

Eolande stared at her a moment longer, then rose to her knees. 'He soon will be,' she murmured, and pushed her way out through the thorny thicket.

Cluaran threw a look of apology at the woman and followed his mother outside. Elspeth saw her own horror mirrored on Cathbar's face. Wyn bent over her son, her shoulders shaking, while the younger woman glared at them.

'I'm sorry,' Elspeth stammered. 'She didn't mean . . . We'd better go.' She took Wulf by the hand and dragged the child after her through the leaves.

'How could you say such a thing?' Cluaran was demanding.

'He could not hear,' Eolande said dully. 'He's gone beyond our voices. And why should she give herself hope, when there is none?'

'There's always hope,' Cluaran insisted. 'A skilled healer could bring him back.' His voice fell. 'There was a time when you would have tried.'

'There would be no point.' Eolande sounded almost pleading now. 'She's lost everything – and the boy would likely die, whatever I could do. Why keep fighting?'

'Would you say that if your own son lay there wounded?' Wyn had followed them out of the cave. 'Will you let him die, knowing that you might have saved him?' Her face was blotched with tears, but she held Eolande's gaze, not letting her look away. The Fay woman twisted her hands.

'I . . . I have some skills I might try,' she admitted at last. 'But there is so little hope . . .'

'Won't you at least try?' Wyn broke in. 'Do you think I'd turn away *any* hope – so much as a feather's worth? I'll fight for Reinhard while there's breath in my body.'

'But if he should die,' Eolande whispered.

The woman's eyes blazed. 'Then I'll fight for my neighbours, and for their children. What else is there to do?'

Eolande closed her eyes for a moment, then let her hands fall. Slowly, she raised her head to look at Wyn, and when she spoke her voice was clear.

'I will try,' she said.

CHAPTER NINE

They carried Edmund by his hands and feet, with a sack tied over his head.

It made no difference to his sight, of course. Even as he flailed and kicked, he was reaching for the eyes of one of his captors to see where they were taking him: away from the road and deeper into the hills. The filthy rag in his mouth was choking him. As he tried to spit it out, he cast his sight behind him, back to the camp. He had always recoiled from using his skill on his own companions, but now, for an instant, he borrowed Cathbar's eyes, and saw Eolande running towards him, weeping.

He managed to get rid of the gag, took a deep breath and yelled with all his strength.

'Help! Cathbar! I'm here . . .'

Something hit him hard in the stomach. At the same time the sacking was drawn tighter over his mouth and nose. Winded and gasping, he kicked out more violently and heard one of the men curse as they broke into a run. Edmund hung between them, jolted at every step, his mouth full of sacking and his head swimming with the smell of mouldy grain.

He did not know how long they carried him. The foul air inside the sack sickened him and he could not draw enough breath into his lungs. He tried to borrow the sight of one of the men, but all he could see was the rocky ground ahead, and his vision was beginning to blur. He flailed his trapped arms as the men began to climb. The grip on one arm loosened suddenly and he fell, the side of his head hitting the ground with a violent blow. He lost his hold on his captor's eyes, and darkness closed over him.

He woke from a confused dream of fire and bloodshed. He was lying on the ground, and for a moment he felt pure panic, not knowing where he was or how he had got there. The figures from his dream still filled his mind: men and women sprawled on the ground, red-lit by the flames burning their homes. He opened his mouth to cry out – but the cry died unspoken when he felt rough cloth over his face.

Memory flooded back. Edmund's head throbbed where he had hit it; he tried vainly to bring his hands up and realised that they were tied together. So were his feet. He could hear voices now: his captors, sitting and talking a little way away from him. He sent out his sight cautiously towards them and saw four bearded men, lounging at their ease on a quiet hillside: grey stone and thin, yellowed grass, with patches of green further down. Edmund suppressed a groan. They were resting: they must be confident that they had thrown off the pursuit. He was alone.

The men talked in low voices, in Dansk, but with a strange, nasal accent that made it difficult to hear what they were saying. Edmund made out a few words: 'boy'; 'our pay'; 'by noon'. One of them grunted and rose to his feet, and the man whose eyes he was borrowing turned to look at a heap of rags and ropes on the ground nearby. The heap shifted – and Edmund hurriedly regained his own sight as heavy footsteps crunched towards him.

The sack was pulled from his head and he blinked up at a scowling face, the beady eyes almost lost between heavy black brows and a bristling moustache. 'He's awake,' the man called. 'Let's go.'

He reached down to cut the rope around Edmund's feet and yanked him upright. 'You walk from now on, boy,' he growled.

They tied a rope around Edmund's waist, pinning his arms to his sides. Two of his captors each took an end, walking on either side of him and pushing him onwards if he slowed. They spoke little to him, apart from curt orders to move faster, and Edmund kept silent. What if the men had taken him as a hostage – could they already know who his father was? If they didn't, they would not find out through him. He could speak passable Dansk by now, but he would not risk being betrayed by his accent.

The men kept up a relentless pace, cursing Edmund when he stumbled, but did not harm him otherwise. But his head pounded, and it was difficult to keep his balance with bound hands, so that as the path became steeper and more uneven he tripped more and more frequently. Before long every step was an effort, and he walked with his eyes fixed on his feet, not daring to look up.

By the time the sun was halfway up the sky, even his captors seemed to be feeling the strain. Some distance up the steepest slope they had climbed, Edmund slipped and fell again, skinning his wrists, and this time the men let him lie. They sat down and took out food and drink, though the moustached man grumbled about wasting time. Edmund, bone-weary, was grateful to lean against a rock and accept the strip of meat and flask of sour ale that they handed him. At least his kidnappers were not savages, he thought: if he found no chance to escape, perhaps he could plead or bargain with their commander for his freedom.

Even if it meant revealing who he was?

The brief rest gave Edmund some of his strength back, but he was relieved beyond measure when they finally reached the top of the hill. No camp was visible in the foothills below, but Edmund, casting his sight down, was not surprised to find men there, laying fires, and plucking freshly killed birds. He wondered who they could be. Surely not the marauders who had ploughed up the road behind them: the scene he had glimpsed seemed too orderly to be a bandits' camp.

Their road was all downhill now. As the sun passed its height, Edmund heard the sound of distant voices, and next moment two armed guards stepped out from an angle of the rock to challenge them. The guards nodded in recognition, and one of them ran ahead while Edmund's captors led him around a final outcrop to a level plain, full of noise and activity.

The camp was set up in the shelter of a sheer, rocky cliff, around a small spring that welled up a dozen feet from the foot of the stone wall. Men were everywhere: guarding the camp's boundary; sharpening weapons; repairing tents. The shelters were made from animal skins and furs, pegged into the ground with metal spikes. Edmund knew that this was no band of outlaws, nor even the retinue of some local lord. He was looking at a king's army.

His captors pushed him forward, and Edmund staggered with exhaustion. They had taken the rope off him, but he knew there was no question of running now: he doubted whether his legs would hold him up much longer.

'I'll be glad to be rid of this one,' said one of his captors, rubbing his arm where Edmund had kicked him.

'I just hope he'll do,' complained the moustached man. 'I still say he's too young to know anything.'

While Edmund was wondering what he meant, the man took him by the arm and propelled him towards the largest of the tents. He stopped at the entrance, cleared his throat and called out in a softer and more respectful tone than any Edmund had heard him using.

'My Lord? It's Viridogard – back with the prisoner.'

Someone answered at once: 'Bring him in. What are you waiting for?' His voice was deep, testy and somehow familiar to Edmund. The moustached man twitched the flap of hide aside and gave Edmund a violent shove that sent him sprawling into the tent. There were three men inside, crowded around a wooden chest with a map spread out on it. An oil lamp filled the air with fumes and blurred their faces.

'Pick him up,' said the deep-voiced man. This must be the chief of the army: even seated, he was taller than the others, and his voice held the ring of authority. The men on either side of him rose, but Edmund hauled himself to his feet before they could reach him, and stood glaring at the shadowed faces on the other side of the lamp. All three men laughed, but when the one in charge spoke again, his voice was dissatisfied.

'He's barely more than a boy. You take a full day, and this is what you bring me?' Viridogard started to protest, but the chief cut him off. 'You'll be paid: I don't go back on my word. Wait outside now.'

The moustached man backed away and left. The chief turned to one of his companions. 'I doubt this one will be able to help us – and that's another day lost, if so. But let's have a look at him.'

Edmund felt as if the ground had shifted underneath his feet. Up till now the man had been speaking Dansk, like everyone else he had met in this land. But the words he had just heard were in English. And the voice was almost as familiar to him as his own.

'*Father?*'

There was a long silence. Then the chief rose from his seat and strode around the chest to Edmund, taking his shoulders with both hands. He was not the towering giant of Edmund's memories, but his shoulders were just as broad and his blue eyes as piercing as the picture he had kept in his mind's eye for more than two years.

'Edmund?' the man whispered. 'What in the name of all the gods are you doing here?'

Heored had dismissed his two captains, and now he and Edmund sat alone in his tent, seated on stools at the king's campaign chest. The map had been cleared away and Heored had sent for food: bread, dried fruit and good ale as well as pigeons his men had been roasting on their fires outside. The camp's healer had plastered Edmund's head with a strong-smelling bran poultice, and a bed of furs had been laid out for him against one wall of the tent. Edmund glanced at it longingly once or twice, but his father still had much to say to him.

'What are you doing here?' Heored demanded as soon as his men had left. 'Why have you left your mother?'

'She sent me away.' Edmund watched his father's face in the smoky lamplight as if re-learning an old lesson: the coppery beard, broad brows and level gaze that he remembered so well. But there were unfamiliar lines around the eyes – lines of age and authority. Edmund faltered for a moment: this was not just his father, but King Heored, ruler of Sussex, leader of one of the most feared armies in Britain.

Heored listened gravely as Edmund told him about the marauders who had raided their home shores, and Branwen's decision to send him to safety with his uncle in Francia.

'It was wisely done,' his father said, but Edmund thought his face clouded for a moment. *I'm still a boy to him*, he thought. *If I'd been a warrior, like him, I'd have stayed to protect my mother, not run away.*

He told Heored of the shipwreck that had stranded him in Dumnonia, his companionship with Elspeth, the boat-master's daughter, and the dragon, Torment, that had hounded them.

His father's eyes widened. 'I've heard of such beasts,' he admitted, 'but I always thought them a fable.'

It was clear that tales of monsters and shipwrecks were not Heored's chief concern.

'So you've been travelling across country, living by your wits and your sword,' he said, approvingly. 'I left you as a child – and now I see a son who can stand by my side.' He summoned a servant to refill Edmund's cup. 'Tell me of the fighting you've done,' he demanded. 'Have you kept up your training?'

'I have,' Edmund said eagerly. 'I'm a fair archer now. I've had plenty of practice in the last few weeks, hunting for food.'

Heored nodded, but Edmund suspected it was not the answer his father had wanted. 'I hope your swordsmanship's as good,' he said. 'There's battle ahead of us, and I'd have you standing with me.'

'I've been travelling with King Beotrich's man, Cathbar. He's a good teacher,' Edmund told him.

He did not explain that it was Elspeth, not himself, whom Cathbar had been training in swordplay. *A son who can stand by my side*, his father had said, and Edmund had felt a pride he had never known before. But could he really be that son?

When he had first gazed at his father's face, so familiar and yet so strange, Edmund had wondered how he must look to Heored. Without thinking, he had borrowed his father's sight, seeing a slight boy with pale, earnest eyes, his wrists and ankles protruding from ill-fitting clothes. For a moment, he had shared his father's amazement at how tall he had grown . . . and something else, a flash of concern, or unease. It happened in an instant – then Edmund had released Heored's sight, overcome by a sense of trespass. He remembered his father's view of the Ripente: he had made use of their help at times in battle, but he had always spoken of the men with disdain, as tools liable to turn in the hand. To Heored, Ripente were not men or women with a skill but a separate race, to be treated with suspicion – and Edmund remembered with a shock that he had once thought the same himself. He would tell his father the truth, but not yet.

There were other things that he was reluctant to talk about, too. He said nothing of Elspeth's crystal sword, fearful that Heored would not believe him. He spoke of Cluaran as their companion and guide on the road, but did not mention the minstrel's Fay blood. And he talked of Loki only as an escaped enemy: a merciless killer and fire-raiser; a danger to the land. His father was fighting armies – how could Edmund tell him that he had been pursuing a god?

Heored listened to his account of the journeyings in the Snowlands with a sort of impatience. It was only when he spoke of their arrival in the land of the Danes that his father regained his interest.

'So you arrived less than a week ago! Was there any fighting in the north of the country? Bands of wandering men?'

'Not in the north,' Edmund said. 'We've seen signs of both since we came south.' He repressed a shudder. 'It's as if it's always happening just ahead of us.'

'They're centred around our camp,' his father said with certainty. 'If I could only draw them to attack us, we might rid the world of a plague! But they'll only prey on the weak – cowards that they are.'

'You know who they are, then?' Edmund was surprised.

Heored shook his head. 'I know not who they are but I know what they have done. After two years of fighting in Northumbria we finally beat back my cousin's enemy and sent them back to Gwynedd. My men and I headed for the harbour at Northumbria, ready to sail back to Sussex, but found that the port was being ransacked by Danes from across the sea.' He smacked one hand into the other. 'We managed to see them off and with half a dozen ships we followed them and played them at their own game by sailing to their shores.'

He had caught up with the Danes when they were almost in their home harbour, he said; had attacked one ship with burning arrows and sunk it. But the rest had escaped; abandoned their boats and fled inland, Heored reported scornfully, to hide from their pursuers in the forest.

'But they fought you,' Edmund said, remembering the battlefield he had crossed only the day before. 'You lost men.'

Heored's face clouded. 'Yes,' he admitted. 'Our men grow restless here; only yesterday I allowed a party of them to go hunting, and the Danes waylaid them as they returned.' He thumped the chest with his fist. 'What kind of men are they? We're invaders in their land! They should be banding together to drive us out . . . yet they hide from us and harry us little by little, like common bandits.'

'Perhaps they are,' Edmund ventured.

Heored was suddenly very still. Edmund felt the weight of his stare as he went on: 'There are many bands of men in this place who are quick to murder their own people for little or no gain.' He told his father about the men who had churned up the road, and the trail of devastation they had left behind them; the murder of the pedlar Menobert and the tales of attacks on homesteads. 'They're not like common brigands,' he said. 'They don't even seem to rob their victims – just destroy everything in their path.'

Heored stood up, upsetting his stool and nearly knocking over the lamp. 'My scouts brought back rumours of this,' he said. 'But they're hired men, from the harbour towns, and not to be relied on. They told tales of an army of madmen attacking the villages, and I told them to bring me proof: capture a man from this army, and let me question him.' His pacing had brought him back to Edmund. 'And they brought you.'

Heored smiled suddenly, and for a moment he was the father Edmund had known as a child. 'And I'm glad of it, Edmund. Tonight I'll gather my captains, and we'll plan what use to make of your news. But for now, we'll toast your return.' A servant stepped forward, but Heored dismissed him impatiently and poured two cups of ale himself, pushing one over to Edmund. 'If what you say is true, we'll maybe not be here much longer. A rabble of madmen!' He drank deeply. 'And when we've beaten them, I'll send to Aelfred in Francia to let him know you're with me. He can reach your mother from there more easily than I can from here.'

'But he's not there!' Edmund said without thinking, and cursed himself. His uncle Aelfred – the sorcerer Orgrim – was someone he had not yet mentioned to his father. How could he tell Heored that his own brother-in-law was a sorcerer who had turned against his king? But there was no escaping it now. As briefly as possible, he told his father what he knew of Aelfred's recent history: his coming to Wessex in an exchange of hostages; his study of sorcery and his attempt to seize power from Beotrich.

'I was there when . . . when his treachery was discovered,' Edmund said. 'He is in prison now. But no one else knows his true name, or his link to our family. He has lost his sight, and I think his reason as well.'

Heored had sunk down on his stool again, and rested his head in his hands. When he looked up his face was haggard.

'I should have guessed,' he said at last. 'I never wholly trusted him, promising though he was. I never told you, Edmund, but he . . . his family . . . have a skill which . . .' He rubbed his forehead. 'Well, the seeds of treachery were always in him. Your mother is the soul of honour, but when I heard she had entrusted you to Aelfred, I confess I had my doubts.'

He said no more, but Edmund felt a coldness descend on him. *He knew!* he thought. *My father knew all the time that Aelfred was Ripente – and he distrusted him because of it.* How could he ever tell the truth about himself now?

'Enough of that!' Heored exclaimed, rising from his seat. 'You're here now. I must make you known to the men, and arm you. I'll not have you going weaponless in enemy territory, even for a day.' He strode to the tent-flap. 'Teobald! Alberich! Nils!' he called. The three captains came up at a run.

'Summon the armourer,' Heored commanded. 'This is my son, Edmund of Sussex. He fights with us from now on. He's to have sword and armour as befits his rank.'

The three men bowed, and Teobald led Edmund to the armoury, where a thickset old man in stained leather offered him a dozen different swords to try.

'It's an honour to have you here, young prince,' the old man said, as he helped Edmund into leather armour and a bulky breastplate. 'Your father's a soldier as well as a king, and it's good to see his young one following in his footsteps.'

'That it is,' Teobald agreed. 'King Heored is always in the thick of the battle,' he told Edmund. 'There's no danger that he won't share with us – and his men love him for it.'

Edmund heard himself clanking as Teobald led him back to his father, a round helmet on his head and the hilt of his new sword hitting the breastplate at every step. He wondered what Elspeth would think if she could see him like this. But his heart lifted to see the pride in Heored's eyes.

'Now you look like a soldier!' his father exclaimed. 'Draw your sword!' Edmund obeyed, and to his amazement the three captains bowed before him.

'Welcome, Heored's son!' Teobald cried, and the other two captains echoed him. Edmund stood straighter inside the cumbersome armour, and raised the heavy sword above his head. *I'm the son of a hero*, he told himself.

'Come with me to inspect the camp,' his father said. 'Tonight we'll hold a council, and these captains will hear what you've told me. And tomorrow I'll send a party of men to bring your companions here. There are women among them, you said? I'll give them safe conduct back to our ships – see them safely on their way before we prepare for battle.'

Edmund almost laughed at the idea of trying to send Elspeth away. 'No need for that,' he told his father. 'My companions are here by choice, all of them. They won't leave until they've found . . . our enemy, and killed him.'

'And how do they expect to do that?' Heored exclaimed. 'Two women and a minstrel?'

Edmund could not answer. He and Elspeth had not discussed what she could do against the demon now that the sword was gone.

'Well, that's as may be,' his father was saying. 'Your place is with me now.' He took Edmund by the shoulders, his face serious. 'I've left your education too much to others. You'll be King of Sussex after me some day, Edmund: it's time you began to learn your duties.'

And maybe it was for the best, Edmund told himself, as he followed Heored to be shown to his men. His father was a great warrior, with an army at his command. Surely, once Edmund had proved himself, Heored would help in the fight against Loki? Whatever it took, he promised himself, he would make his father proud of him.

CHAPTER TEN

Eolande made them move Wyn's son into the open and take him downhill, to where grass grew. Cluaran and Cathbar could not avoid jolting the young man as they carried him, but he was too deeply unconscious to notice. Elspeth, following behind with Wulf, hoped they were not too late.

'Leave us now,' Eolande instructed them, as the men laid Reinhard under a group of stunted trees. She knelt at his head, with Wyn beside her. 'Cluaran – if he wakes, we'll need a dressing for the wound in his chest.' Elspeth looked back as Cluaran led them away: the Fay woman was bending over the young man, her hands cupping his head, murmuring something too quiet to hear.

Cluaran asked Elspeth and Cathbar to fetch more water, while he and the young woman, Sigrid, went further downhill to look for medicinal herbs. They dared not light a fire for fear of alerting their enemies, and when Cluaran returned with yarrow leaves, moss and bark, there were no utensils but his cooking pan and a stone to use as a pestle.

'How did your mother get her skill at healing?' Elspeth asked, as Cluaran showed her how to shred leaves and bark into the pan. 'I thought the Fay were never ill.'

'That's as may be,' Cluaran answered. 'But my father was not Fay, and nor am I . . . no more than half. Her knowledge of herbs, which she gave to me – she learnt that from the women of Hibernia, where I was born.' He began to pound at the mixture in the pan. 'This will be no use to him unless she can find his spirit and coax it to return to his body. That's a much rarer skill.'

'And may she succeed,' said Cathbar. He was standing nearby, sharpening his sword. 'But come sunset, Cluaran, we must leave her here, and go after Edmund.'

'I'm coming too,' Elspeth put in, as Cluaran nodded. She glanced over at Wulf, who was playing one of his interminable games with pebbles, watched by Sigrid. Maybe they could leave the child here as well. They might only have the one chance to rescue Edmund. Suddenly it seemed unbearable to be sitting here while her friend was still in danger. 'How far is the camp from here?'

'Close,' Cathbar promised her. 'Over the next ridge.'

They did not have to wait until sunset for Cluaran's mother to finish with Reinhard. The sun was still visible over the southern ridge when Eolande came up the slope, her steps slow and her face white and drained. Elspeth stared at her, suddenly cold – but when she saw them, the Fay woman smiled.

'He's awake,' she said.

Cathbar and Cluaran carried him back to the shelter of the hawthorns. The young man was too weak to talk, but there was colour in his face, and Elspeth saw him smiling at his mother and Sigrid as they dressed his wound with the poultice Cluaran had made.

Wyn rose from her son's side to take Eolande by the hand. 'Is there anything I can do to repay you?'

'Nothing, thank you,' Eolande told her. 'Only take care of your son.'

Wyn nodded, but did not release Eolande's hand. 'Mistress,' she said, a little uncertainly, 'may I ask your name? I'd have my son know who it was who saved him.'

The Fay woman hesitated a moment. 'It's Eolande,' she said. 'But if I have saved him, it was in part-payment of a debt that I owe. You are not beholden to me.'

The woman shook her head. 'I shall never forget you, Eolande,' she said. 'May our friendship always go with you.'

They crouched on the ridge, looking down on a landscape of rough pasture dotted with woodland, with the road a hazy line over to the east.

'Their camp is behind that hill,' said Cathbar, pointing. 'There are sixty or more of them – and they've posted guards all around, so go carefully, and don't speak. Understand, Wulf?' he said to the child, who nodded. He had refused to stay behind with Wyn and Sigrid – as Elspeth had known he would.

The journey down was faster than the way up, even with the need for caution. Cathbar led them down a gully to the west of the camp, which would shield them from the sight of any watcher below.

'The tents are all close under the cliff,' he told them. 'They have sentries on the hill, and what looks like a sheer drop on the side nearest the camp. The road's to the east, with trees between it and the camp: they've sentries in the trees as well. To the south and west it's all open fields. They patrol the edges, but we could slip past in the dark.'

They hid in a tiny copse, one field away from the camp. Elspeth could see the closest tents and the faint light of cooking fires. She strained her eyes, but she could catch no sight of Edmund: only heavy-set men in dark cloaks, turning spits or unrolling packs. Above them, on the hill, she could see the little figure on look-out duty, and in the fields before the camp, two sentries patrolled, crossing and recrossing. The scene was brilliantly lit by the low sun.

'If we go in from the west,' Cluaran murmured, 'we don't have to wait till dark.'

They made their move as the sun was setting. They had agreed that Eolande and the boy would stay behind, and as the other three removed their furs and took out the blankets from their packs, the Fay woman took firm hold of Wulf's arms. She paled a little as the child wriggled and protested, but did not let go. Then, as the sinking sun emerged from the clouds to send streaks of gold across the field, and into the eyes of the man on watch, Cluaran stepped forward.

'Go as soon as he comes after me,' he whispered, and as soon as the man raised his hand to shield his eyes, the minstrel slipped from the trees and moved silent as a shadow around the edge of the field. In the next field, sheep were grazing, and as Elspeth and Cathbar waited, sword at the ready, they heard a commotion from the animals: a chorus of bleats and a ragged pounding as the flock bolted. The man on top of the rise peered in the direction of the noise and started towards it, calling to his companions.

'Now!' whispered Cathbar, and he and Elspeth darted over the rough grass to the bushes at the base of the hill.

On the other side of the camp they could hear running feet and curses mixing with frightened bleating. They moved cautiously around the bushes, but there was no sound of alarm from the camp. Then Elspeth gasped as branches were pushed aside behind her and a hand was laid on her arm.

It was Cluaran – bright-eyed, and not even breathless. 'Waiting for me?' he murmured. 'Better move now: they'll be coming back.'

They reached the edge of the camp, and lay in the long grass peering in. The first of the men were indeed returning, a little shamefaced as they told their companions that they had found nothing but skittish sheep.

'Wait here,' Cathbar muttered. 'I'll find where Edmund is and come back.'

He wrapped his blanket around himself in imitation of the men's dark cloaks, leapt to his feet and strolled into the camp. As soon as he was a few paces away, he was almost indistinguishable from the other men milling about: not only in build and colouring, but in the assurance of his walk, as if he belonged there. Only the watchers saw how he avoided looking anyone in the face. He headed straight for the row of tents against the cliff, and disappeared among them.

Elspeth peered through the grass stems, seizing on every slight movement and wishing she had Edmund's Ripente sight, to look inside the tents. Then Cathbar was striding back, ducking down quickly as he reached them.

'He's in that one,' he said, pointing at a tent at the end of the row. 'Not bound, and only two men with him. Come on!'

Cluaran and Elspeth wrapped themselves in their blankets, and they walked the twenty paces with Elspeth between the two men, not stopping to see if anyone glanced at them. No one had challenged them when they reached the tent. Cathbar ripped up one of the pegs in a single movement, and they burst in, swords drawn.

Edmund looked up in astonishment. He was sitting on a stool with a wooden cup in his hand, dressed in unfamiliar clothes, and looking a great deal neater and cleaner than Elspeth had seen him since their arrival in the Snowlands. One of the men with him had just filled his own cup from a pewter jug of wine. The other was seated by Edmund, a tall, bearded man with fierce blue eyes and thick yellow hair.

The blond man leapt to his feet, his hand on his sword hilt. Edmund jumped up too, and stayed his arm. 'There's no danger, Father!' he cried. 'These are my friends!' He turned to them, his eyes shining.

'This is my father,' he said. 'Heored, King of Sussex.'

They were quickly made welcome, seated in the king's tent and offered food and shelter as honoured guests while Cluaran fetched his mother and Wulf. Elspeth was given a seat by the entrance, apart from the others. After a courteous greeting, Heored had ignored her, addressing himself almost entirely to Cathbar.

Edmund came to sit by her. 'I was going to send men to find you tomorrow. I should have known you'd get here first!' he said. Elspeth was touched by his obvious pleasure at seeing her, as well as his pride in his father. But there was something else at the edge of his smile: an anxiety which she could not explain. He bent to fill her cup, and as his face came near to hers he whispered to her, quick and fierce.

'Say nothing of Ripente!'

Elspeth stared at him, startled. Now the anxiety was plain in his face, and his eyes pleaded with her not to give him away. She nodded, and Edmund's face cleared.

He told her how his father had come in pursuit of the raiders who had invaded his cousin's lands; how Heored had learned of the attacks on the villages and tried to capture one of the attackers, and how Edmund had been captured by mistake.

'I told him about the men whose tracks we saw: the ones who killed Menobert,' he said. 'He's heard the same stories that we have: of a band of madmen who destroy everything in their path.'

'They're true!' Elspeth cried, and told him of the devastated settlement they had passed, and their meeting with Wyn.

'We must tell him that, too,' said Edmund, looking at his father, who was still deep in conversation with Cathbar. 'He held a war-council just before ... before you arrived, and they've agreed to go in search of them, to defeat them once and for all.'

Listening to him, Elspeth felt a growing unease.

'They're a significant band of men, if the stories are true,' Edmund went on, 'but they've never faced swordsmen before, only unarmed villagers, and we know they have no discipline, and no leader. We'll be more than a match for them. If my father is right, we'll be rid of the threat to his cousin – and we'll free this land of the marauders.'

Heored was having a similar conversation with Cathbar. 'We expect to attack in no more than a day,' the king said. 'Our scouts are already finding the marauders' location. We'd welcome another good man or two,' he added invitingly.

'You honour us,' Cathbar said, 'but I fear we must move on. We're chasing a different quarry.'

'Yes,' Heored said. 'Edmund told me something of the sort.' Every line of his face betrayed his displeasure. 'Though I'd have thought that the men who've been wreaking havoc all around us – and attacking our own shores – would be a better target for your sword than a single warrior, however powerful. Well, captain, you know your own business, of course – but Edmund will stay here and fight with me.'

'Edmund?' whispered Elspeth, and to her horror, she saw that her friend was nodding.

'I'm sorry, Elspeth,' he said. 'My place is with my father now. This is the duty I was born to.'

Heored called an end to the meeting when he heard that one of his scouts had returned. Elspeth walked out of the tent not knowing where she was going. *Of course Edmund has a right to stay with his father!* But it felt like a betrayal, as though she had lost her only friend.

She heard rapid footsteps, and looked around to see Edmund pounding after her. He stopped when he saw her face.

'Do you really mean to leave us?' she asked him.

Edmund's voice was not quite steady. 'My father needs me here.'

But I need you! Elspeth wanted to cry. How could she succeed in her task without him? She said nothing; only stared in silence at Edmund, who met her gaze defiantly. He had grown in the last weeks; he was taller than her now, and there was an authority in his face that she had never seen before. For so long now – throughout the long, uncertain journey – Edmund had been her loyal companion; the one who had never doubted her no matter what she did. Her friend. Now, for the first time, she saw him as something entirely different: a prince, and Heored's son.

'I know you have to find Loki,' he said. 'But I will be fighting him as well by stopping these men from burning more villages. They'll continue to kill more people if they're not stopped.'

People like Wyn and her neighbours, Elspeth thought, nodding in spite of herself.

'My father says I must start to learn kingship,' Edmund added. 'And what should a king do, if not this?'

Elspeth nodded again, slowly. 'All right,' she said. 'But if you're going to fight with him, you should tell him about your skill. He needs to know you as you are.'

'I'll tell him, of course I will.' Edmund dropped his gaze. 'Just . . . not yet. He's only just heard about Orgrim.'

'You're not your uncle!' Elspeth burst out. 'You have a gift, that's all. If he thinks that makes you a traitor, he's a fool!'

Edmund flinched as if she had slapped him. 'I'm sorry,' she said quickly. 'But you told me your father has used Ripente before now. He must have trusted them.'

'*Used* them,' Edmund echoed, and there was a note of bitterness in his voice. 'Not welcomed them to his court as his friends, or allies.'

They had reached the edge of the camp, passing a pile of empty barrels and a straw target on a stand. Elspeth stared across the fields. Edmund was right. Wasn't it better to do some immediate good than to go on wandering while all around them people burned along with their homes?

Until now, she had never doubted that she would find Loki – that he was only a little way ahead of them, growing closer all the time. The faint voice of the sword had come to her, enough to urge her forward; reassuring her that when the time came, she would find the means to defeat him. Now . . . she glanced at her right hand, feeling its emptiness. There was no voice in her head now: not so much as an echo. When had she last heard it? And how far could she go without the sword, and without Edmund?

Some of her despair must have shown on her face. 'Stay with us, Elspeth!' Edmund begged. 'You and the others. You can help us in the fight. I'll convince my father – he'll soon see you're a better fighter than I am. And you can search for Loki just as well from our camp.'

'Thank you,' Elspeth said. She could not imagine being able to continue her search from the camp, but she could see how much Edmund wanted her to stay. 'I will think about it,' she promised.

She let him take her back to the tent that had been set up for the visitors. Two or three men saluted him respectfully as they passed, while shooting looks of curiosity at Elspeth.

In the tent set up for the visitors, the others had already settled down for the night. Elspeth stepped over a snoring Cathbar and found a space between Eolande and Wulf, who grumbled sleepily as she squeezed in beside him. She lay very still, trying not to disturb the others. *It would never work,* she told herself sadly. She must leave Edmund with his own people, and pursue her search without him. She was sure that Cluaran and Cathbar would go with her.

But where would she lead them?

Tired though she was, it was a long time before she could sleep.

CHAPTER ELEVEN

Edmund did not sleep at all that night.

He walked back to his tent feeling uncomfortable, as if he had said something disloyal about his father to Elspeth. But he had only told her that Heored did not trust the Ripente – and why should he? He was a king: he knew the dangers of treachery better than others. Elspeth could not be expected to understand.

His father was poring over the campaign map, laid out on a chest. He looked up as Edmund entered the tent. 'Your friends are all settled? Good. Come and look at this.'

The map was crudely sketched on a single sheet of vellum. 'It's not accurate,' Heored warned. 'Look – he's drawn the road far too close to the hills. I should have brought a draughtsman with us. But it gives us a fair idea of the terrain.'

'Where is the enemy's camp?' Edmund asked, bending over the map.

'Our scout says it's here, by the road.' Heored jabbed at the vellum, leaning forward in the smoky yellow lamplight until his head was next to Edmund's. 'Where the forest starts up again – see? So we wait for them here, in the trees, and send some men around behind them, to flush them towards us.'

Warmed by his father's closeness and his confidence in him, Edmund nodded as Heored went on.

'My other two scouts are going in closer to see what preparations they're making – but the word is that they've already been attacking and plundering villages. There are two at least that they could reach from there.' He stabbed at the map again. 'If they're like most bandits, they'll make a foray, then retreat to their camp. And if we can catch them as they return . . .'

'No!' Edmund cried. 'We can't just stand by while they're killing more people!'

Heored frowned, plainly unused to being interrupted.

'Please, Father,' Edmund insisted. 'If we come on them when they're attacking a settlement, we'll defend it, won't we?'

'You've a sense of responsibility, boy,' Heored said. 'That's good: a king should protect the innocent. If we can help the villagers without foolish risk, we will. One way or another, we'll have battle before too long.' He looked down at the new sword which Edmund now wore at his side. 'How does the blade handle?'

'Very well,' Edmund said quickly. In fact it felt heavy and unwieldy to him after Cluaran's bow, but he put his hand to the hilt and tried to look confident.

'Show me what you can do with it!' Heored ordered. He strode outside the tent, and Edmund followed, dreading that he would disappoint his father so soon after he had shown his trust in him.

Most of the king's men were in their tents by now, but the embers of a dozen cooking fires gave enough light to see by, and the men on guard watched curiously as Edmund drew his new sword and showed his father the moves he recalled from his old life in Sussex. It seemed impossibly long ago, like a life recalled in a dream, but Edmund remembered the thrusts and slashes well enough, and managed to parry when Heored drew his own sword to fence with him.

'Not too bad,' his father said at length. 'You need not have been so cautious, Edmund: I'd not have let you hurt me. Still, that last blow was well returned. Remember to step sideways, not back, when your enemy thrusts at you – and keep your guard up!'

Edmund nodded gratefully, leaning on his sword for a moment.

Heored looked at him with a flicker of concern. 'Go in and sleep now. I'll join you as soon as those two laggards return with their news.'

Edmund felt as taut as a bow-string and could not imagine sleeping, but he followed his father's instructions. It was a relief to unbuckle the sword-belt and shrug off the heavy cloak. He had only just lain down when there was a hubbub outside the tent.

'About time!' came his father's voice. 'Both scouts, or just one?'

'Both, we think, but the guard could not tell for sure, my lord,' a man replied. 'He says they're approaching very slowly.'

'I'll give them slowly!' snapped Heored. 'Send them to me as soon as they get here. We've waited long enough for them.'

Why would the scouts be so slow? On an impulse, Edmund sent his sight out to the field below the camp. He found a man's eyes almost at once: moving slowly, as the guard had said; seeing the lights of the camp through bushes. And there was his companion: Edmund made out a second figure close by. Neither seemed to be wounded: their movements were slow and deliberate, and he could feel nothing but stealth behind the eyes.

Then the man turned to look behind him – and there were more shadowy figures: five of them; a dozen . . . clad not in woollen cloaks but in rough, bulky furs.

These were no returning scouts! Edmund found himself on his feet, heading for the opening of the tent to shout a warning – but he checked himself. How could he make his father believe him, without revealing his Ripente skill?

Heored was standing in a little knot of his men. 'Our scouts are returned at last,' he said as Edmund came up to them.

Edmund took a deep breath. 'How do we know they're our scouts, and not some of our enemy?'

Heored stared at him for a moment. Then he nodded and gave a bark of laughter. 'Hark at my son, reminding me of the rules of caution!' he said. 'You, captain,' he ordered, 'have someone go to the edge of the camp and give them the signal.'

The man ran off, and a few moments later Edmund heard a low whistle. After a pause, the whistle was repeated – and then there was a flurry of talk, growing louder as the speakers approached the tent.

'They're not answering, my lord,' the captain reported, his face suddenly tight.

Heored flashed a look at Edmund which he could not decipher. Suspicion? Or was his father proud of his alertness?

Then the king was on his feet and issuing orders. 'Wake the camp. Each man is to be outside his tent and armed by the time of my call. The guests . . .' he shot another glance at Edmund before he continued. 'Arm the men if they need it, and escort the women and the child to the north side of the camp.'

Edmund wanted to tell his father that Elspeth would fight too, but Heored had already turned away, and in another moment the camp was full of hurrying men. Edmund ran to the visitors' tent. Elspeth was leading Wulf out, but as soon as she saw Edmund she placed the boy's hand in Eolande's and whispered something to her. The Fay woman nodded, and Elspeth slipped away from their escort and ran to join Edmund.

'No! Elsbet!' Wulf cried, but Eolande took him away, while a guard marched at her side.

'I'm fighting with you,' Elspeth declared.

'I thought you would,' Edmund said, and added, unable to help himself, 'But take care!' She still held her sword in her left hand.

'You too,' Elspeth replied, and he saw concern in her eyes. *Even left-handed*, he reminded himself, *she's still better with a sword than me.*

There was a gathering noise from outside the camp. At first it was a low grumble from the south and east that made Edmund think of cattle lowing. Quickly, the sound became shriller and closer: men's voices, a chant from many throats at once. Then the first of them were in the camp: lumbering, fur-clad men brandishing swords and axes, their mouths wide with yelling.

Heored faced the invaders, the embers of the fires around him glinting red off his sword. 'To me!' he cried, and there was an answering roar as his men rushed forward.

Edmund was jostled and pushed as he forced his way through the throng. He could hardly see where he was going, but he had to reach his father's side!

There was Heored, a head taller than the men around him – and there, facing him, was a man like a bear, his huge axe swinging. Heored struck a mighty blow with his sword, knocking the axe from the man's hands, and Edmund saw how far his father had held back when he had fenced with him earlier. *I must show myself his son*, he vowed.

But he faced what seemed a wall of fur-clothed men, all sweeping down on him, teeth bared, swords and axes whirling. A blade swung towards him; Edmund parried clumsily, and the jarring shock numbed his arm for a moment. He whirled to face another heavy-set man, sidestepping as a sword whistled down a finger-width from his ear. The man ran on without pausing, nearly knocking Edmund off his feet.

He ducked and slashed, was shoved from behind and dodged blows from above. His arm ached with the weight of the sword, and there was nothing around him but reeking fur and murderous iron. He struck against another man's blade with such force that he saw sparks, but the sound was lost in the roaring and clashing that filled his ears. A huge axe-man took a swing at him, and as he twisted away he caught a glimpse of Elspeth out of the corner of his eye: sword raised, fighting back-to-back with Cathbar. Edmund spun back, bringing his sword up to deflect the next stroke. The axe glanced off his breastplate with a force that sent him stagger-ing – but his assailant had fallen back too, his face distorted with pain as blood welled from a gash along his axe-arm.

Edmund found he was yelling aloud in triumph as he pressed forward, raising his sword for another blow, but the man was already running from him. Cheated, he pulled up short – and saw that all the invaders were retreating, fleeing beyond the borders of the camp. Some of Heored's men raised a cheer, but the king was grim-faced.

'It's too quick a retreat,' he said. 'We've not killed half a dozen of them!'

He was right. The man who had charged at Heored lay dead, and two or three others, but no more. None of their own men had fallen, though several were wounded; the king's healer was bandaging the worst hurt.

'They've drawn back, not run away,' one man declared. 'It's as if they were just trying our mettle. There's no saying they won't return.'

'True,' said Cathbar. 'From all I've seen, there are many more of them than this. If they have a leader, he'll be planning to surround this camp and pen us in. I'm for moving out.'

'The men you saw by the road outnumber us?' Heored asked a third man. Edmund recognised him as the scout who had returned earlier that evening. The man nodded.

'Then we're agreed,' Heored said. He turned to the three captains. 'We retreat from here. To the west: give the word. Each man to take his pack and his armour.'

As the men ran off, the king gestured to a servant to bring his pack and Edmund's from his tent. He watched approvingly as Edmund wiped his new sword on the grass and sheathed it.

'Well, Edmund, you've begun sooner than I thought,' he said, as they took up their packs, 'but none the worse for that, it may be. Tell me now: you've seen the map; where are we headed?'

Edmund looked at Heored's calm face and for a moment felt like laughing: even while running for their lives, his father would pursue his education! But he made his own face calm as he answered. 'We should seek higher ground, but the hills we came from are too far. A river? The one we forded today: it widens towards the west, doesn't it? And there's a bridge that we could guard.'

'Well done!' his father cried. 'The bridge is less than a league away. The map's right about that, at least; our scouts have seen it. If we reach it quickly we can hold off all comers.'

They broke camp immediately. Heored's most trusted captain led the retreat, walking fast but silently westwards through the first field. Eolande and Wulf were in the second group, escorted by guards on both sides, both of them easily keeping pace with the men. Eolande seemed as calm as if she were going to dinner, while Wulf skipped between the armed men, darting glances around him as if he could barely contain his excitement. Edmund looked about for Elspeth or Cathbar, but could not see them in the crush. The mad excitement of the battle had receded and he found he was shaking; he hoped Elspeth was unhurt.

A group of archers would be the last to leave the camp; among them Cluaran. Edmund begged Heored to let him join them, knowing that he was better with the bow than the sword, but his father would not hear of it.

'They'll most likely come up on our flank,' he said. 'That's where I'll need you.'

They moved out, stepping as softly as they could on the uneven ground, alert for any sign of pursuit. Almost at once, Heored turned to Edmund with a finger to his lips, and pointed to the row of bushes on the far side of the field. 'In there,' he breathed. 'Be ready.' Nothing moved in the foliage. Edmund sent out his sight to check – and saw humped tents, dimly lit, and a column of men moving stealthily away from them. One figure near the back of the column was looking directly at him: shorter than the rest, with pale hair under his round helmet . . . Edmund drew back quickly and turned away. He looked at his father with admiration: how had he known?

Heored signalled to a man behind him, pointing into the bushes. The man nodded and slipped back to warn the archers.

'It's what I'd have done myself,' the king murmured to Edmund as they moved on. 'They meant to come round and attack us from all sides. Now they'll try to cut us off as soon as we reach the hedge.'

The first party of Heored's men had almost reached the end of the field. Edmund's heart was in his mouth as he watched them, expecting an attack at any second, but none came. The men were through into the next field . . . then the group with Eolande and Wulf.

'But they're waiting there – I know they are!' Heored muttered, and kept his hand on his sword as his own party moved forward. As they came alongside the bushes that bordered the field, Edmund heard movement in them, and his heart began to thump so loudly that he thought his father must hear it. Behind him, he knew every archer would have an arrow fitted. Only half a dozen paces to the hedge . . . then four . . . then two . . . and they were through to the next field.

Heored was giving quiet orders to another man, who sped off to the front of the column. 'The river's two fields to the north of us, but we'll need to cut off to the north-west to reach the bridge,' Heored whispered to Edmund. 'But they must know where we're heading! They're following us now: what are they waiting for?'

'Could it be a trap?' Edmund whispered back.

'I've just sent word to Teobald at the front to be on his guard. But it may be that they're fewer than we thought, after all – or afraid of our archers.'

Maybe, Edmund thought as they headed north-west. But the attackers had not seemed afraid up till now, nor badly organised, for all his father's scorn of them. Could there be some hazard ahead that the map did not show? He closed his eyes, feeling his way over the tussocky ground. He found mice first, scurrying from the approaching heavy footfalls. He stumbled and wrenched his sight back for a moment, squinting at the ground ahead of him, then closed his eyes and searched again. There was an owl, scanning the grass below for any sign of movement, its eyes seeing the ground far more clearly than Edmund could in his own body. The bird stooped; missed and pulled itself up with an angry jerk – *but I saw sheep-droppings down there*, Edmund thought; *that ground must be firm enough*. Then the bird wheeled and Edmund saw the river, a wide loop of grey in the starlight, and over to the west, a glimpse of the bridge.

The ground seemed firm, but perhaps the bridge was broken? Edmund willed the owl to fly further westwards, but it turned away. Frustrated, he cast out in the direction of the bridge, looking for another night-flying bird.

There was nothing; and no animals, either, when he searched lower down. He felt still further – and froze.

'Edmund! What ails you, boy?'

Edmund staggered, and found himself staring into his father's startled face. All around him the column of men had halted, and murmurs of complaint and query were growing as the men peered through the darkness to see what was holding them up.

'Well?' The concern in Heored's eyes was beginning to turn to annoyance.

'Father – tell the men to stop! We can't go to the bridge. It's a trap! They have men waiting on the other side.' The sight still filled Edmund's mind: the mass of bulky figures, the glittering eyes and gleaming blades; but above all, the ferocious anticipation he had felt behind the eyes he had borrowed. 'There are dozens of them. They'll wait till we begin to cross, then attack from both sides.'

Heored was standing very still, his eyes fixed on Edmund's. 'I won't deny I feared something like this,' he said slowly. 'But you speak as if you've seen them. How can you be so certain?'

It was too late to stop now.

'I did see them,' Edmund said. 'Maybe sixty or seventy armed men, dressed like the ones who attacked the camp.' The words came out heavily, like stones dropped into water. 'I used the sight of one of them. I am Ripente.'

CHAPTER TWELVE

Heored's eyes seemed very dark as he stared back at Edmund, but his face did not change expression. He was silent for a moment. Then he nodded and turned away. He did not speak to Edmund again, but sent a messenger to the front of the column and stood staring after the man as if willing him to greater speed.

Edmund jumped when he felt a hand on his shoulder, and looked round to see Cluaran. The minstrel said nothing, but his narrow face was sombre, and Edmund wondered if he had heard the whole conversation.

One of Heored's captains rushed up, followed a moment later by a second. 'Halt your men!' the king barked. 'The bridge is guarded – it's a trap. Bring the men behind me in fighting formation and retreat north to the riverbank. We'll make our stand there, where they can't surround us.'

'By your leave, my lord, I have a better idea.'

It was Cluaran. 'We should head downstream, to where we can ford the river. There's a steep rise of ground just beyond where we can hold them off.'

'We'd never get there in time!' the king argued. He had gestured the captains away, and the men were already beginning to file back. But over the field that they had just crossed, there was movement. Even in the dimness, Edmund could see the hedge at the field's end stirring, seeming to grow taller.

'Quickly!' Heored called to his captains. His men were re-forming in a square behind him, waiting for the order to start the retreat. But over the field, the hedge had become a solid wall of men moving towards them. A new sound rose through the darkness: the low growling that Edmund had heard at the start of the last attack.

'Let your father start the retreat,' Cluaran said in Edmund's ear. 'But take your cue from me.'

As Heored's men began to move off, Cluaran stepped forward to face the oncoming horde. He stretched his hands in front of him, palms out. The enemy were closer now; Edmund could make out pale blurs of faces, and the low growl was becoming a roar. Heored reached out with an oath to drag Edmund after him, but behind them, Cluaran stood his ground.

A breeze sprang up, stinging Edmund's face. As Heored pulled him on, through the archers he had set to cover their retreat, a gust of damp air swept over them. Edmund cast a glance over his shoulder at Cluaran: the minstrel was surrounded by pale, whirling motes, whipped up by the wind. He stood motionless, seemingly unaware of the wall of men approaching him – much closer now; their harsh chanting filling the air. Edmund slipped his arm from his father's grasp:

if Cluaran's plan should fail, he would not leave the minstrel alone.

The motes of light thickened, streaming together until he seemed wrapped in cloud. The wind was howling now, almost drowning the chant of their enemies. Abruptly, Cluaran spread his arms wide: the cloud seemed to flow from his fingertips, spreading on the wind to cloak the advancing men in thick wet mist.

The chanting faltered. Edmund could see Cluaran clearly again: a slender black shape outlined against a solid bank of fog. For a moment he stood, statue-like. Then he turned and ran towards Edmund, through the astonished archers.

'Don't waste your arrows!' he cried. 'The fog will follow them as long as it lasts. My Lord – look behind you,' he added, as he reached Edmund and his father. For the first time Edmund saw how pale the minstrel was: his face was slick with sweat and his voice shook.

Heored stopped at last, and turned to look at their pursuers. There was nothing to be seen but roiling fog, filled with confused shouting and the clash of weapons.

The king was silent for a moment. Then he gave a piercing whistle which made every man turn to him. 'We head downstream!' he shouted.

They forded the river less than half a league to the east, and did not stop until they had scaled the higher ground beyond. Below them, across the water, the fog still hung over the land like a curtain, swaying and buckling as their enemies tried to find their way out of it. Some of the king's men cheered when they saw their pursuers still mired below, but most were too tired: foot-sore, chilled and damp. Heored stationed guards and ordered his men to take what rest they could. Cluaran threw himself down on the ground and was asleep at once, but Edmund could not rest. His father seemed to be avoiding him, only muttering, 'You should sleep now,' as he walked past – but Edmund was dreading the next conversation they must have.

He sat on the ground by Cluaran, gazing into the darkness. After a while Elspeth came up to sit beside him.

'You fought well,' she said, and when he did not reply, 'Do you think they'll attack again tonight?'

They looked down at the fog-bank, and Edmund realised that it was thinning: he could see dim figures within the mist, but they moved confusedly, in all directions.

'I think we're safe now,' he said. 'Thanks to Cluaran.' He said nothing about his own part in alerting his father.

The morning star had appeared before the fog lifted completely. By then, the fur-clad men were gone, leaving only a churned mess of footprints behind them. Heored took no rest all that night, as far as Edmund could tell: he moved among his men, checking weapons and equipment; he consulted again with his captains and relieved the guards. Elspeth slept after a while, and Edmund waited for his father to summon him.

But when the sun finally rose, Heored had not said one word to him.

The ground was cold beneath Elspeth when she woke, and her pack dug into her neck. Squinting against the morning light, she opened her eyes. Somewhere behind her, she heard the sound of deep voices: Heored was in conference with his captains. She pulled herself up on her elbows. Eolande lay near her, still sleeping deeply, with Cluaran and Cathbar a little further off. There was no sign of Edmund, and she guessed he must be with his father.

Wulf! She looked around with sudden exasperation. She was sure the child had been curled up between herself and Eolande, but he was not there now. 'Why can he never stay where he's put?' she muttered, scrambling to her feet.

The flat top of the hill was no more than fifty feet wide, and Elspeth stepped carefully between men who slept crouching, knees drawn to their chests or slumped against each other. She skirted the hastily thrown-up tent where Heored and his men still talked, and headed for the edge of the plateau, but Wulf was nowhere to be seen. How far could the child have wandered this time? She found herself at the edge of the makeshift camp, staring down the hillside to the river and the field beyond where their enemies had massed the night before. It was deserted now: the faint yellow glow from the east showed only a plain of churned mud. The fog had dispersed, leaving wisps of vapour hovering over the ground. There was still no sign of Wulf.

Someone was standing guard a little lower down the hillside, his hood pulled up against the chill morning breeze. It was unlikely that he would have seen the child and not stopped him, but Elspeth walked down to ask him anyway. He turned as she approached, and she saw that it was Edmund.

'I couldn't sleep,' he said. 'I told the sentry I'd take his place.'

'I thought you were with your father,' she said – and stopped in alarm, his face was so white and unhappy.

'He didn't call me,' Edmund said. He looked away from her, down the hill. 'I told him last night, Elspeth. Told him I was Ripente. I don't know if he'll forgive me.'

'Forgive you!' she echoed. 'What does he have to forgive you for? That's foolish talk,' she insisted when he did not answer. 'I've seen how proud he is of you! He just needs time to understand.'

'Maybe,' Edmund said, but he did not look back at her.

Following his gaze down to the misty field, Elspeth said, 'Have you seen Wulf? He's wandered off again.'

'Again!' Edmund turned sharply. 'Has the boy no sense at all?'

They found Wulf easily enough on the other side of the hill, picking up stones on the slope behind Heored's makeshift tent. He waved at Elspeth, and seemed surprised when she scrambled down to him and grabbed him by the arm. 'I was bored,' he explained innocently when she scolded him.

'There are bad men around here, Wulf!' she said as she led him back up the hill. 'You must stay close to us!' But the child only stared at her blankly.

The voices inside the tent rose as they reached it.

'We must fight them!' Heored was saying. 'They've killed two scouts and attacked our camp. They must learn that the men of Sussex are not to be treated so. And there are my cousin's injuries still to avenge.'

'By your leave,' protested one of the captains – Elspeth thought she recognised the voice as Teobald – 'we've no proof that these are even the same men. What if the raiders of Northumbria have gone back to their homes, and these are just bandits – or even barbarians from Frisia or Saxony?'

'They're the same men.' Heored's voice was grim. 'They attack defenceless villagers. They kill women and children. It sticks in my throat that such villains have escaped punishment for so long.' As another captain raised his voice to object, they heard a crash from inside the tent, and the wall nearest them shook as if Heored had jumped to his feet.

'No more talk,' the king growled. 'We attack today.'

Edmund took Elspeth's arm and walked swiftly away from the tent. 'Last night, I asked my father to protect the villagers,' he said.

'You see!' Elspeth exclaimed. 'He does trust you – he listened to you.'

But Edmund shook his head. 'Not any more.'

'Rouse up, all!'

Heored was striding towards them. 'We move against the marauders today! Collect your packs and sharpen your weapons!' He turned to Edmund. 'Here, boy.'

Elspeth saw hope flare in her friend's face: perhaps Heored had seen reason already, realising how useful a Ripente might be to them in the planned attack. But all Heored said was: 'You'll command a group of archers: we must play to our strengths today. Look to your bow.' He gestured to where a few bowmen were assembling at the camp's edge, and turned away with a brief nod.

Edmund stared after him for a moment, his face stricken. Then he squared his shoulders and walked towards the bowmen before Elspeth could speak to him.

No one paid Elspeth any attention. She found Eolande and asked her to take care of Wulf. She expected the child to protest: the Fay woman always seemed a little awkward with him, and he had made it clear he preferred Elspeth's and Edmund's company to hers. But now he made no complaint, and Elspeth guessed he was sulking with her for having dragged him away from his game.

The camp was suddenly full of movement and shouted orders. Elspeth found a spot at the very edge of the summit and made a few practice feints with her sword, testing the grip. The weapon felt easier in her hand now, and she knew that she was gaining in skill, even left-handed. Last night, fighting side by side with Cathbar, she had matched his speed, if not his strength, and after the men had fled he had clapped her on the shoulder and called her a fine pupil. If there was fighting to be done today, she told herself, she would be part of it again, even if Heored did not choose to give her orders.

She remembered Wyn and her son, and their devastated village: there were more reasons for this battle than the honour of Heored's kingdom.

The king had already sent a small group of men to retrieve weapons and supplies from their camp, and two more to follow in the footsteps of yesterday's scouts and find their adversaries' encampment.

'Go carefully,' the king warned them. 'We can't lose any more good men.'

You could use Edmund's skill and not risk anyone! Elspeth thought in frustration. But Heored did not even look at his son.

There would be a delay while they waited for the advance party to return, and Heored allowed his men to break out breakfast rations. But they had hardly started eating when they heard a cry from the foot of the hill: the scouts had returned.

'Enemy men approaching, my lord!' one of them called.

Elspeth joined the general rush to the hill's edge. A small party of men were crossing the muddy field towards them. As she watched, they splashed through the river which separated them from the hill. She grasped the hilt of her sword, and felt the men around her doing the same. She saw that Edmund already had an arrow fitted to his bow, and so did most of the archers with him, but the king held up a hand to halt them. One of the approaching men held a spear, and attached to it, a fluttering rag of white.

There were five of them, all dressed in the same furs that their attackers had worn last night – but these men walked smartly, in formation. As they drew closer Elspeth heard one of the captains draw in his breath sharply.

'The king was right,' he said. 'They *are* the men we followed from Northumbria – look at that shield-boss!'

Each of the five men held a round shield as well as a sword, and each shield was embossed with the shape of a leaping wolf.

Heored walked to the edge of the hill as the party approached, forcing them to stand lower down, looking up at the Sussex men. The spear-holder, a tall man with a handsome, arrogant face, seemed unconcerned. He planted the spear in the ground, its pennant bobbing like apple blossom, and waited for silence before he spoke.

'I bring word from Olav Haaksen, earl of all the lands south of the river,' he said, his ringing voice as arrogant as his face.

Heored inclined his head: *Speak.*

'Earl Olav bids you to a parley,' the man went on. 'Invaders though you are, he wishes no quarrel with you.'

'A strange message,' Heored said coldly, 'for a leader who only yesterday killed two of my men and sent his followers to sack my camp.'

'That was a group of hotheads, acting without orders,' the messenger replied. 'But you cannot deny that your presence is a threat to our land.'

'Our presence!' Heored echoed. 'Your peace-loving earl has been massacring his own villagers!'

'Not so.' The messenger's voice was calm. 'Some of our villages have been sacked by bandits; these are dangerous times. It is Earl Olav's business to deal with the marauders on his lands, and none of your concern.' Heored glared at him, and the man gazed impassively back. 'What answer shall I give the earl?' he asked.

'How do I know your master can be trusted?' Heored demanded.

'There is a sacred hill east of here,' the messenger said, 'with a temple dedicated to Freya. By long custom, no weapon may be borne there. If you agree, you can meet there in peace.'

Elspeth heard a murmur among the men surrounding her. A truce sworn at a shrine was binding, whatever the god involved.

'Very well,' said Heored. 'When does Earl Olav wish to meet?'

'At once,' came the reply.

CHAPTER THIRTEEN

The whole of Heored's army followed the messenger eastwards along the river. The king still feared treachery, and would not split his followers, and the men walked with their swords and bows at the ready, casting suspicious glances around them. Edmund, remembering the hedges alive with men last night, was glad of the bright sunlight which showed the fields empty in all directions.

He found himself walking beside his father at the column's head. Heored walked in silence, and Edmund, with so much that he wanted to say to his father, could not find the words.

Then Heored turned to look at him.

'Your friend, the shipman's girl, fought well yesterday,' he said. 'And the minstrel saved us last night, with those arts of his. But these are strange companions for a king's son! A girl who battles alongside soldiers . . . a man who charms the weather . . . And now you say you are Ripente.' He sighed. 'I don't understand the paths you're taking, Edmund. I fear I've neglected your teaching: I should have taken you with me sooner.'

'How could your teaching have stopped me being what I am?' The words burst from Edmund before he could stop himself. 'Father – I am Ripente. I'm sorry it grieves you, but I'm no traitor, and nor are my friends. I would trust Cluaran or Elspeth with my life; I have done.' His throat was too tight to continue.

'We'll talk of this later,' Heored said. 'That must be our meeting-place.'

They were approaching a low, rounded hill, bare of trees and so regular in shape that it might have been a giant burial mound. On top was a simple wooden building: square, with a pitched roof. Clustered around the foot of the hill was a small crowd of men, dressed identically in leather armour and breastplates.

The soldiers parted to let another man through, taller and stockier than the others, dressed in a long fur cloak. His face was weathered, with a great hawk-nose above a curved blond moustache.

'Earl Olav,' said the messenger walking on the other side of Edmund's father, 'I bring to you King Heored of Sussex, his son and his liege men.'

It was agreed that no more than twenty on each side would attend the parley in the temple, while the rest of the Sussex men waited a respectful distance below. Cathbar would be one of those at the parley, Edmund saw with relief, and after some thought his father included Cluaran as well. Both of his companions were still dressed in the armour of the Sussex men, though the armourer had clearly taken fewer pains with

Cluaran's gear than he had with Edmund's: the minstrel's breastplate was too big for him, and the cloak too long.

When Edmund stepped up as well, his father at first shook his head. 'You'd do better waiting down here,' he said, and Edmund saw an unfamiliar flash of anxiety in his eyes. 'There's something about this earl that I still don't trust.'

'I don't care,' Edmund said stubbornly. 'My place is with you.'

Heored nodded, laying his arm for a moment around his son's shoulders. 'Keep your wits about you, then.'

As the party started towards the hill, Edmund saw Elspeth walking at the back, half hidden between Cathbar and Cluaran. He smiled a little: his father would disapprove if he saw, but it warmed his heart to know that his friend would not be left behind.

They unbuckled their sword-belts and laid the weapons on the ground, while the Danes did the same a few feet away. Then, on an order from the earl, they began the ascent.

The path they used was narrow and deeply worn, and in places Heored's men had to ascend in single file. Edmund sent his sight to the top of the hill, looking for an ambush. But he found no human eyes there at all; borrowing the sight of a circling bird, he saw only the empty shrine, and the worn grass around it.

When they reached the hilltop Olav Haaksen and his men were waiting in front of the temple. It was a simple construction, little more than a platform the height of a man's shoulders, holding three high walls with a pitched roof above. The fourth wall was part-open, with two great doors pulled back. A flight of wooden stairs led up to the raised entrance. Inside the structure, oil lamps had been fixed to each of the supporting pillars, casting a garish yellow light that made the space behind them hard to see, but Edmund could make out an altar, and on it a large central statue flanked by two smaller figures.

'That'll be Freya, their goddess, and her children,' Cathbar said in his ear.

Elspeth and Cluaran came up beside them as Heored halted his followers by the steps. Haaksen stepped forward, gesturing to Heored to do the same, and the two men climbed the steps together to stand within the temple.

Heored spoke first, holding up his hands to show that they were empty. 'I've come unarmed to your temple, as you asked me. Now you are bound to hear my demands.'

'Speak on, Heored of Sussex.' The earl's voice was calm and faintly amused.

'First,' Heored said, 'do you deny that you and your men sailed to Northumbria and ransacked the port there?

'I do not,' Haaksen said. 'Though I might do; for I did not sail myself, and you have no proof. But we are in my temple. It was indeed some of my men who despoiled your cousin's port: lesser lords, and younger sons without land or wealth of their own. I knew of their undertaking, and encouraged them, having no lands or wealth to give them.'

There was a muffled exclamation from the men around

Edmund. Was their quest over, and so simply? The earl had admitted responsibility; bound himself, surely, to make amends. But Haaksen had not finished.

'So here is my word,' he said, and raised his hand in pledge. 'In the presence of my god, I bind myself and all who follow me never again to sail to your lands for spoil; nor to your cousin's lands, as long as my life lasts.' He let his hand fall. 'So much for your demands. Now you must hear what I require of you.'

'Our demands are not yet done.' Heored's voice was steely. 'Your men murdered some of my cousin's people; reduced others to poverty. What reparation will you make to them?'

Haaksen's eyes glittered. 'You will see my reparation,' he cried. He lifted his hand again and brought it down in a chopping motion.

Instantly, half a dozen of his men leapt up the stairs of the temple, while the rest threw themselves in front of the platform, blocking it off. Heored, roaring with fury, grasped Haaksen by the throat – but the earl's followers had already surrounded him. One of them reached behind the images on the altar, and Edmund saw a flash of steel. Next moment, the men were passing bright swords from hand to hand.

'Treachery!' Cathbar bellowed.

The Sussex men surged towards the temple, throwing themselves on the Danes who stood in their way.

For an instant, Edmund was frozen with horror. He saw Elspeth beside him, opening and closing her right hand, mouthing 'Ioneth!', her face crumpling when no sword appeared. Cluaran had snatched a stone from the ground and was using it as a weapon against a man a head taller than himself. Cathbar had knocked one man down and was trying to clamber on to the platform, kicking at two of Haaksen's men as they pulled him back by the legs.

Above him, Edmund heard his father cry out – and he could move again.

He dodged between the fighters, ducked under the outstretched arms of one of Haaksen's men and through the legs of another. He was on the steps – then inside the temple. And in his belt he still had his little hunting knife.

For a moment he could see only the ring of men advancing on their prey, swords gleaming dully in the yellow light. Then he caught sight of his father.

Heored was bleeding from several wounds, but was still on his feet. He had his back to the rear wall of the temple, beside the great central idol, and had picked up one of the flanking statues, a thick wooden pole half the height of a man, with a face carved at the top. He held the statue in both hands, swinging it like a club.

Edmund darted forward, drawing his knife. The swordsmen around his father were moving warily, but they were still closing in. With a yell, Edmund stabbed at the man nearest him, catching him in the sword arm. The man grunted and swerved. Heored looked towards him, and saw his son.

'Edmund – no!' he cried, and for the first time in his life Edmund saw fear in his father's eyes. 'Go back!'

But Edmund could not obey. One of the assailants had seized on Heored's distraction to lunge at his throat. Edmund struck without thinking and buried his knife in the man's back. The attacker dropped without a sound, the knife still in him, and Heored grabbed at his sword as it fell.

Then Edmund felt himself seized around the waist, his arms pinioned, and dragged away from his father. He howled and struggled, twisting around in the iron grip.

Olav Haaksen's face grinned into his. 'You can't save him, foolish boy!' he cried, and threw Edmund from the platform.

He fell hard against one of the men below, who staggered. Edmund hit the ground on hands and knees. For a moment all he could do was crouch there, winded, while lights flashed before his eyes. Then his sight cleared and he looked up, as a heavy grinding noise sounded above his head.

The great doors of the temple had been closed. Edmund screamed, but he could not pull himself up through the press of bodies. He could still hear shouts and the clanging of metal behind the heavy wooden doors. Haaksen stood before them with a bloodied sword in his hand, slashing at any man who tried to come close, until the sounds died away.

'It's over!' the earl shouted exultantly.

The men around Edmund had stopped fighting. Haaksen called up two of his followers to open the temple doors again. Inside, nothing moved. One of the lamps had fallen and gone out. The dim light from the other showed only a confused heap of bodies.

'Sussex men!' he cried. 'There's no need for any more to die. Go home now, and my word to you will stand.'

'Your word!' shouted Teobald, his voice breaking. 'You broke parley – you murdered our king!'

'His life was forfeit, for leading his men to this land,' Haaksen said. 'And our god required it. He fought well,' he added, looking with a little regret at his dead men on the platform. 'But that makes the sacrifice more worthy.' He beckoned to some of his men on the ground. 'Take up their bodies,' he told them, 'but leave the king for his own people.'

Cathbar looked at him with contempt. 'You've defiled your own goddess's temple!' he said coldly.

'This?' Haaksen laughed. 'Freya and her kind are dead! We worship a new god. This will be his temple from now on, consecrated with blood and fire. Look!' He leapt on to the platform again and took up the remaining torch, bringing it to light the giant statue. For the first time Edmund saw that the face of the goddess had been defaced with sword-strokes. Over it was scrawled a new face: narrow eyes, a savage grin, and hair and beard of flame.

'The burning man,' Haaksen said, and there was reverence in his voice. 'He heals when he will, and kills when he will, and his eyes are upon us now and for ever. He comes with the thunderbolt, and his veins run with fire.'

'And his name,' Cluaran said softly, 'is Loki.'

To Edmund, standing in the ruins of his world, it seemed as if he had known it all along. *Loki . . . who destroyed Elspeth's father, and Cluaran's, and now mine. Who unleashes dragons and burns villages. What else could he be but a god?*

'Your father is dead, little king,' said Haaksen. 'Go home, and I'll kill no more of your people. The Burning One will need many warriors when he comes to spread his rule over your own land. But it will not be my men who bring him to your shores. You'll embrace him yourself before long.' He smiled. 'As all do in this land. Even the ones who spread his word in blood and fire – burning the homes of those who will not praise his name.'

The bodies were being carried out of the temple, leaving only one behind. Olav Haaksen turned on his heel, closely flanked by his men, and strode away down the hill.

Edmund ran to where his father lay sprawled on the altar beneath the grinning, mocking face.

Heored opened his eyes as Edmund raised him and looked at his son with the ghost of a smile. 'You came to me in a good hour,' he whispered. 'You saved me from the death of a trapped animal, let me die with a sword in my hand.'

'Don't leave me, Father! Please . . .'

'No more of that!' Heored interrupted, with some of his old impatience. 'You're a man now . . . A king. Listen to me, Edmund – take the men home, do you hear me? Go and comfort your mother.' He broke into a racking cough, gasping for breath, while Edmund clung to him as if his father were a leaf being whipped away in the wind.

'I'll do everything you say,' he promised, trying to keep his voice steady. Heored nodded. When he spoke again his voice had faded to a breath, so thin that Edmund had to bend his ear to his father's mouth

'Whatever skills . . . the gods have given you . . . you're still my son, Edmund. Be a king.'

'I will, Father! I'll be worthy of you, I swear it.' Edmund's voice caught in his throat. 'And I'll avenge you on the one who did all of this. I'll destroy the Burning Man.'

He did not know if his father heard him. Heored's eyes stared at him unseeing, and his head lolled back. Edmund lowered his father to the ground and looked up. Men were standing around him, waiting for him to speak. Cathbar looked down at him gravely. Behind him, Cluaran was silent and Elspeth's eyes were full of tears.

Edmund felt tears run down his own face, but he did not stop to wipe them away. He bent to close his father's eyes, then rose to his feet.

'King Heored is dead,' he said, amazed to hear how steady his own voice sounded.

Teobald nodded and knelt down by Heored's body. When he stood up, he held the king's signet ring, the great ruby that Edmund had never seen off his father's hand. The captain took Edmund's right hand and slid the ring on to his middle finger. Then he knelt again.

'Hail,' he said, and around him the other men joined in, their voices rising in chorus.

'Hail, Edmund: King of Sussex!'

CHAPTER FOURTEEN

There was no getting near to Edmund that afternoon. He was given no time to mourn, Elspeth thought with sympathy: the captains surrounded him, pledging their service, and asking his instructions for the disposal of the camp, and the place of his father's burial. There was work to do, too. Some of Heored's men had been wounded by Haaksen's followers. Two had died, and several others needed all the help that the camp healer and Eolande could give them. The Fay woman kept Elspeth busy improvising splints and tearing bandages, and then, after the wounded and dead had been carried back down the hill, set both her and Wulf to fetching water.

Elspeth was glad to be occupied. Whenever her hands were idle, Haaksen's words came back to her: *The Burning Man . . . his eyes are upon us now and for ever.* She remembered the grinning face she had seen scrawled across defaced shrines throughout her journey. The demon's image had followed her across the country, but she had not recognised it until now. Perhaps Loki truly was everywhere.

She shivered, looking over her shoulder – but there was only the activity of the camp: men lighting fires, cleaning their weapons, and further away from the hill's foot, building a pyre.

They held the funeral just before sunset. Teobald and the other two captains laid Heored's body on the bier with his two slain men on each side. Their three swords were laid beside them. It was Edmund who set the lighted torch to the wood; then all the men stood back while the flames rose and the thick smoke coiled upwards, turned a lurid red by the dying sun.

Edmund looked very small and slight among the men, and his face was wax-pale in the light of the flames, but he held himself as straight as a spear.

'I pledge my father's memory,' he declared, and there were answering cries of 'Heored!'

'Before he died,' Edmund went on, 'my father charged me not to spend the life of a single one of his men on needless revenge. Tomorrow you will start back for Sussex.'

There was a loud murmur among the men; Elspeth suspected that but for the sorrow of the occasion, it would have been a cheer. She looked at her friend, who suddenly seemed remote from her: a leader of men. Would he go home, too? And if he did, how would she manage without him?

It was a black night, without even a moon. Elspeth walked through the sleeping camp. The burial mound had been completed: it stood stark and bare, abandoned except for Edmund, who sat alone, keeping watch over his father for one last night.

He looked up as she approached, his face twisted with misery. In that moment she forgot that he was a king and ran to him, throwing her arms around him.

'Oh, Edmund, I'm so sorry . . .'

Edmund leant against her, his shoulders shaking with sobs. They held on to each other fiercely for a few moments; then Edmund pulled back and brushed the tears from his face, struggling for calm.

'I'll be better tomorrow,' he said. His voice was slow and rough, as if the words hurt him. 'I know what it is I have to do, and my father's . . . the captains will help me.'

'*Must* you go back?' Elspeth had not intended to say it, but the words flew out of her. 'If Loki wins, we've all lost. There won't be a kingdom for you to rule!'

Edmund turned to her, and she recoiled from the anger in his face. 'I'm lost already,' he said. 'It was Loki who killed my father, not Haaksen – he was just the tool. Up in that temple, I swore to destroy him – but I don't know how. We can't even find him!'

'Maybe we can,' Elspeth argued. 'We know now that he's getting followers . . . worshippers. They're killing in his name: the Burning Man. He must have won them over somehow – maybe their leaders have met him. If we can find some of them, and talk to them . . .' she shuddered, 'maybe pretend that we believe in him too, we can find out where, and what form he took.'

Edmund was staring at her. 'As he did in the fishing village in the Snowlands, you mean? Making them see him as a miracle-worker?'

'Yes, and the healer in Alebu. If we talk to people, just as travellers . . .'

But Edmund was looking away again, the hope dying in his face. 'It's no good,' he said. 'I have a duty to my men. What would they think if I abandoned them? I have to be a king now.'

He did not look like a king, Elspeth thought. Sitting here in the dark, his thin arms around his knees, he was more like the boy she had first met on the *Spearwa*: lost and afraid. And he bore the weight of everyone's expectations, on top of his grief. She could not burden him with more demands.

'Father told me to take them home,' Edmund said, very low.

'That's for tomorrow,' Elspeth told him. She put an arm around his shoulder, and he sagged against her. 'You should rest now.'

He nodded slightly. In a few moments his head fell forward and his breathing became soft and regular. Elspeth lowered him to the ground and wrapped his cloak around him before creeping away.

In her dream that night, Elspeth stood on a steep hill, ankle-deep in snow. A chasm gaped at her feet, its depths rumbling

with unseen fires – and from the far side, someone was calling to her. She made out a tiny, distant figure; black-haired, clothed in white.

Ioneth! she shouted over the ravine. The little figure answered, gesturing downwards at something. Try as she might, Elspeth could not make out the words: only the faint, sweet sound of Ioneth's voice. She ventured closer to the chasm's edge, but the roaring from the depths grew louder, drowning out all other sounds. Ioneth seemed further away now, her frantic warning fading into the distance. And in the chasm, something stirred: something fiery and raging, too huge to be contained. An answering jolt of fire shot down Elspeth's arm and burst painfully from her hand.

She started from sleep. Her hand tingled, but she could not tell whether the jolt had been real or imagined. Light from a blue sky stung her eyes, and the makeshift camp was filled with quiet bustle as the Sussex men rolled their blankets. Elspeth pulled herself up, reassured by the bright light and the orderly preparations. Then she saw the freshly made grave-mound, and remembered. King Heored was dead – and today Edmund would leave to take his men home.

Teobald and the other captains were calling the men into marching order. Elspeth looked for Edmund but did not see him. *It's probably best*, she told herself. *We said all we needed to say last night.* She tried to shake off the heaviness that dragged at her, and set off to find Cathbar and Cluaran. She

would tell them her idea of using the Burning Man's converts to lead them to Loki.

But she still had to find a way to fight Loki. She remembered her dream: Ioneth's fading voice, and the impossibly huge distance between them as the fire rose against her. *I won't let you vanish!* she vowed, clenching her right hand.

Cluaran came striding towards her, propelling Wulf by his shoulders. 'I found the imp playing around the king's grave,' he said. 'We're nearly ready to go, if you are.'

Elspeth nodded. 'We should say farewell before we go.'

Cluaran gave her an odd look. 'Edmund's here now,' he said.

Edmund was running up to them, his face touched with colour. He was no longer wearing the fine clothes his father had given him, but his old fur cloak and heavy boots. He looked better, Elspeth thought; no longer lost as he had seemed last night.

'I wasn't sure if we'd have the chance to say goodbye,' she greeted him.

'I'm not saying goodbye,' he told her. 'I'm coming with you.'

Elspeth stared at him.

'You were right,' he said. 'While Loki lives, there's no safety for my people, or for anyone. We have to fight him.'

'And what of your promise to your father?' Cathbar asked.

'I promised him I would send our men home, and I will. Teobald will lead them back to Sussex, and bear a letter to my

mother. Father charged me not to waste any more of our men's lives, but he didn't forbid me to attack Loki myself. You may think I'm a fool, but I have to try.'

Cathbar looked serious. 'I don't know how you'll succeed,' he said, 'but I won't call you a fool, Edmund Heoredson.' He turned to Elspeth. 'Well, my girl, our party is complete again – and it seems our task is to catch the wind and tie up the lightning.' He swung his pack to his shoulders. 'So we'd best make a start.'

CHAPTER FIFTEEN

They started by returning to the road.

Both Cluaran and Cathbar approved of the idea of looking for the god's followers. 'I thought of something of the sort myself,' the captain said. 'But we'll have to watch our words, and lie skilfully.'

'Trust me for that,' Cluaran said.

The trees by the roadside were in full leaf, and loud with birdsong. The fields that they passed seemed deserted, and Elspeth began to fear that it would be a long search for anyone they could question. But the road was still churned up with footprints, and Cluaran, inspecting them, said that some at least were recent.

It was mid-morning when they found their first opportunity. Cathbar, who was up ahead, stopped and called back to them. 'Over there!' he said, pointing.

Just visible down the road was a thin plume of smoke. It came from a settlement a little way from the road: small, poor, and apparently deserted. All the people they could see were gathered in the field at the roadside. There were around two dozen of them, all poorly clothed. Near the road, a scrawny donkey cropped the grass. Its cart had been set up in the middle of the field, with a small fire lit in front of it. A man stood on the cart to address the crowd, who listened with rapt attention.

'And he shall come to them in flame!' the speaker shouted. 'Then all shall know his glory. He will rule over all the earth. From east to west, there shall be none but the Burning Man!'

There was a clumsy response of 'Praise him!' The listeners were mostly young men, with a few women and children at the back. Elspeth guessed that most of them were from the village, but a few of the men, and two women, stood in a separate group close to the cart, leading the responses. They were even more ragged than the rest of the crowd: beggars, Elspeth would have said, but for the fierce pride on their faces.

'Who will come with me?' the speaker cried, his voice rising almost to a scream. 'Who will join in the work, and spread the word of the Burning One?'

The group near the cart cried out together, and some of the young men among the villagers joined in, but not all.

'What about our fields?' called one woman, and an old man near the back spat disgustedly.

'Load of nonsense, if you ask me,' he shouted. 'Leave my crops to go traipsing round the countryside? Be off with you.'

'You talk of fields?' the preacher cried. His voice dripped scorn. 'What are cabbages and corn to the glory of the spirit? Our god can nourish us with a word.'

'Have you tried eating your own?' the old man jeered. There was a nervous laugh among the listeners. Three of the men by the cart detached themselves and made for the back of the crowd.

'We will rise up with him!' the preacher vowed. 'No more poverty, or hunger, or disease. The Burning Man will heal all ills for those who truly believe in him. We have seen it!'

'We have seen it!' echoed his followers by the cart. The three who had moved away were making their way purposefully towards the old man now, and Elspeth saw the flash of knives in their hands. She cried out, but Cathbar had already started forward.

'But the scoffers,' the speaker's voice was suddenly deeper, 'those who will not take him into their hearts, they will be cast out.' As if on cue, the three men raised their knives – but Cathbar was there in front of them, taking the bewildered old man by the elbow and propelling him away from the crowd. One of the men gave a roar of anger, and all three started after Cathbar, but Cluaran stepped into their path.

'He was not worthy to hear your words,' the minstrel said. 'Speak to us instead.'

The men stopped, looking bewildered. Eolande stepped up to join her son, and Elspeth followed with Edmund, holding Wulf tightly by the hand.

'Who are you?' one of the knifemen asked suspiciously. The preacher on the cart had stopped speaking and all eyes were turned on them.

'We're travellers,' Cluaran replied. 'We passed this way by chance, and were caught by your leader's golden words. Tell us more!' he called to the preacher.

But the man on the cart scowled. 'Beware of the stranger,' he warned the crowd. 'Beware of those who invade our land from outside, bringing evil customs. Let no such man into your midst!' The villagers began to mutter, and one or two of the men turned threatening stares on Cluaran.

'Praise the Burning One!' It was Eolande's voice, loud and piercing. 'Praise him, night and day! Tell us your words, and save us!'

The women by the cart joined in: 'Save us!' and the crowd turned back to the preacher. After a moment the man began to speak again. Elspeth shot a grateful look at Eolande.

The next time the preacher demanded that his listeners follow him, the men all yelled as one, punching the air and stamping in their eagerness to volunteer. Elspeth joined in the general clamour, and worked her way around the side of the crowd until she reached one of the ragged women standing by the cart.

'Now we follow the Burning Man, where will he lead us?' she asked.

The young woman turned to her as if in a trance. 'We follow the preacher's word,' she said. 'We go wherever he does.'

'But where?' Elspeth persisted. The woman seemed to consider her question for a long time.

'South . . . west, maybe . . . Some will sail to other lands. What does it matter? The Burning One is here; he's all around us.' She looked at Elspeth with bright, vague eyes. 'Can you not feel him?'

Elspeth had to repress a shudder. While she tried to think of a reply, the young woman took hold of her arm. 'Why do you ask so many questions?' she said. 'Are you with us? Only call on him – he will put an end to all your searching.'

He might, at that, Elspeth thought with a flash of panic. Suddenly she wanted to be away from these people. She thanked the woman and returned to the back of the crowd.

'It's useless,' Edmund sighed. 'I asked one of them if they were going to meet this Burning Man, and he told me that he is everywhere. They don't know where he is, Elspeth.'

Elspeth nodded. 'They say they might go south, or west – and to other lands. There was nothing useful.'

'The men who attacked the villages were heading south,' Edmund said. 'I'm for carrying on that way – but not with these madmen.' Elspeth nodded vehemently.

'In that case, we should leave now, while they are distracted,' Cluaran said quietly.

He pointed to a clump of trees on the other side of the road, where Cathbar was standing, signalling to them. The preacher's voice had risen to a shriek, and his hearers were shouting back at him. Elspeth grabbed Wulf by the hand and the five of them walked quickly into the trees, the preacher's fervour fading behind them.

Elspeth's mind raced as she walked. They had risked their safety and gained nothing useful. If only they could find someone who had met Loki – who could describe how he looked now!

Cluaran was behind her, speaking animatedly to Eolande – no, arguing. His voice was irritated; his mother sounded anxious.

'There are those among them who have the power, certainly,' Eolande was saying. 'But you know they don't want to get involved this time.'

'But what about Ainé? Surely she . . .'

'She least of all!'

'She fought Loki before. And her loss was no greater than yours,' Cluaran insisted. 'She would listen to you, if you asked her.'

'No,' Eolande said, and her voice was choked. 'You can't ask that of me. I cannot go back.'

Cluaran shrugged. 'Then I'll go myself,' he said.

'What are you planning, Cluaran?' Elspeth asked when they stopped to rest. 'Do you know of someone else we can ask?'

She could not read Cluaran's expression as he looked back at her. 'You heard that, did you?' he said.

'Well, do you?' she persisted. 'If there's someone who can help us, we have to find them!'

'It would not be as simple as that,' Cluaran said. 'But yes, I may have a better way to find Loki.'

Edmund and Cathbar looked up from laying the fire, and even Wulf put down the stick he had been shredding.

Cluaran looked pointedly at Eolande, who sighed and nodded. 'My mother and I have . . . countrymen who might help us, if they choose,' Cluaran said. 'We will have to continue through the forest for another day.'

'Do they live there?' Elspeth asked, surprised that he had not mentioned kin living among the trees before.

'Let's just say that I can reach them more easily from there,' the minstrel said.

Cluaran led them rapidly through the trees, heading south. 'We're looking for water,' he said.

The sound of running water drew them to a muddy trickle which Cluaran followed upstream until it joined a wider brook. They followed the brook while the blue sky overhead gradually paled and the sun sank out of sight below the tree-tops. At last they came to a river: still narrow enough to jump, but flowing swiftly between deep banks. Cluaran struck his hands together in satisfaction and quickened his pace.

The ground began to rise as they tracked the river to its source, and the trees around them were smaller and more widely spaced. Soon the water was bubbling over broken stones. Then they were climbing beside a small waterfall. As they reached the top of the rise Cluaran exclaimed in triumph.

It was a rocky outcrop, flat-topped and ringed with hawthorn bushes instead of trees. Standing on the bare rock was a small ring of stones, smooth and round, and within them a larger, flatter stone with some kind of design scratched on it, worn almost away with age.

'This will do well,' Cluaran said.

Eolande was still tense and silent, but she came up to examine the stone, running a light hand over it. 'The Water Maiden?' she asked, and Cluaran nodded.

'I think so.'

They camped nearby, on the thin grass beside the ring of stones. As the others laid out their bedrolls, Elspeth went to inspect the design on the flat stone. The lines were so faint they might have been accidental scratches, but when she stood where Eolande had been, she could see an image in them: a long-haired woman, who was pouring water from a pitcher.

Wulf came running over, looking at the stone with interest.

Cluaran looked up from his pack. 'Come back over here,' he said sharply. 'There is still much to do before nightfall.'

Elspeth exchanged a puzzled glance with Edmund. They would only be staying here one night; what more was there to do beyond setting out bedrolls? But she left the stone and took Wulf by the hand to lead him over to the half-built camp. Wulf dragged his feet, glancing over his shoulder at the scarred stone.

'When will you meet your friends?' Edmund asked Cluaran.

The minstrel did not look up. 'Tonight, if they are willing,' he said.

It was evening now: the circle of sky above their little rise had turned the colour of slate, and the light was reddening through the trees to the west. A chilly breeze had sprung up, and Cathbar grumbled as he pulled his cloak more tightly around him.

'It'll be draughty when the night winds blow,' he complained. 'Still, no doubt we're safer from the wild beasts up here. Any wolves about, Edmund?'

Edmund stiffened. 'I won't be using the gift again,' he said.

'Not using it!' Elspeth exclaimed. 'Why?'

'Because I gave my word,' Edmund replied. 'I promised my father to act like a king.'

'And that means never using your skill?' Elspeth was incredulous.

'Yes! The Ripente serve kings – they don't rule.'

That was your father's belief, not yours. And he was wrong! But she looked at Edmund's unhappy face and held her tongue.

'It's men we have to fear, not beasts,' Cluaran said. 'And the ones who threaten us most will not come here. This is a shrine: a very old one,' he explained. 'There are hundreds of years of faith here: even Loki could not turn this place to his own worship all at once.' He stood up. 'It's time for me to go. I'll return tomorrow before sunset. Wait for me here, and if you have to leave this spot while I'm gone, stay close to the river.'

Cathbar stood too, and offered to go down into the trees and hunt for some supper.

'I'll go with you,' Edmund said, and Elspeth offered to take Wulf to collect firewood. As she followed Wulf back into the trees, she heard Cluaran speaking to Eolande in tones she had not heard from him before: almost pleading.

'There are many there who still miss you: they would welcome you back.'

'No,' Eolande said. 'I don't belong there any more.'

'Where do you belong, if not there?'

'I don't know.' Eolande's voice faded behind her, but Elspeth could hear the sadness in it. 'Maybe nowhere.'

Wulf seemed eager to run deep into the forest, but Elspeth stopped him, collecting their sticks as close by as she could. When they returned, Eolande was leaning against one of the round stones and gazing blankly at the ancient image in the centre of the ring.

Cathbar and Edmund returned late, with a single small bird. 'All the animals seem to be elsewhere tonight,' Cathbar said lightly, but he did not look at Edmund, and Elspeth wondered if he blamed her friend for refusing to use his gift to help with the hunting. Edmund said nothing at all.

They lay down around the small fire. To Elspeth's surprise, Eolande offered to keep watch, saying she could not sleep. She sat straight-backed beside the shrine, and Elspeth's last memory before she slept was of the Fay woman's dark eyes looking at her intently. *Or as if there's something about me she fears.* She was wondering what it could be when sleep overtook her.

They woke hungry and chilled. After last night's unsuccessful hunt, their food rations were running low, and after their sparse breakfast of dried meat Cathbar set off to try again. He did not ask Edmund to come with him.

Elspeth sat with Edmund, looking out through the trees. They had made up their packs and scattered the ashes of the fire, and now there seemed nothing to do but wait. She could not remember when she had last been so idle.

'I wonder how Cluaran visits his people,' she said.

Edmund considered. 'I think there's a secret entrance to their kingdom somewhere. But it's best not to try to find it – from all I've heard, they're prickly people.'

Elspeth nodded. 'Do you think they'll really be willing to help us?'

'Eolande's helping us,' Edmund reminded, looking over to where the Fay woman still sat by the shrine. As if she had heard her name spoken, Eolande looked up.

'Where is the boy?' she asked, her voice uneasy. 'We should stay close together.'

'Wulf? He's by the river,' Elspeth reassured her, getting up to check. She stopped at the edge of the little outcrop, just above the spring. The water bubbled out near her feet and spilled into the stream below, surrounded on both sides by bushes, and further away by beech and linden trees. Wulf was nowhere to be seen.

'I don't know why you chase after him like this!' Edmund complained as they trudged through the forest. 'He's been nothing but trouble since he joined us.'

'Wulf doesn't see danger the same way we do,' she said.

'I think he's used to foraging for himself,' Edmund said. 'The people he was with before plainly took no care of him.'

'But they were his family!'

'Perhaps not.' Edmund's face was thoughtful. 'He said they were traders. We know they had a cart, and goods to sell. Could they not have afforded proper shoes for their own son, living on the road, in such cold weather?'

Elspeth thought of Wulf: his mischievous smile and boundless energy. But Edmund was right: when they first met him he had been a scrawny, shivering waif, with pitifully thin clothes and rags around his feet. 'You think he might have been a slave?' she said.

Edmund nodded. 'Some traders keep them. And it would explain why Wulf never talks about his family.'

'Perhaps you're right,' Elspeth admitted. *Perhaps he never even knew his family!* she thought, with a stab of pity for the outcast child.

'I think we've found him,' Edmund said. In the soft ground by the water's edge was a small footprint. Next moment, Elspeth heard a skittering from the bushes nearby and saw the boy's face peering at her through the leaves.

'Wulf!' she cried. 'Why must you keep running off?'

'But I found berries, Elsbet! Come and see!

'They can't be eatable, Wulf,' Edmund said. 'It's still spring.'

'Come and see!' the boy insisted. Elspeth and Edmund exchanged a glance, and followed him.

Wulf led them away from the river. 'We can't go far, mind,' Elspeth warned him.

Wulf nodded. He moved his head stiffly, Elspeth thought, and as he turned back to his path she was sure he winced. 'Is something hurting you, Wulf?' she asked. The boy did not answer, but his hand went up to his neck.

Elspeth stopped. 'Let me see,' she ordered.

The sides of Wulf's neck were chafed raw. The thin little chain he wore had become twisted and it was cutting into his skin.

'I'm sorry, Wulf,' she began. 'I know you love this chain . . .'

'No!' the boy said. 'I hate it.'

'But didn't your father give it to you?'

'The father put it on me, yes,' Wulf said. His face clouded. 'He was bad to me, Elsbet. So was his son. The real son.'

Elspeth let out a long breath. It looked like Edmund had been right. Wulf was a slave, and a poorly treated one.

'They shackled him!' Edmund exclaimed, behind her.

'We'll get it off him now!' Elspeth said fiercely. The chain looked flimsy; with a thin blade, they could surely snap a link.

'Here.' Edmund was already at Wulf's side, drawing his knife. 'Hold still, Wulf.'

But Wulf ducked his head and backed away, wailing. 'No!' he insisted. 'Let Elsbet do it!'

Edmund shrugged and handed the knife to Elspeth. As she took it, she felt the same sense of wrongness that had run through her with the sword Cathbar had given her. *But this isn't a sword*, she told herself – and an almost forgotten shock ran down her arm, from shoulder to fingertips.

Ioneth?

Was there a stir of response? She felt a thrill of joy: if Ioneth was returning to her . . . But she must focus on the task now. *Help me, if you're here!*

Wulf tilted his head to one side and narrowed his eyes as she touched the point of the blade to one of the links, trying to avoid his raw skin. The jolt shot down her arm again, painfully this time, but she ignored it.

'Be brave, Wulf!' she told him. 'You'll be free in a moment.'

'Yes,' the boy whispered.

His rough shirt was in the way of her hand, and she waited while Edmund fumbled at the fastenings and pulled it open.

'I wonder if his owners did this to him as well?' he muttered.

Elspeth looked down at the boy's chest. A scar ran from shoulder to navel, deep red against the white skin. Something about it seemed familiar . . . and then the pain came to her again, so fierce that she almost dropped the knife. A scene flashed before her eyes: fire and stone; a chained figure, and the white light as she struck with the crystal sword. And then Loki: the chain still around his neck; his chest slashed with red.

'No,' she whispered. 'No. I did this myself.'

She snatched her hand back and thrust the knife behind her, away from the chain. The little figure before her stood like a statue – and for a moment she could not make herself move. 'Edmund,' she said, as clearly as she could, 'take the knife and run. Get back to the shrine.'

'But what . . .'

'Just run!' she cried, her eyes still fixed on the boy's face. It was without expression, but the narrowed eyes had turned the colour of candle flame.

Elspeth turned and ran with Edmund. She did not dare to look back, but Edmund cast a glance over his shoulder as they pounded through the trees.

'Elspeth . . . Wulf . . . he's changing. He's growing taller!'

'Get to the river!' Elspeth sobbed. Her legs would not move fast enough.

No thunderous footsteps came after them. Instead they heard a rush of air, and a crackling that grew louder and fiercer as they ran. They were almost at the river when smoke billowed over them, and a terrible heat knocked them to the ground.

CHAPTER SIXTEEN

Eolande had known that something like this would happen.

When she heard the distant cries, and saw the smoke billowing above the trees further down the river, her first response was guilt. She should not have kept the children here. Now they might all die: the strange, empty-hearted little boy; the young king, with all his promise . . . and Elspeth.

She used a skill she knew to cast her sight down the river. Two of them were in the water: Elspeth and Edmund. She drew a quick breath of relief. The flames were creeping towards them, but they would not consume them – not yet.

So she could still help them. And after all, she would have to return.

She walked into the stone ring, summoned her sense of the place and drew the doorway in the air. It came to her touch as if she had made the journey only yesterday: three lines of faint light, the air between them shimmering like the skin on water.

She took one step towards it, and halted. She must tell them she was going, if she could. She called down the flow of the water, not knowing if she could make them hear.

'Elspeth! Run upstream! I'll fetch help.'

Then she stepped through the opening.

They had thrown themselves headlong into the water: Edmund was wet to his hair. Just downstream of him, Elspeth was still on her hands and knees. He splashed over to her and took her arm to pull her up. The face she turned to him was ashen.

'He's Loki!' she gasped. 'All this time, when we walked together . . .'

'We have to move,' Edmund said, dragging at her hand.

'He slept beside me . . .' Elspeth moaned, but she ran with him.

The roaring of the fire kept pace with them. On the bank, flames leapt at the edge of Edmund's vision, and he could hear the crackling as the fire spread to the bushes at the water's edge. Smoke poured over their heads. They bent low as they ran, but Edmund's throat was soon rasping and his chest tightened painfully. Beside him he could hear Elspeth wheezing. He concentrated on putting one foot in front of the other, forcing his way through the muddy water that swirled about his knees. His mind filled with what he had seen in that single backward glance: the child standing beneath the trees, his body billowing like smoke; then suddenly, impossibly tall.

His hair had turned to flames, his eyes had glowed and his face flickered as if his whole body were filled with fire. And the branches which brushed his head had instantly begun to smoulder.

The flames were closer now, leaping higher than the bushes they consumed. Behind them, Edmund thought he could hear crashing, as if something huge were pushing over trees to get to them. 'Faster!' he muttered, but the water dragged at him, and his feet slipped on unseen stones.

Elspeth was ahead of him now; she grabbed his arm as he stumbled. 'Listen!' she panted.

Had she heard the sounds of pursuit as well? Edmund did not dare glance behind him again. But his friend was looking upstream; and he saw a sudden flash of hope on her face. 'I think it's Eolande,' she said.

Edmund blinked through the smoke-haze and peered as far along the stream as he could. It vanished into the trees ahead – but there, surely, was the distant froth of the waterfall, and above it, a tiny grey figure. Then a hot wind hit them, bringing more smoke, and the figure was hidden.

'Get down!' Elspeth screamed. She shoved him in the small of his back and he staggered forward, landing on all fours with his face an inch from the water. But the smoke was lighter here, and he could breathe again.

They crawled forward side by side, forcing their way against the current. The water became clearer, and the shock of its cold against Edmund's skin was reviving at first. When he looked up he could see the waterfall ahead of him, closer already . . . but the flames were closer, too. They burned right up to the water's edge; nearly as tall as he was, and racing ahead though there was nothing growing here for them to feed on.

The riverbed was growing steeper and narrower. Edmund's left shoulder scraped against the bank, and he and Elspeth were wedged together as his jerkin caught on a rock. He pushed Elspeth in front of him and tore the wet cloth loose.

The water was no longer cold on his skin. And when he next looked up the fire burned on both sides of the stream, right up to the water's edge.

Ahead of him he heard Elspeth shout in triumph – and then she was standing against the waterfall, bathed in its spray, while flames leapt higher than her head on either side. The water's clamour mingled with the roaring of the fire to drown out what she said, but she pointed upwards. The shrine was just above her, its grey stones bare and empty. The fire had not touched it – but there was no one there to help them.

'We can climb up!' Edmund heard her shout as he scrambled up to join her. 'Come and help me!' Now he saw where she was pointing. The fall was not a sheer drop but a steep slope over uneven rocks, with a rubble of boulders at the base. About halfway up a couple of projections stuck out, the water cascading around them. If Elspeth could stand upright on the rocks at the base she might clamber to the lower spur, and then if she could hold on against the water's force . . .

There was a laugh behind them, low and clear as a bell, ringing effortlessly through the noise of fire and fall. Edmund could not help it: he turned, drawn to the sound, and felt Elspeth doing the same.

They looked out over a landscape of flame. The riverbanks were burning on both sides as far as Edmund could see. Further downstream the two lines of fire met behind them: it seemed the water had been consumed entirely. To their left the blaze had caught the nearest trees, which burned like torches. To their right there was a sea of fire stretching into the distance, covered with oily black smoke. A few taller, more stubborn trees still blazed above the wavering clouds.

And Wulf, for whom they had searched so hard, no longer existed – had never existed.

A figure emerged from a clump of fiery trees. It seemed wrapped in black cloud and as tall as the trees themselves: their sparking tops made a halo around its head. The fire parted before the giant shape as it approached, leaving a path of cinders.

It took two steps – and something changed in its scale. It was no longer a giant in the distance, but a tall man standing before them, black-cloaked and fiercely beautiful, his face and hands glowing like flame.

Loki.

'Well, Elsbet.' Wulf's lilting accent still sounded in his voice, and when he laughed, Edmund saw an echo of the child's face. 'Will you free me now?'

Elspeth moaned and covered her face with her hands. The demon's body rippled again, the cloudy stuff of his cloak floating out and collapsing in on itself. When it cleared, the child Wulf was standing there, his arms outstretched.

'They treated me so ill!' he whimpered. 'Both of them: the minstrel and his father. They chained me. They bound me to a rock. You can put right the wrong they did, Elsbet!'

'*Leave me alone!*' Elspeth screamed.

Edmund pushed her behind him and pulled out his knife. 'Come any closer and I'll add to that scar of yours!' he yelled. Behind him he heard Elspeth scrambling away.

Wulf gazed at him for a moment – and then he was Loki again, fire-lit and grinning. 'She'll come to me in the end,' he said, and his beautiful voice had nothing of the child in it now. He turned on his heel and the flames leapt up to hide him as he walked away.

Edmund turned to Elspeth. She had climbed on to the boulders at the foot of the waterfall, but she had stopped, gazing around her in horror. The flames towered on either side of the pool they stood in, high as the top of the waterfall. Water still bubbled from the gap in the rocks, but above it more fire danced, cutting off their view of the shrine. Behind them the river had vanished; the banks had collapsed, and the two fires had met and merged. They were surrounded by walls of flame.

'It's all illusion!' Elspeth cried suddenly. She stood on tiptoes on the highest boulder, reaching up to grab the projecting spur. 'Help me up!'

Edmund hesitated. The water around his knees felt hot, and steam was rising from the surface. 'But if it isn't?'

'It's not real fire!' Elspeth insisted. 'He did this to us before, Edmund. Remember, in the cave beneath the mountain? We thought we would be consumed in flame, but there was nothing there. He can't catch us like this!' Without waiting for his help she leapt, caught the lower spur and hauled herself up, thrusting her arms through the flames to pull herself on to the ledge.

And screamed.

For a dreadful instant she hung there, still screaming; then she dropped. Her arms and hands were blazing as she fell back into the pool. Edmund flinched from the heat as he tried to catch her – and then the two of them were sprawled in the steaming water, the flames on her skin mercifully extinguished.

Elspeth was on her knees, sobbing with pain, holding both arms out into the water. They were burned dark-red, and her right hand was bent into a claw. Walls of flame encompassed them on every side, moving closer as the water dwindled. Already the air around them was so hot that each breath scorched Edmund's throat.

There was a clap of thunder. Edmund looked up, bewildered, as clouds raced to cover the tiny patch of sky which was all they could see above the leaping flames. The thunder bellowed again – and then there were drops of water on his skin, blessedly cold. The drops thickened to rain, and then to a downpour heavier than the waterfall. It pounded on their heads as he and Elspeth looked at each other, wide-eyed. Edmund realised he was shaking with relief as he knelt beside her in the churning water, taking deep breaths of the cool, wet air.

There was sizzling and steam all around them as the fires went out. The rain began to slacken, and Edmund heard familiar voices. Cluaran was leaning over the edge of the rocks above the waterfall, with Eolande behind him. Cathbar was running towards them from the far bank, sparks scattering around his feet. He stopped in horror at the sight of Elspeth's arms, then splashed into the water to lift her with surprising gentleness. She cried out as he raised her, and breathed in gasps as he carried her up the ash-strewn slope.

Cluaran leant down to pull Edmund over the waterfall. Black soot disfigured the rock before the shrine, and all around the ring of stones the ground was charred and blackened – but the circle within the stones was untouched.

'You should never have left this place,' Cluaran said to Edmund as they helped to lay Elspeth down against the central stone. She moaned, and the minstrel gazed in dismay at her arms. 'Did you meet him?'

Edmund nodded dumbly. Cluaran had gone pale, and his face worked as if in fury, or dread. But he said nothing more. After a moment he shook his head and turned away.

'But don't you see?' Edmund called after him. 'All that searching, and Loki was with us all the time. And he promised to come back.' He looked down at his dearest friend in the world, who had her eyes shut, the lashes sooty against her white skin. He knew the demon would keep his promise, because they had the one thing he needed to be free.

Elspeth.

CHAPTER SEVENTEEN

Pain eddied and swirled in Elspeth's hands, engulfing her arms before it spread through her body like a neap tide, higher and higher, drowning everything, choking her . . . Her ears were filled with screaming. She could hear Cathbar trying to quiet her, but he sounded so far away, and didn't he realise that it was Ioneth screaming, not her?

Hush, she tried to tell her. *We're safe now: he's gone.*

'Is there nothing we can do?' It was Edmund's voice, distraught as she had seldom heard him. 'She's in such pain . . .'

'This tonic should help.' That was Eolande again. 'But she must be calm enough to take it.'

What did they mean? Elspeth tried to tell them that she was quite calm enough to take medicine – that it was Ioneth they must help. But no words came out, even though her mouth was moving. She was the one screaming after all. With an effort she made herself breathe out, close her throat to the terrible shrieks of pain. Somewhere deep inside her, Ioneth quietened too.

'There,' Eolande said. 'Raise her a little.'

She felt herself being lifted very carefully. Then a cup was at her lips and something warm and bitter-tasting in her mouth. Her throat was burned dry and cracked, but she managed to swallow.

After a few mouthfuls the pain was further away, and Elspeth thought she might be able to breathe without a scream coming out. She opened her eyes. Edmund was cradling her head against his shoulder and staring down at her in alarm. Eolande knelt beside him, offering the cup with the last dregs of the medicine.

'Where's Loki?' she tried to ask. But the words would not come; not yet.

Edmund laid her back down and she strained to listen as the voices of the others swam in and out of her hearing.

'She cannot be moved!' Eolande insisted. 'It will be days before she can walk any distance.'

'Then we'll stay here,' said Edmund. 'The shrine will protect us, won't it?'

'Not enough,' Cluaran said. 'Loki could ring it with flame, and we could not stop him. It took all my power, and Eolande's, to raise that storm, and we barely contained the fire. Sooner or later, he would find a way in.' He gazed down at Elspeth and his eyes were dark with grief. 'Loki has tried to play with her like a cat with a mouse, and he has failed. He will not try so gentle a way again. If she will not cut his last bond, then he will kill her. Elspeth is his only hope and his greatest enemy. He will have that sword – by whatever means.'

'But if just two of us stay here,' Eolande said. 'I can weave a protection around us – keep her safe until she's healed.'

'For days?' Cluaran demanded. 'And then how would you reach us? No – I have a better idea.' He dropped his voice, and for a while Elspeth heard only murmuring, and an exclamation of protest from Eolande. She strained to listen, but the sounds of their talk began to fade, and she knew she was slipping back into darkness.

'Elspeth!' It was a sharp whisper, right by her ear. Cluaran was looking down at her, his face not quite in focus. 'Loki will come after you again, and soon, while you're still weak. Do you understand?'

Elspeth nodded.

'I know of a safe place,' Cluaran went on. 'He will not be able to touch you there – but I can't take everyone; only you. Will you come with me?'

Elspeth opened her eyes wide, trying to convey her dismay. 'Edmund . . . who will keep him safe?'

Cluaran's face was very still. 'Edmund will be safe as soon as you are gone,' he said. 'Loki has no interest in him.'

'We'll meet again when you're healed.' Eolande was bending over her now. 'We'll wait at the coast for you; then take ship for Wessex. There is a place there where . . . where we might be safe together.'

Their faces were beginning to blur again. Elspeth tried to move – and felt the pain at the edges of her consciousness, ready to rush in and overwhelm her. Ioneth had started to sob again, and it was hard to hear what the others were saying.

'Yes,' she croaked.

'Then it's done.' Eolande's voice faded. 'Sleep now . . .'

'You'll take her where?' Edmund demanded. He had not abandoned his men to have Elspeth snatched out of his sight, not when Loki had revealed the extent of his power.

'To our people's country,' Cluaran said. 'Mine and Eolande's. Elspeth will be hidden there; she'll have the time she needs to heal.'

'But how will they receive her?' Eolande's voice was anxious. 'You know how little they love strangers.'

'We have no other choice,' Cluaran said. 'The sword must be saved, if we can save it.'

'You mean, Elspeth must be saved!' Edmund broke in, glaring at him.

The minstrel returned his stare levelly. 'And Elspeth too, of course,' he said.

There was little preparation to do. They filled their water flasks, and Cluaran shared his food between the others, saying that the Fay would provide for him.

'You must go straight to the coast and take ship to Wessex,' he said. 'We've no need to chase Loki from now on. He'll come to us. All we can do is choose the battleground. Eolande will lead the two of you, and Elspeth and I will follow.'

Cathbar and Eolande waited at the edge of the stone ring while Edmund bent over Elspeth to say goodbye. She seemed on the edge of sleep: her eyes were half-closed, and her breathing had slowed. She murmured something as Edmund spoke to her, but did not open her eyes.

'I'll meet you again, Elspeth,' he vowed. 'Go with Cluaran, and be healed.'

Then he followed Eolande and Cathbar down the ridge into the ruined trees. He looked back just once: Cluaran stood within the circle, his hand raised in farewell, while Elspeth lay unmoving at his feet.

They headed west, back towards the road, putting the river behind them. Edmund breathed more easily when they were among green leaves again – but the stink of burning followed them for a long time.

'I'll be glad when we're out of these trees,' Cathbar muttered to Edmund as they pushed through a thicket. 'We'll get on properly when there's a good road under our feet.'

Edmund nodded, but in truth he hardly cared how fast they went, nor where. He had left Elspeth behind – every step took him further from her, and he could not convince himself that he was doing the right thing.

It seemed an age before they reached the road again. The low sun showed the track stretching behind and before them, its surface rutted with wheels and men's feet, though there was not a soul nor a dwelling in sight. Cathbar strode forward to take the lead. As he had predicted, they made good progress: Edmund reckoned they had covered well over a league, leaving the forest far behind them, before night fell.

'We must be near the southern edge of the kingdom,' Cathbar said. 'We'll be in the Saxons' lands in a day or less, and after that, the Frankish kingdom – we can take ship for home from there.'

They slept in the shelter of a hedge at the roadside, and woke to a mild, grey morning – and the road full of travellers. Old men and women weighed down by bundles and families with handcarts and small children passed them as they rolled their blankets and ate a hasty breakfast, and were passed in their turn as Cathbar set the pace for their day's journeying. About mid-morning they overtook a large group, leading goats on strings and a donkey-cart loaded with chests, stools and blankets. Like the others, they shuffled forward with eyes bent to the ground, and would not answer when Cathbar hailed them.

There were no settlements near the road here. Edmund guessed that many of these people had been walking all night. The roadside was dotted with the remains of shrines to different gods, but no one stopped to honour them. All had been overthrown, the little statues cast down and broken, or daubed with the grinning features of the Burning Man. Edmund thought he recognised some of the broken images from his mother's shrines at home, and after the first few, he tried not to look at them.

Before midday they came to a wall: roughly made earthworks as high as a man, extending over the fields to each side of the road.

'I know of this place,' Cathbar said. 'King Harald had it built for protection against the Saxons, and lately against the Franks.'

When they reached the barrier it was not guarded. The heavy wooden gate fixed across the road was swinging open, and there was not a man in sight.

'Strange times,' Cathbar said uneasily.

When the sun finally emerged from the clouds, they were passing a cart at the side of the road, the donkey cropping grass while the driver sat nearby, propped against one of the wheels. He was so still that Edmund was seized with dread, remembering the pedlar Menobert, murdered at the roadside. But the carter stirred as they approached and nodded to them. *Just taking a rest in the sun.* For a moment Edmund almost envied the man, scrawny and ragged though he was. What must it be like to have nothing to think about but the next meal?

The road was bordered by hedges now, with a few trees dotting the fields behind them. Edmund heard Eolande give a small gasp, and followed her gaze to see another roadside shrine, almost hidden by hawthorn and brambles. For a wonder, it had escaped destruction by the worshippers of the Burning Man, perhaps thanks to its thorny veil. Edmund looked closer at the little goddess who smiled out from between the thorns – and stared.

It's Branwen! he thought, astonished. *Or another just like her.* His mother's namesake, the goddess who ruled over water and the sending of messages. The same flowing hair, the same broad-winged bird hovering above her.

'Stop a moment,' he said.

He had no wine for a libation; not even beer, but he took the last of his father's wheat bread from his pack and crumbled it before the feet of the little image. Heored had never been greatly concerned with honouring the gods – he had always preferred to trust to his own strength and the loyalty of his men. Still, Edmund sent a brief, silent prayer to any power that might be listening for his father's soul, and for his men's safe journey over the sea to Sussex.

And keep my mother well, he finished, as he touched the statue's feet. *Keep her in good comfort until I return to her.*

'What's going on here?'

It was a man's voice, sharp and commanding. Edmund spun round to see a group of nine or ten: all burly, all in thick furs, and armed with clubs and axes.

'Looks like we missed one!' their leader declared, his gaze flicking from Edmund to the shrine. 'Stay where you are, idol-worshippers! We'll show you the power of the one true god!' He pushed past Edmund and raised his axe above the little image.

'Leave her alone!' Edmund grabbed at the handle of the axe, deflecting the man's aim so that it carved a swathe through the hedge and stuck fast in the woody stems beneath it. The man tugged ineffectually at it, shooting a murderous look at Edmund. Then he turned to his men.

'Take them!' he ordered.

Edmund drew his sword. Cathbar was already at his side, his weapon in his hand, and Eolande had raised her arms, muttering the beginning of a charm. But their backs were to the hedge, and the men had surrounded them, brandishing their long-handled axes. They grinned as they advanced.

There was a terrified braying behind the attackers. A moment later the men scattered as a wild-eyed donkey burst through their ranks, the cart it drew careering behind it. The beast swerved crazily as it reached Edmund, and juddered to a halt that sent the cart skittering sideways, knocking several of the attackers off their feet. A man yelled down to them from the donkey's back; it was the skinny carter they had passed a while before.

'Climb on the cart! Quick!'

The frightened donkey's hooves kept the men at bay while they scrambled up. Cathbar lifted Eolande bodily and landed her in the cart with little grace. The Fay woman said nothing. They huddled together, Edmund and Cathbar slashing at any of the bandits who came too close, as the driver urged his mount into another wild turn and sent him galloping down the road.

Edmund clung to the back of the cart, slammed against the wood with every jolt, while the yelling men pounded after them. One hurled his club to the ground and started to throw stones; Edmund ducked as a pair whirred past his ear. He twisted round to see the road ahead, willing their cart to go faster. The donkey was running flat out, its ears laid back. The driver crouched over its neck. When Edmund looked back, more of the pursuers had fallen behind. Soon, only the leader was still in view: a small, furious figure with fists raised. His shouts followed them down the road.

'You! Carter! I'll know you again. You're a dead man!'

The carter gave no sign that he had heard. Half a league further on, he let the donkey slow and stumble to a halt; then he climbed stiffly down and patted the beast's steaming side.

'We're not built for that kind of travel, are we, Longears?' he said wryly. His voice was deep, with a trace of accent that Edmund found familiar.

Cathbar jumped down from the cart, and came to shake the man's hand. 'We owe you a debt,' he said. 'A double one if we've brought trouble on you from those men.'

The carter shrugged. 'They'll have forgotten me long before I come this way again. It would have been the business of any decent man to stop them.'

'Well, we're grateful that you did,' Cathbar said. 'And if you're not overtired of our company, Master Carter, would you consider taking us further down the road? We'll pay you well.' He had taken out his silver-pouch as he spoke.

'Keep your money,' the carter said. 'I'd welcome your company. I'll be stopping to give this brave fellow a drink –' he slapped the donkey's side again – 'and after that we head south-east, to the coast.'

Edmund felt hope flare inside him. Perhaps the goddess Branwen had heard him after all. The carter would take them straight to where they wanted to go. Where they could wait for Elspeth, find a ship, and sail for home.

CHAPTER EIGHTEEN

It was quiet when Elspeth woke. She gazed up at a pale-grey sky, fringed with leaves. Someone was sitting beside her, perfectly still. She tried to raise herself and gasped as pain flared in her hands – not the agony of the sword, but a savage pain that snatched the breath from her.

Cluaran bent over her. 'How is your hand?'

He did not say 'hands', Elspeth thought. It would be Ioneth who truly concerned him. She looked down. Below her wrists, her hands were an angry red and mottled with blisters. Her right hand curled on itself like a singed spider, and when she tried to open the fingers the pain made her cry out. Another cry sounded in her head at the same instant.

Cluaran was watching her, his expression almost pleading.

'She's still alive,' Elspeth said. 'The fire hurt her, but she's still with me: I can hear her.'

Cluaran turned his face away. 'We must leave as soon as possible,' he said. 'Can you walk?'

Elspeth was so tired, she thought she could sleep for a moon. But she remembered what Cluaran had said about Loki coming to find her – to kill her – and she knew the time for rest would not come for a while. 'Where are we going?' she asked.

Cluaran looked down at her, and his face was expressionless once more. 'We're going to my other people,' he said. 'To the land of the Fay.'

Elspeth stared at him in dismay. 'No! I have to stay here. If Loki comes after me, I need to be ready for him.'

Cluaran shook his head. 'We have no choice. It is our only chance of healing your wounds.'

'It's Ioneth, isn't it? You are doing this for her, not me! Well, it's me Loki wants to kill. Ioneth is dead already!' Elspeth stopped, panting and aghast at the anguish that pounded behind Cluaran's eyes.

'To us, yes,' he said quietly. 'But she lives on in the sword. And that is our only hope of defeating the demon-god.'

He helped Elspeth to her feet, holding her tightly when she swayed and nearly fell down again. The fire in her hands filled her ears and hands, and she had to wait for it to clear before she could see where they were. They were standing in the stone circle, starkly grey in the blackened forest. The sky was bright above them; it must be close to midday, although the sun was hidden behind clouds. Or maybe smoke.

Cluaran released Elspeth and stepped away from her. He raised his arms above his head, his fingers coming together in a pinching movement as if pulling something towards him. He held still for a moment, then moved his hands apart, bringing them down in a wide arch around his body. A faint line of light followed as he bent to touch the ground. The air within the arch shimmered like the skin on still water. The trees on the other side suddenly looked further away. Then the air seemed to thicken, and the arch was filled with a pearly haze, shot with soft colours like the gleams inside an oyster shell.

Cluaran straightened and turned to Elspeth, taking her arm. 'Keep close beside me. Stay on the path, and speak to no one, unless I speak first. Are you ready?'

Elspeth nodded, and they stepped through the arch.

The haze enveloped them. Elspeth couldn't feel the ground beneath her feet, and for a moment she flailed in panic. But Cluaran's hand was firm on her arm. 'Keep to the path,' he said softly, and she moved one foot forward, then the other, as the pearly light flowed around her. A few paces further she thought she could make out a path ahead, grassy and lined with taller growing things that faded into the haze. The path was faint and bleached of colour, as if seen by moonlight or through mist, and she still could not feel it beneath her feet, though Cluaran drew her along it steadily, till Elspeth thought they had been walking for ever. There was a roaring like wind in her ears, but when the minstrel spoke his words seemed to drop into a huge silence.

'We're here.'

Colour and sound returned as if she had surfaced from underwater, and Elspeth blinked, shaking her head to clear it. She could hear birdsong again, and the sound of her footsteps. They were walking down a forest track, through trees that were smaller and wider-spaced than the ones they had left. There was a soft, pale light, gold-tinted like dawn or evening. There was no sun visible through the trees, and none of the long shadows of evening; no shadows at all that Elspeth could see. She wondered how long they had been walking – and with the thought, her legs buckled and pain surged back into her arms.

'Steady,' Cluaran said as she staggered against him. 'You can rest soon, I promise.'

They emerged from the trees into a meadow full of summer flowers and loud with the sound of water. A stream ran through it, widening to a pool at the far side. A tall, slender figure in a green dress was walking towards them across the grass.

'Cluaran!' she cried, and ran to embrace him, talking rapidly in a language like birdsong and falling water, and the wind in leaf-heavy trees.

Cluaran replied, indicating Elspeth. The young woman turned to her, but without looking at her face or giving any greeting. Instead she took both Elspeth's hands in her own and bent over them. Elspeth winced, but the woman's touch was cool and gentle as she ran her finger over the blistered skin.

After a moment she released Elspeth's hands and said something to Cluaran. She was pointing to the stream that ran nearby: Elspeth thought the gesture included her, and turned to Cluaran for a translation.

'You can talk to her, Roslyn,' he said. 'In her own tongue.'

The woman's face stiffened, but she looked Elspeth in the eyes for the first time. She had a long, narrow face, not unlike Eolande's. Her eyes were clear, the colour of water over pebbles, and her skin had a faint greenish tint as if it reflected the grass. 'Follow me,' she said. She led them across the meadow to the pool. 'Cool your hands in the water, child,' she urged. Elspeth could still hear the murmur of leaves in her voice, like an accent beneath the words.

Elspeth knelt by the water's edge. The water was clear to the stones at the bottom, rippling with the pattern of the clouds above. She told herself that Cluaran obviously knew the Fay woman well, trusted her to help. She leant over and let her burned hands slip through the skin of the pool. At once, she felt icy fingers stroke her, clutching at her scorched skin until she couldn't pull away if she wanted to. For a moment she thought of the tortured water spirits beneath the frozen lake in the Snowlands. But this was different: she didn't want to take her hands away. Instead, she wanted nothing more than to kneel beside the pool for ever with her hands clasped by the water.

A hand rested on her shoulder. Elspeth looked up and saw Cluaran, outlined in gold against the sky. 'That's enough,' he said, and the gentleness in his voice showed he knew how much Elspeth wanted to stay.

Reluctantly, she sat back on her heels. Her hands slipped free of the water with a shower of droplets, a tiny rainbow captured in each one. The pain had gone; she felt as if she were wearing gauntlets of coolest silk, or grass woven soft against her skin.

Behind her she could hear Cluaran in animated discussion with the woman, Roslyn.

'Use only words she can hear,' he said. 'I'll keep no secrets from her now.'

'But she's not . . .' Roslyn's voice was shocked, and she lapsed into her own tongue again. Cluaran interrupted her.

'Neither was my father! But you played with him as a child, so I was told.'

Elspeth looked up, startled. Roslyn seemed barely older than herself, and far younger than Cluaran, with her brown curls and clear eyes. The Fay woman nodded, her face suddenly stricken. 'I miss Brokk, too,' she murmured. 'Your mother's loss is shared by more than she knows.'

Cluaran's voice was gentler now. 'I already owe Elspeth a debt, Roslyn. If she succeeds in her task, our people will owe her even more. I'd have my own kin honour that debt, even if no one else here does.'

There was a long silence. Elspeth heard a soft footfall behind her, then Roslyn knelt beside her, holding a wooden bowl filled with water and strips of moss.

She gave Elspeth a cautious smile. 'Give me your hands, and I'll try this remedy.' She wrapped Elspeth's hands in the damp moss, and bound them with threads as fine as spider-silk. As she worked, she and Cluaran talked, but in Elspeth's language now. 'And so I've seen Eolande again,' Roslyn said, smiling a little sadly, Elspeth thought. 'Cluaran – can you not persuade her to come back to us?'

The minstrel looked grave. 'It would be best for her,' he said. 'But too much has happened.'

Roslyn sighed. 'When you see her again, say that her sister misses her.'

Elspeth's hands felt wrapped in countless layers of cool and softness, and she let herself slip into drowsiness. As her eyes closed, she thought she could hear Ioneth's voice again: calmer this time, murmuring words that she could not make out.

She awoke to find that someone had moved her further from the pool, and laid her head on a folded cloak. The golden light was the same as it had been when she fell asleep, and the sky was still blue; she raised her head and looked in vain for the sun.

The Fay woman bent over her, smiling. 'You've slept a long time,' she said. 'See how your hands have healed.'

The moss had gone, and they were covered in some green-ish salve now. Under it the skin of both palms was still red and sore, but the blisters had gone, and her right hand had lost its rigid claw-look. She flexed it: there was no burning pain; just a deep throbbing. Was that Ioneth's voice in her head again, whispering a greeting?

Cluaran had come up and knelt beside her. He smiled, as Roslyn did, but there was a new tension in him.

'How long have I been asleep?' she asked.

'Two days, as we measure time here,' Cluaran said. 'As the world outside goes, much longer.'

'How much longer?' Elspeth tried to get up, but her limbs were too stiff. She pushed herself clumsily to her knees. 'We must go, Cluaran! Edmund and the others will be waiting for us at the coast.'

Cluaran shook his head. 'I told Eolande to wait no longer than three days. They'll have gone by now.'

Elspeth stared at him in horror. 'You told them to leave without us?'

'I had to.' Cluaran's face was so grave that Elspeth fell silent. 'Elspeth – the most important thing was for you to heal fully. In this land you are hidden from him. As soon as you cross the boundary, he'll come after you. Would you really choose to meet him before you could use your hands?'

'But how will we find them again?' Elspeth tried to keep the tears from her voice.

'Eolande and I have fixed a meeting place in Wessex,' Cluaran said.

'How will we get there?'

'You said no secrets, Cluaran.' Roslyn's voice held an edge of reproach, and she placed a hand on Elspeth's shoulder. 'If you're sending this child to fight the Burning One, should she not know all your plan first?'

'I'm not *sending* her!' Cluaran snapped. 'And you don't know the dangers we face – neither of you do. Outside our boundaries, Loki could have heard anything I told her. He could take any form, or make any creature his spy. Out there, nothing we say is safe from him. Even this land won't keep him out for ever.'

'What do you mean?' Roslyn exclaimed. 'He couldn't come here – no gate would open for him!'

'And that would stop him, you think, if he had his full power?' Cluaran's voice was scornful. 'Let him free himself of that last chain, Roslyn, and he'll need no gate. He'll break through the wall like bursting a bubble.'

Roslyn's face was white. 'But how can Elspeth fight him?' she whispered.

'There is a place in Wessex, a stone circle of great age, so ancient that men have long forgotten the time of its first building.' He looked at Elspeth. 'Your people call it the place of the Hanging Stones. It's been turned to the worship of a dozen gods – but Loki was never one of them. If any place can block his power, it's there.'

'But how will we reach them in time?' Elspeth demanded. 'If they've already embarked, and we're still here? They can't wait there for days while we follow them.'

'You are not in the kingdoms of men here,' Roslyn said softly. 'We have many gateways that lead to Wessex.'

Cluaran narrowed his eyes. 'You told me . . . Ioneth was still with you,' he said. 'Will she be ready?'

Elspeth gazed at his face and Roslyn's, her eyes pricking. She shook her head. 'She hasn't spoken to me since we left the Snowlands. I can feel that she's there, but I don't know how to call her.'

Cluaran reached out suddenly and took her right hand between both of his. Elspeth felt a surge of energy shoot down her arm to her burned palm. She let out a small cry, but Cluaran seemed not to notice.

'Ioneth!' he whispered. His voice seemed to echo around her, and an answering whisper sounded in Elspeth's head. 'Ioneth,' he said again. 'Come to us – help us! This is what you gave yourself to do.' His voice fell until Elspeth could barely make out the words. 'This is why you left me.'

And the voice was in Elspeth's head, clear for the first time since Loki's cave.

Cluaran! I'm here . . .

Cluaran gasped and dropped Elspeth's hand. For a moment she thought he must have heard the voice too – then she saw where he and Roslyn were looking, open-mouthed.

Her hand was glowing. White light spilt from the palm, stretching towards Cluaran. It grew longer, defining pale edges, forming the shape of a blade. For an instant, Elspeth held the crystal sword again: translucent; almost solid. Then the light faded to the merest shimmer in the air, and was gone.

CHAPTER NINETEEN

They must be halfway to the coast already, Edmund thought.

It was a different journey, now that they had transport. The donkey, recovered from his bolt after a rest and a rub-down, took to the road with a will, apparently unworried by the extra burden in his cart.

'He had full crates and barrels to drag on the way up,' the carter explained. 'You three won't tire him.'

He was not as old a man as Edmund had thought at first: his hair and beard were mostly black, though streaked with grey, and his movements were vigorous. But he was thin to the point of emaciation, unkempt and poorly clad, in strange contrast to his trim cart and well-conditioned animal.

They had told him that they were travellers heading to the coast to take ship to Wessex. The carter introduced himself as Fardi.

'You're Frankish, then?' Cathbar asked. 'That name means "wanderer", doesn't it?'

The man's face closed. 'It's what my master calls me,' he said. 'All the wandering I do nowadays is along this road, to sell his wares.'

By early evening they were approaching a more populated area: a rise in the road revealed cultivated fields and rooftops in the distance. Around the next corner was another ruined shrine. The wooden statue of the god had been smashed to splinters and dust, and the face of the Burning Man was scrawled on the one wall still standing.

'It's a danger to believe in anything, these days,' Fardi said quietly.

'Do you have a faith, Master Fardi?' Edmund ventured.

'Not any more,' the man said shortly. He slowed his donkey to an amble and led it off the track, on to a patch of rough grass adjoining a sheep-pasture and backed by woods.

'It's not safe to travel after dark,' he said. 'We'll stay here tonight.'

He went into the trees to hunt for supper, taking Cathbar with him. Edmund and Eolande collected branches, then Edmund built a fire while the Fay woman searched the hedgerow for early berries.

'A strange man, our rescuer,' she remarked, laying out her small haul on a cloth while Edmund coaxed sparks from his flint.

Privately Edmund agreed, but he said, 'He saved our lives. And he's been good to us: he didn't have to take us all this way.'

Eolande nodded. 'He does seem like a good man. But there's a darkness in him.'

The men came back with a hare, and Edmund forgot his uncertainty in skinning the beast and improvising tripods of sticks to balance the spit. But later, as they sat around the fire beneath the cold stars, he found himself watching Fardi. The carter ate little and said less, and he seemed ill at ease when asked about himself. He worked for a fisherman in the coastal town of Harofluet, he told them, selling the catches from his master's boat and the ale his mistress brewed. He was a bonded man, tied for life to his master's service. Cathbar exclaimed at this.

'A lifetime is long to spend as a slave!' he protested. 'And you have the air of a freeborn man, Master Fardi. Would this master of yours not allow you to earn your liberty again?'

'I gave it of my own free will,' the carter replied. 'I owe him my life, such as it is.' He bent his head over his meat, and the talk turned to other things.

As they prepared to sleep, Edmund took Cathbar aside and told him what Eolande had said to him earlier: that Fardi was keeping something from them. The captain seemed unperturbed.

'Well, and what if he is?' he said. 'A man has a right to his privacy. Do you mistrust him, after he saved our lives and shared his food with us?'

'Wulf found us food, too,' Edmund pointed out.

Cathbar frowned. 'So we must suspect every stranger we meet, in case he's . . . that one in disguise? But that's what he wants – to set each man against his neighbour. Go down that road, and how can we unite against him?'

'At least say nothing of Elspeth or Cluaran while we're with him,' Edmund urged. 'Even if Fardi is truly helping us, there's no saying who might overhear.'

'There's sense in that,' Cathbar agreed. 'We've spoken of Wessex already – but not of who we'll meet there, or why.' He turned away to lay out his blanket, and Edmund thought his face looked troubled.

The carter was no more talkative the next day, though Edmund caught the man looking at him once or twice: sidelong glances which Edmund could not read. He told them all to stay on the cart, sending the donkey along at a brisk pace. The heavily trodden mud at each side of the track, and the whiff of burning that came to them when the wind changed, told them the marauders were still around them. At one point, as they approached a bridge over a river, Fardi made them lie flat on the fish-smelling boards while he covered them with sacks. But it seemed the bridge's guards were local men, known to the carter; Edmund, lying still in the reeking darkness, heard friendly-sounding voices and laughter before the cart rolled on again.

Fardi released them from hiding further down the road. 'We're in the Frankish kingdom now,' he told them. 'The border guards say that some of those cursed wreckers got over the bridge, but nothing the emperor's men can't contain.'

'I wouldn't be so sure of that,' Cathbar muttered.

Edmund crouched at the back of the cart, watching the road unroll behind them. The road grew wider and for the first time they passed a number of other carts: one or two of the drivers greeted Fardi. The track veered to the west, and suddenly Edmund could see the pearly haze of the sea.

'We'll be there before nightfall,' Cathbar said, and Edmund felt his heart lift.

Harofluet was the largest settlement they had seen since Alebu, and like that town, all its life eddied around the harbour. Many of the houses were caulked with tar to protect them from the biting sea-winds, and the sharp scent mingled with the smell of fish as they rattled past. Fardi halted the cart outside a house that was larger than most and introduced them to his master, a red-faced elderly man who spoke only Frankish. Cathbar seemed to understand the language well enough, but Edmund could pick out only a few words.

Both the fisherman and his wife looked nervously at their unexpected guests, and the man drew Fardi aside to ask him rapid questions in Frankish. But the carter must have given his master and mistress a good account of them, for at the end of the conversation the old woman turned to them with a smile, and beckoned them into her house for a meal of fish soup and ale. As they sank gratefully on to wooden stools by the fire, Eolande asked Fardi to pass on their thanks.

'You told us your master owns his own boat,' she added. 'Do you think the three of us might buy passage on your next voyage? We're anxious to return to our homeland of Wessex.'

'No!' Edmund started to protest, but Eolande shot him a warning look.

As Fardi relayed the request the old fisherman's face fell, and when he replied his voice was angry. Edmund tensed, wondering if they had given offence. But Fardi, too, was grim-faced as he translated.

'My master says he would gladly help you,' he said, 'but he has no men. A week ago a band of rabble-rousers came to the town, recruiting for a cult, and many of the young men joined them, stealing boats to set sail with their new companions. His fishing boat is still here, but half of his crew have run off with the madmen.'

The old man clapped Fardi on the shoulder. Edmund guessed he was praising the carter's loyalty and bewailing the untrustworthiness of the runaways. Edmund did not even pretend to follow what was said. Fardi had said that some of the men stole boats – might they be in Sussex by now, attacking his home? He had a sudden urge to jump from his seat; to use his father's name and money to get them a boat at once. But how could they rush home when he had promised to wait for Elspeth?

There was no opportunity to talk to Cathbar or Eolande while they were under the fisherman's roof, and Edmund felt he was on fire until they could leave the next day. Eolande seemed to share his urgency. At first light, she thanked the old couple for their kindness. 'We must not add to your burden,' she said, ushering Cathbar and Edmund to the door.

Once outside, she led them towards the seafront. Edmund saw Fardi looking up from his wood-chopping to watch them go. Eolande took them past the harbour, along a deserted stretch of sand where no boats were tied. When the last hut was out of sight she turned to them. 'Edmund,' she said, 'I want you to use your sight now. Make sure that nothing over-hears us – not so much as a bird or a beetle.'

Edmund was so startled by her tone of authority that he obeyed without protest. When he had checked in all directions and nodded, Eolande went on.

'Cluaran told me to wait only three days for him and Elspeth to join us – three days from the time we left them. If they're not here today, we must take ship tomorrow.'

'But how could they possibly catch us up in that time?' Edmund cried, outraged.

'They don't follow us on foot,' she said. 'If we are not here when Cluaran arrives, we have agreed to meet in Wessex.'

'Where in Wessex?' Cathbar asked, but the Fay woman shook her head.

'It's best not to name it. We think that the Chained One can tell wherever Elspeth is when she's in the world of men. He'll attack her as soon as he can. This is where we mean to draw his attack: to a place where his power will be weakened. He must not know where we're going until we are there.'

She turned and began striding back towards the harbour.

'You coming, lad?' Cathbar said to Edmund. 'It goes against

my nature to be led blindly, but if you think what the creature might do to stop us if he knew where we were going . . .'

Edmund thought of the sea journey that lay ahead. Loki had nearly drowned him once; would he try again? But this was his best – his only – hope of seeing Elspeth and his home again. He nodded and followed Cathbar down the beach.

They found Fardi waiting for them at the harbour with Eolande. He called to Cathbar as they approached. 'My master has a smaller boat that could make the voyage with only six oarsmen, and three of his crew are still here and in need of work. If you and the boy would be willing to take an oar, he says he'll hire you boat and men for a good rate.'

'It's a generous offer,' Cathbar said. 'But that's only five rowers.'

The carter spoke stiffly. 'I've served my master without pay for half a year now, and gladly. When he saved me from drowning, I swore I'd never go to sea again. But the truth is, he never wanted me as a bondsman. He says he'll release me if I wish to go. And I can handle an oar.'

Cathbar looked astonished. 'You'll go back to sea? We'd be grateful to you, of course – but man, we're strangers to you!'

'He'll likely have no work for me anyway, until all this trouble blows over,' the carter said. 'But the truth is, it's this boy here.' He gestured at Edmund, who looked at him in bewilderment. 'Maybe he reminds me of someone . . . I've a wish to see him safely home, that's all.' When Cathbar did not answer at once his strained expression turned to a scowl. 'If you don't trust my seamanship . . .'

'No!' the captain said hastily. 'We'll be honoured to have your help, Master Fardi.'

'It's settled, then,' Fardi said. 'I'll fetch the men, and my master will show you the boat. When do you want to leave?'

'At dawn,' said Eolande.

Beneath *Eigg Loki*, the fire dragon writhed.

Smoke hung about the mountain and cloaked the ground for leagues around it, and still the fires poured forth. The dragon roared flame; spat rage and frustration, and yet his prison would not be consumed.

But something was changing, out there in the world beyond the coils of smoke. The fiery point that was his master was always there, darting at the edge of the dragon's awareness. Now there was a pull – a voice that tugged him towards that distant point – and for the first time since he had awakened the dragon felt the sense of freedom just above him, limitless space, waiting for the flames to burst out and fill it.

The rock was still there over his head, hateful and solid. But there would be a time when the rock would melt. The dragon would fly upwards; he would take the air to himself, and fill the world with his fire.

Not yet, the voice whispered. *But soon.*

CHAPTER TWENTY

Elspeth stared at her right hand, disappointment weighing in her stomach like a stone. The crystal sword had not reappeared since that first explosion of light, and Ioneth had not spoken again, for all their calling.

'We've stayed too long already,' Cluaran said. 'Our companions will be on their way to Wessex, and we must meet them.' He stood up. 'We'll visit Ainé before we leave,' he told Elspeth. 'She's one of the three who left the Fay to join the fight against Loki when he last freed himself. She knows what it is we face: she may have some help for us.'

He embraced Roslyn as they parted, and to Elspeth's surprise the Fay woman kissed her as well.

'Greet my sister Eolande for me, child,' she told her. 'Tell her I long to see her again.'

'I will,' Elspeth promised. 'And thank you for healing me.' Her hands no longer hurt, though since the momentary return of the sword her right hand had been filled with a strange prickling.

Cluaran took her back into the trees, where the green foliage of summer was mixed with silvers, yellows and reds. The trees seemed to stretch around them for leagues in all directions, but only a few hundred paces later they emerged into fields again, with rolling hills in the distance. At the foot of one of the hills a small lake reflected the blue of the sky. A group of young men and women were swimming in it and lazing on its banks; the first people Elspeth had seen here, aside from Roslyn. She thought they might greet Cluaran, but they paid him no attention, and he hurried Elspeth past them.

'Don't draw attention to yourself,' he said in a low voice. Elspeth shot a nervous look behind her, but the bathers were already a long way behind, well out of earshot. The hills were suddenly behind them, too: like the woodland, they had appeared much wider while she was passing them. *Everything here is smaller than it seems. I wonder how far we've really come?*

She thought it must be half a day at least since she had awakened, but there was no day or night here; no sun or shadow; nothing but the steady, golden light of a perpetual dawn or early evening. Only the smallest white clouds drifted over the sky; only the mildest breeze ruffled the surface of the pools and lakes they passed.

'It's so beautiful here,' Elspeth said. More green hills were unfolding around them now, dotted with purple and white flowers. She wondered how Cluaran could bear to leave it behind.

'Yes,' he agreed. 'But we have no seas, Elspeth; no snowlands or deserts. . . and no journeying.'

Ahead of them the grass stretched out in a rippling plain that seemed limitless, but suddenly figures appeared on the distant horizon and moved towards them, far too quickly.

It was a group of young men, talking and laughing. Cluaran pulled Elspeth closer to his side. 'Keep your eyes down,' he murmured.

The men had seen them, and one of them raised a hand in a half-greeting. His gaze fell on Elspeth and he let his hand fall back. One of his companions spoke to him in a low voice, his face twisted in distaste. Then all four turned to walk in a different direction, shooting glances of hostility at Cluaran as they went.

Elspeth glared at their retreating backs. 'What had we done to them?' she demanded.

Cluaran laid a finger to his lips. 'Outsiders are forbidden here,' he said. 'Unless they're brought as infants, as my father was – and even then, many do not tolerate them. You'll meet the same reception, and worse, in the place where I'm taking you. They won't offer you violence – most would not lay hands on you – but many will be angry. Do not look them in the eye, don't speak unless someone speaks to you first, and return courtesy even to rudeness. Do you understand?'

Elspeth had transferred her glare to Cluaran, but the seriousness in his face quietened her, and she nodded.

Something else had appeared on the horizon now. Elspeth thought of ships' masts until she saw that they were buildings:

slim towers, some straight and others at strange angles. As they approached she saw that they were made of pale wood, gold- or silver-coloured, with generous shutterless windows which must let the wind in cruelly at night. Someone was sitting in a window at the very top of a tower, his legs dangling down; he did not look their way, but gazed out through the other towers. Elspeth could hear the sound of water splashing, and somewhere far off, someone singing.

There was no palisade around the settlement: they could simply walk in, over the springy turf that stretched to the very doors of the houses. Elspeth looked through an arched doorway to see a sleeping-pallet and a slender-legged table holding a cup.

'Don't stare!' Cluaran snapped, dragging her forward.

But Elspeth still gazed about her: she could not help it. They passed houses with brilliantly coloured flowers and leaves growing from the walls, or festooned with vines. Others were covered with carvings of swirling lines, or images of beasts, birds and human faces. There were no people about, though: even the man she had seen at the top of the tower had vanished, and the singing had fallen silent. Cluaran was almost running now, his hand gripping her arm.

'Remember what I said!' he hissed at her, as they rounded a house grown about with glossy green bushes and came on to a wide grassy space.

It looked like a town square. The tall houses surrounded it, and in the centre was a fountain ringed with smooth white stones. And there were people here: half a dozen men and women standing in front of the fountain and glaring at them.

Cluaran had stopped dead and placed himself in front of Elspeth. An angry buzz came from the Fay and one of them, a tall, dark-skinned man, stepped forward and addressed Cluaran.

The language of the Fay sounded harsher in his mouth than it had in Roslyn's. Elspeth could not understand a word he said, but the anger in his face and his sweeping hand gestures made it clear that he wanted them to be gone. As his voice rose, more Fay came into the clearing by twos and threes, until there was a crowd around them, all facing Cluaran, their faces set in various expressions of anger and disgust. None of them looked at her, Elspeth realised; there were just a few furtive glances, quickly withdrawn.

The speaker paused for breath and Cluaran spoke, his voice soothing. He gestured towards Elspeth and towards a point behind the crowd, and held up his hand, palm out.

The tall man strode forward and grabbed Cluaran by both shoulders, shouting into his face. The minstrel stared back at him calmly, and the man's voice became a roar. His hands moved to grip Cluaran by the throat.

Elspeth gave a small cry, but before she could move Cluaran threw his arm out to block her. He was on tiptoe now, pulled upwards by his assailant's grip. His face was turning red, but he made no move to defend himself. The crowd was yelling almost as loudly as their leader.

There was a flash of white light, and then silence. The tall man's grip slackened and Cluaran crumpled to the ground, gasping and clutching his throat.

The crowd parted and a woman walked through. She wore a long cloak with a hood, and was shorter than most of the people there, even shorter than Cluaran. She came over to the minstrel and raised him to his feet. She made a small sound of concern as she looked at his face. Then she pushed back her hood, and Elspeth saw with a shock that she was old: grey-haired and wrinkled, with deeply sunken eyes. No one she had seen in this land had been anything other than young and beautiful.

The crowd had begun to melt away. The woman turned to the man who had attacked Cluaran and snapped a few words at him which made him duck his head and stalk off without a word. She called after him, something that Elspeth took to be a warning. Then she turned back to Cluaran.

'Well, Ainé,' the minstrel croaked as she shook her head at him, 'you took your time. Another moment and I would have had to fight.'

'I came as soon as I heard the racket,' the woman said. 'You must allow an old woman to move slowly.'

Cluaran snorted. 'You don't need to be old, Ainé!'

'No,' she agreed levelly, 'I don't. I choose to show my years.'

She turned to Elspeth. 'So this is the girl. You're welcome here, child – by me, if by no one else.'

She took them to a house on the edge of the settlement, a lower and simpler building than the others. She sat them on stools in a corner, out of view from the outside, and offered them oatcake and berries.

'Take your fill,' she said when Elspeth hesitated. 'I know there are some who claim that our food harms outsiders, or gives them uncanny powers, but I've never known either to be true. Eat: you'll need all your strength in the days to come.'

Elspeth realised she was ravenous. As she filled her mouth with the sharp-tasting berries, the old woman looked at her appraisingly.

'It was not wise, bringing her to the town,' she said to Cluaran. 'I could have met you at the gateway. But it's true that time is short. The Chained One gathers strength as he draws men's belief to him.' She looked searchingly at Elspeth. 'You've been hurt, child; I fear you're not yet at your full strength. Do you feel ready to meet him?'

'No,' Elspeth admitted.

She heard an exclamation from Cluaran, immediately bitten off.

'And why is that?' the old woman asked.

'I don't have a weapon!' Elspeth burst out. 'How can I fight him with no sword?'

'Ioneth has come back to you!' Cluaran protested. 'We saw her today.' Ainé looked at him enquiringly, and he told her how he had called on Ioneth at the pool, and how the sword had reappeared.

'But it was only for a moment, Cluaran.' The hope in his face filled Elspeth with a dull anger: didn't he think she'd know if it had truly returned, the sword that had once been as much a part of her as her own arm? She looked up at Ainé, willing the Fay woman to understand. 'I couldn't make her stay – I couldn't even feel the sword in my hand. It wasn't really there.'

'Let me see,' said the old woman. She did not take Elspeth's hand, but continued to look into her eyes. 'Ioneth,' she murmured, so softly that Elspeth had difficulty hearing her, 'are you awake? Do you know me?'

There was an answering murmur inside Elspeth's head. 'Ainé . . .' Beside her Cluaran drew a deep breath: the faint glow was forming again around her hand and arm.

'We can help you, Ioneth,' the old woman went on. 'I'll give Elspeth all the protection I can, and Cluaran will not leave her side. But the final stroke must be yours. Do you have the strength?'

The glow was brighter now, stretching again into the shape of the crystal sword, but still pale and insubstantial. Elspeth stared at the blade, willing it to take solid form, but it remained little more than a thin edge of light.

'It's no good,' she whispered. 'This isn't the sword. It's just . . . just seeming. I can't fight Loki with this!'

'You're wrong,' Ainé said. 'You could not fight any human enemy. But Loki is not a man.' She leant forward, her face intent now. 'Don't you see? He has form and substance only because he makes them for himself. He was bound to his human shape by the chains we put on him – but even so, he could never be killed by iron alone.'

Elspeth recalled the being she had met in the cave, straining against his chains. She had been able to wound him then: his shriek of pain still rang in her mind.

Ainé smiled and rose to her feet. 'Ioneth is still with you,' she said, and reached out a hand to pull Elspeth up, too. 'She poured all her life into one purpose: to destroy the Destroyer. It's that strength of purpose alone that will kill him. But we must move quickly.'

She led them out of the house, heading for the fields beyond the settlement. 'I have a warning for you, and a gift,' she told them as they hurried across the springy grass. 'I'll give you both as we go to the gateway.'

She walked with long strides, faster than Elspeth could have believed, speaking over her shoulder as she went.

'Loki is still bound by the one chain that he could not break. He seeks to cast off that chain so that he can abandon his physical form and become a god again. If he does – if he regains the world of pure spirit – nothing will be able to kill him. We have always believed that only the sword can sever that final chain – or Elspeth's own hand, which still holds the sword.'

'He tried to trick me into cutting it,' Elspeth said, remembering Wulf with a shudder.

Ainé nodded. 'But what he may not know – what we must keep from him at all costs – is that there may be another way for him to free himself. Beneath *Eigg Loki*, he tried to drain the life from you, Elspeth, and afterwards he was able to break one of his bonds himself. It may be that he no longer needs your hand to free him. He may try instead to consume you; to take your soul and Ioneth's together.' She stopped to look at them, her small figure suddenly commanding. 'So my warning to you is this, Elspeth. Strike at his heart, but whatever happens, do not allow him to touch you. And, Cluaran: tell Eolande to keep his fire from touching her.'

'Rely on us,' Cluaran said, and his eyes blazed.

'She must rely on you,' Ainé said. 'On all her companions. She will not succeed without you.' She held his gaze for a moment longer, then became brisk again. 'And now we are here.'

She raised both hands above her head, and suddenly there was a shimmering line in the air. She pulled her hands down a little way. Through the opening came a sound Elspeth had not heard for many weeks, but which made her eyes prick with its familiarity: the crash of waves on shingle.

'This isn't the place!' Cluaran exclaimed. 'We need the Hanging Stones, Ainé!'

'The stone circle is less than three leagues away,' the old woman told him. 'But this is where you should be now.' She turned to Elspeth. 'There's little enough I can give you, child. Less than you deserve. But I can offer you the company of your friends, at least until the circle, and show you something you thought lost. Take this for your protection.' She handed Elspeth a stem of mistletoe, dotted with white berries like pearls. 'Wear it until you reach the stone circle,' she said. 'It has a charm of concealment on it: the Chained One will not find you until it withers.'

Elspeth's hands trembled as she took the little sprig. Ainé smiled at her once more, then put her hands on Cluaran's shoulders and kissed him. 'There's nothing I have to give you but a word, Eolande's son,' she said. 'When the time comes, you'll know what to do. And your name will be honoured here.'

She returned to the gateway, bringing her hands down swiftly until the misty opening stood outlined in the air. Cluaran looked as if he wanted to ask her something more, but she stepped away from the opening, raising her hand in farewell. He shrugged and took Elspeth's hand. Together they stepped through the doorway, the mist closing around them, while the sound of the waves pounded in Elspeth's ears.

The fighting had reached Wessex. Aagard, chief war-adviser to the king but too old to wield a weapon himself, fought back despair as he turned from his fire. The charm was spent, and he had found no trace of Elspeth or the sword – nor of the Chained One, who commanded their attackers. Edmund was on his way home, with Cathbar and the Fay woman, but what could those three do, however brave, however skilled, against the armies who besieged their coasts? And there was the grievous news of King Heored's death. His men had returned just ahead of the enemy, and had given great service in repelling the first wave of invaders. But how would they hold against the next attack, and the next? Already some of the marauders had landed further up the coast, in Kent and Essex, and were spreading their cult of the Burning Man.

The fire spat out one final spark. He turned to extinguish it – and stopped, appalled. Something was stirring in the depths: something white-hot and malevolent. As he watched, the fire leapt up again and roared out at him, a huge mouth. For an instant it filled the room with flame, throwing Aagard on his back. The fury raged around him: *Coming! Coming now!* And then it was gone, leaving only a ringing echo.

And far to the north, beneath *Eigg Loki*, the final bond snapped. The great dragon soared into the air, his mouth gaping in a scream of rage and joy. Flame blossomed around him as he gained height and turned, crackling like lightning, to obey his summons to the south.

CHAPTER TWENTY-ONE

After more than two days at the oar, Edmund decided he would never understand Elspeth's love of the sea. They had started in choppy water, dodging around a great number of other boats, from fifty-oared cargo ships to fishing boats barely larger than their own. All the vessels seemed headed for Sussex and Wessex, and in such numbers they put Edmund in mind of an invading fleet, raising new fears for his mother and their household. One hulking vessel had come so close it had nearly rammed them. It had taken all the oarsmen's skill to avoid the looming hull, and then to keep from being capsized by the wake. As they frantically bailed, Cathbar cursing beside him, Edmund had looked after the vast ship to see the image of the Burning Man painted on its sail.

After that the boat-master had steered them south, out of sight of land. It was not until they reached the open sea that Edmund realised how tired he was. The other oarsmen tried to take slack for him – the carter Fardi, in particular, who had placed himself behind him, and showed an unexpected strength and skill at the oar – but Edmund was determined to pull his weight, and by nightfall he was so weary, and his hands so blistered, that he could think of nothing else.

The next day's work came more easily, but now the wind dropped and the sun began to beat down. There was no refuge from the heat – and no refuge, he could not help thinking, if a storm should break out of that clear sky, as it had done before, and a dragon appear again. The sense of exposure, of being watched, weighed on Edmund, and he did not look up as he rowed.

The sea was so still by the second night that they shipped their oars and slept, leaving two men on watch, and the next morning a smudge of land had appeared to the north, which the boat-master said was the island of Wiht.

'Take us west of there,' Eolande told him. 'I'll show you the place.'

The sight of land restored Edmund's spirits, and when Eolande finally steered them to a cove and they brought the boat safely in, he felt a wash of relief that made his hands tremble on the oar. It weakened his legs as they scraped on to the shingled beach and jumped out into the foam.

They were dragging the boat on to the shore when Eolande gave a cry, pointing up the beach. There, only a hundred yards away, were two small figures: a slightly built man, and a black-haired girl.

'Elspeth!'

Edmund raced across the shingle, his tiredness forgotten. Elspeth started at the sound of his voice, then gave a cry of delight and ran towards him, leaving Cluaran behind. She threw her arms around him, and he saw that her hands were healed.

'It's so good to see you,' she gasped as they hugged one another. 'And is that Cathbar with you, and Eolande?

Edmund nodded. 'Where did Cluaran take you? How did you get here so fast? I never thought . . .'

He stopped as Elspeth's face froze. She released him abruptly, her hands falling to her sides, and stood gazing at their boat as if in horror.

'Elspeth?' Edmund faltered. 'What's wrong?'

She seemed not to hear him. Slowly, as if she was unsure on her feet, she walked past him towards the little knot of men tying up the boat.

One of them had left the group and was standing alone, watching her. It was Fardi, and after a moment he came forward to meet her. His eyes were wide, his gaunt face suddenly as white as foam. After a few paces he stopped and held out a hand, as if he was feeling his way through darkness.

'Elspeth?' he whispered.

She gave a sob, then hurled herself forward. 'It is you,' she cried. 'It's really you this time, Father.'

There was little time for explanations. Edmund waited while Elspeth wept and told her father some of what had befallen her since the wreck of the *Spearwa*, but Cluaran soon came up to interrupt them.

'We can't stay here,' he said bluntly. 'There's a place we must reach. It's some leagues away, and the sooner we're there the better.'

Elspeth looked down at a pin she was wearing: a mistletoe twig that Edmund had not noticed before. 'Cluaran's right,' she said. 'We must go.'

There was a settlement a short distance inland, where they left the other sailors with thanks and silver. The men tried to persuade Trymman – the real name of Elspeth's father, formerly known as Fardi – to stay with them to rest and toast his new-found good fortune, but Cluaran would not wait.

'We'll likely be walking through the night as it is,' he said. 'We must be there by tomorrow – our protection will not last much longer.'

Elspeth held on to her father's arm as they walked, and he gazed at her as if he could never look enough. He had the same thick black hair as hers, and maybe the same shape of face, though it was not easy to tell, he was so thin. But now that Edmund knew who he was, he could recognise the master of the *Spearwa* as he had last seen him, with his keen gaze and bristling brows.

The man must have felt Edmund's scrutiny: he turned to him with a lopsided smile. 'You were my last passenger, the boy who was heading for Francia,' he said. 'I thought you seemed familiar. You've grown taller, and your face is older, or

I'd have known you before. I'm glad I could finally take you where you were going – more glad than I can say.'

They travelled for most of the day, only halting when the sun was low in the sky. They stopped at a farmhouse near the road for milk and barley cakes, and for news of the region. Edmund, thinking of his kingdom and his mother, asked about the road to the east, and the farmer shook his head: marauders were attacking further down the coast, he had heard, and a Kentish pedlar who passed this way yesterday had told stories of a heathen cult that had overrun the eastern kingdoms, making converts by force and burning villages as sacrifices to their god.

It was a subdued party that took up the journey again. The farmer's stories had left Edmund sick with worry. *Let us meet Loki soon!* he prayed. *We have to stop this – to try, at least.*

Ahead of him, Cluaran reached the brow of a hill and stopped, with Eolande beside him. Edmund ran to join them.

'There it is,' Cluaran murmured.

It was still a long way off: maybe a full league. A great temple open to the air stood on the distant plain: a round structure of standing stones, topped with flat slabs in an unbroken ring. Inside it were taller stones in pairs, each pair holding a third slab like the lintel of a doorway. The doors stood dark against the red evening sky; forever open; leading only to each other.

The stone circle.

Elspeth clung to her father's arm: it still felt as if she might lose him if she let go. Every now and then they would gaze at one another and smile – but her father's smile was so tremulous still that it wrenched her heart, his face gaunt and lined with grief. It was how she had known, almost at once, that he was not another vision come to torment her. When Loki took the shape of her father he had been beautiful, holding out strong arms to her and laughing. What did the Chained One know of sorrow?

'When they pulled me from the water I wanted only to die,' he said. 'I'd lost my ship; I'd let my good men drown – I'd drowned you, as I thought, dearest in all the world. I lay in that fishing boat and prayed for death, and when it didn't come I made myself a bondsman. I was a worthless man.'

'Don't talk so!' Elspeth protested. 'It wasn't your fault the *Spearwa* sank!'

Edmund called to her from ahead. The others were standing at the top of a slope, and when she and her father joined them, she saw their destination on the plain below: a great ring of stones.

'We won't reach it before nightfall,' Cluaran said. 'Does your little branch still live, Elspeth?'

She looked down at the mistletoe. The leaves were beginning to dry and the berries to wrinkle, but it still kept its white and green. 'I think it'll last till tomorrow,' she told him.

'We'll camp below the hill, then,' he said.

They were too tired to build a fire. Elspeth's father lay close beside her. Asleep, he looked less ravaged; more as she remembered him. She sat watching him and listening to the soft breathing of the others until the restlessness grew too much for her, then got up as softly as she could and stared out into the night. The plain stretched before her, featureless beneath the thin moon, but she could make out the tall stones at the edge of vision.

A mad urge came over her to go there now, take off the protective charm and face Loki alone, away from her friends and her father. But how was she to fight, with nothing but a light in her hand? She had felt Ioneth's presence ever since Ainé had called to her, but only as a murmur on the edge of hearing, and a faint tingling in her palm. And she remembered the thing that Wulf had become: the blazing, grinning giant who could change his shape with a thought, and make flames spring up with a gesture.

Don't let him touch you, Ainé had said. *Keep even his fire away from you.* It was like telling a sailor to avoid the waves.

Edmund had come up behind her, his face a pale blur in the darkness. 'Cluaran thinks he'll come tomorrow,' he said.

She nodded, showing him the charmed spray of mistletoe pinned to her shirt. 'They say he can find me wherever I am. This keeps us hidden for now, but it's withering.'

'Oh.' He started to say something else, but stopped, and they sat in silence for a while. 'And the sword,' Edmund said at last, 'has it come back?'

Elspeth did not know how to answer. 'It did appear,' she said. 'I saw it in my hand, and I heard Ioneth speak again. But it wasn't real – not solid. Someone I met in . . . in the land of the Fay said it might be enough.' The fears she had been forcing down took hold of her all at once. 'Edmund, I don't know what I'm going to do. I can't protect any of you!'

He stared at her – but it was astonishment she saw in his face, not fear. 'Why should you protect us?' he said. 'We'll look after each other, won't we? That's why we're here.'

He was quite serious. She knew that he had always planned to stand with her against Loki, but now that they had both seen what the demon was . . . 'Edmund,' she said quickly, before she could change her mind, 'don't come to the stone circle tomorrow. Take the road back to Sussex.'

'What are you talking about?' he began, but she pushed on, although the words were like stones in her throat.

'If the sword fails, he'll kill me and everyone with me.'

It was almost a relief to have said it out loud. Edmund's face was as pale as the moonlight and his eyes stretched wide, but he was still shaking his head.

'Think, Edmund!' she insisted. 'You have a kingdom that needs you. You can still fight him after tomorrow; you'll have armies.'

'I have thought,' Edmund said. 'I know I have to be king. When this is over I'll go back, and I'll rule as well as I can. But not tomorrow.' His voice was not quite steady, but as stubborn as she had ever heard it. 'You're the best friend I've ever known, Elspeth, and I'll not leave you to fight without me. Don't even think it.'

Elspeth stared at him for a long moment. 'Then . . . thank you,' she said at last. I'm glad you'll be with me. Even if we fail . . .'

'We won't fail!' he told her. 'I don't plan on dying – nor on letting you die. Whatever happens, we'll find a way to destroy Loki.'

CHAPTER TWENTY-TWO

Cluaran woke them before dawn, and as the first red streak appeared on the horizon he was already leading them across the plain.

The red stain on the horizon spread and brightened, and something appeared through the glow: the shape of hewn stones, blurred by the morning mist. They pushed through the wild grasses, watching the stones grow closer and more distinct, while the line of light behind them grew more brilliant. As the sun's rim appeared, they came to the stones.

There were maybe two dozen uprights making up the great circle, each five times the height of a man. Above them ran an unbroken ring of stone like a giant's necklet, without seam as far as Edmund could see. Within the circle were more stones set in a horseshoe, five pairs each with a cross-slab on top: the doorways he had seen last night.

'Who could have made this?' Master Trymman breathed.

'Come on,' Cluaran called, leading them forward.

They had to climb down into a ditch, then scramble up a

steep bank on to a circular plain of grass. Cluaran led them forward at a run – and then they were among the stones, the dawn touching them all with fire.

Grey walls towered above them on every side. Among the great central structures were countless smaller stones, some planted upright, others fallen; the shortest of them was twice Edmund's height, except where some of the fallen ones had cracked and turned to rubble. As the rising sun streamed through the outer blocks, the stone ring above them seemed to float suspended, and each of the five great gateways was filled with light.

'It's called the place of the Hanging Stones,' Eolande said. 'Even the Fay don't know who built it. But the stones hold the power of all their history. If any place can protect us, it's this.'

'So what do we do now?' Trymman asked, still gazing about him in awe.

'We wait,' Cluaran said.

Elspeth walked to the middle of the circle, through the central doorway. She stood for a moment bathed in red-gold light, between two bars of shadow. Then she bent and laid something down on a stone at her feet: the sprig of mistletoe, twisted and brittle now, the leaves crumbling to dust.

'It won't be long,' she said. 'He knows I'm here.'

Edmund could not stay still. Elspeth sat with her father, and not wanting to disturb them, he wandered through the stones alone. Eolande was standing at the very edge of the circle, gazing out to the north. Further along, Cathbar leant against a fallen slab and sharpened his sword, while Cluaran sat nearby with his knees drawn up, watching the sunrise.

'They're too young for this,' Cluaran was saying.

'That they are,' Cathbar agreed. 'But they'll do their part, both of them.' He sheathed his sword and stretched out more comfortably against the slab. 'War is no respecter of age. I was twelve when I first had to fight.'

'I was nineteen,' Cluaran said. He stared ahead of him, looking thoughtful. 'Tell me,' he said, 'do you ever get used to it? Looking at your companions before the attack, wondering which of them . . .'

'You think too much,' said Cathbar shortly. 'And that's a question you don't ask.' He clapped the minstrel on the shoulder. 'Your comrades are your best hope of leaving the fight alive, and you're theirs. You don't go killing them off, even in thought. Bear up, lad.'

'Lad!' Cluaran protested. 'I'm three times your age at least.' But he let the subject drop.

Edmund moved quietly away from them, and saw Elspeth standing in the horseshoe of stones, her right arm outstretched. Even through the low sunlight, he could make out the shimmer around her hand, but she lowered her arm as though dissatisfied.

There was a cry from the edge of the circle. Eolande had turned to them, her face in shadow, her arm lit red as she pointed into the northern sky.

'He's coming!'

Edmund ran to her, peering vainly upwards.

'Use your skill!' she snapped at him.

I'm not king yet, he thought, and closed his eyes, casting out to the north. There was nothing there . . . He felt further off . . .

It hit him without warning. One moment there was nothing; the next his head was full of fire, and a fury so vast he could not contain it. It crackled from him as he soared and swooped, pouring out red flame on the earth below for the sheer joy of destruction.

Edmund wrenched his eyes open. He was lying on his back, the others gazing down at him in horror.

'He's a dragon,' he gasped. 'A dragon made of fire . . .'

Elspeth leant down to help him to his feet. 'He'll attack from above, then,' she said, her voice steady. 'Eolande, can you and Cluaran make rain?'

The Fay woman nodded. 'For a time, at least. And when Loki was bound last time, we cast a protection around the fighters. There were four of us then, but I'll shield you all I can.' She turned to Edmund. 'You must help us, too.'

'How?' he said, bewildered.

'By matching fire with ice,' she said, 'as you did once before. You woke the dragon of the glacier to help you defeat Torment. Call her now!'

'But it was hundreds of leagues away. I can't reach her from here, Eolande!'

'You can,' she insisted, and took both his hands. 'Try, now!'

Edmund stretched out his sight again. It was harder than before: part of him quailed at the memory of the raging fire that had possessed him a moment ago. He felt himself nearing the scorching presence again, and flinched.

'Go on,' Eolande whispered, and he cast further, not stopping until he found a seabird flying low over grey waves . . . a rocky shoreline . . . a pine forest, trees dripping in the spring thaw . . . His sight was a string pulled impossibly taut: he felt it must break, or snap backwards.

'Go on!' came the voice again.

A wind seemed to catch him and blow him further . . . further still. There were the snow fields again, their whiteness giving way to patches of grass. He rode a hawk, high up, scanning the landscape. There were hills, their tops still white . . . and there – there was the shape of *Jokul-dreki*, the ice dragon, curled in sleep around the highest peak.

Her mind was like skeins of cloud, so huge and drifting that he could get no grip on it. There was darkness and a dream of the snow fields, endless and far below, and a memory: a tiny, persistent figure, warning of danger . . .

He reached for the memory; clung to it and added his own voice. *It's here now – the fire that will burn your land! We need your help, one more time.*

The huge mind twitched as if to throw him off like a buzzing insect. That fight was in the past: there was safety now, and sleep . . .

No! he screamed, and called up the vision he had just seen: the blazing fury and the inexhaustible fire streaking towards them, leaving nothing but ashes in its wake. The remembered terror hit him, and he felt himself falter . . . Then it was all dissolving, the dragon's mind slipping from his hold as he clutched vainly at empty air.

Only, just before he was swept away, he caught a flash of brightness as the great eyes opened, and felt the cracking of ice above his shoulders.

He came back to himself, weak and shaken. He had fallen to his knees, and Eolande stood beside him with her hand on his shoulder. 'I think I woke her,' he started, but the Fay woman did not turn to him; she was staring fixedly over his head. Edmund climbed to his feet. Cluaran was standing nearby, his head thrown back, murmuring to himself and moving his hands in shapes Edmund had seen once before, when they were hiding in the forest from Orgrim. Storm clouds streamed towards them from the west, to gather in a grey pall over their heads.

Elspeth was still in the centre of the circle, among the stone gateways, with her father and Cathbar. All three were gazing to the north.

The sky there was clear, but Edmund saw a flicker of lightning stabbing at the horizon – and above it, a black speck, outlined in a corona of fire.

Torment looked out from his cramped cavern as the lightning died away to the south. It had gone, the thing that had taken his lair. It had burst from the stump of his mountain, pouring out fire, while he was taking sheep from an upland meadow, and he had been forced to retreat to his cave half-fed. But now . . . he lumbered to his feet. He would find more prey, and he would fly back to his mountain. Maybe it had cooled. Maybe there was still a lair for him . . .

And then, without warning, the voice was in his head again, sweet and clear, compelling him: *Fly south. There's killing to do.*

As it spoke a picture rose before Torment's fractured eyes: the quarry retreating before him, his claws outstretched to rip and rend. *Now is the time,* it said.

Screaming his delight, the blue dragon spread his wings and flew.

It's now, Edmund thought, trying not to panic. *He's really here.* The dragon was approaching faster than the storm clouds. From a distance he had looked slender, almost snake-like, save for the beating wings. Now he seemed nearly as big as the stone circle itself – and all made of flame. His outline flickered. The shadow he cast on the ground beneath was red-tinged. He swooped lower, and the grass beneath him turned black, fires springing up on each side.

'Keep together,' Eolande said. 'I'll shield you for as long as I can.'

Elspeth seized Edmund's hand for a moment. 'Look after my father,' she breathed.

'I will,' he whispered back. 'Good luck.'

She turned from him, throwing out her right hand. 'Ioneth!' she cried. 'Help us now!'

The white light burst from her hand as the thunder sounded.

The sun was suddenly cut off. A scorching wind rushed over them and the circle was roofed with flame. Overhead, the creature was too big to see: a looming, fiery darkness, crackling with white sparks.

There was light again for an instant as he passed over – but he wheeled with another thunderclap and dived towards them. Edmund caught a glimpse of the black, cavernous mouth before flame poured over them, flame in a waterfall, to drench and overwhelm. He threw his arms over his head – and the flame was gone, scattered by an invisible barrier as the dragon soared over them again. Elspeth stood her ground, the crystal sword fully formed in her hand. The blade was pale, but it held its shape as she raised it high over her head to slash at the monster.

Coward! Edmund berated himself, drawing his own sword. He ran to stand beside her. Cathbar was already there, and as the dragon swooped for a third time, all three stabbed upwards together.

They could not reach him. Flame poured all around them – Edmund could feel the scorching heat even through Eolande's barrier – but his sword met no resistance.

'I have to get higher!' Elspeth shouted. 'Help me climb up!'

'No!' Trymman protested, but she had already run to one of the smaller standing stones and was trying to scale it one-handed.

'Let her,' Eolande cried, her arms outstretched. 'I'll shield her!' Cathbar lifted Elspeth on to his shoulders and helped her scramble to the top of the stone. She stood up, balancing precariously, as the thunder crashed and the sky darkened again. The great mouth swooped towards them – and she raised the sword high, not slashing now but holding it steady.

A whistling shriek rang through the after-echoes of the thunder, and the monster wheeled and shot straight upwards. His fiery tail thrashed on the ground, as broad as the stones themselves. Edmund darted over and cut at it; once, twice, feeling no resistance at all, before it writhed upwards and away – but next moment he yelled and threw the sword from him. The blade glowed red-hot, and his hand was blistering where he had held it. Fat drops of rain splashed around him, and sizzled and steamed on the fallen sword.

Someone grabbed him and pulled him violently back-wards; it was Cluaran, his face tight with strain. 'Stay inside the shield, you fool!' he hissed, and turned back to his rain-making. Edmund's face felt suddenly sore, as if sun-burned. He put up a hand to feel his cheek: the whole sleeve of his shirt was scorched and blackened.

Elspeth was still balanced on top of the stone, holding the sword aloft. The blade looked brighter now, and more defined, as if it had gained strength from the blow it had struck. But the dragon had not dived again. He hovered above them, blocking out the sun. The great body looked almost black between the blazing, outstretched wings. His head tilted so that one eye looked directly down on Elspeth.

The malice in that long, flame-yellow eye called back a memory to Edmund: Loki, walking away from them through the burning wood, smiling: *She'll come to me in the end*. He started forward, crying a warning, as the dragon sent out a jet of white-hot fire directly at his friend.

For an instant the fire enveloped Elspeth. She staggered and fell, sprawling across the top of the stone block. Edmund howled and ran to her – but she was not screaming, or burning, and as he reached her she pulled herself up with a groan. Eolande stood at the foot of the stone, pale with exhaustion: the charm had held. This time.

But the dragon was pulling his head back for a second attack. Trymman and Cathbar rushed to pull Elspeth safely down, and they huddled beneath the stone doorways as the flame poured around them.

'How much longer can you hold the protection spell?' Cluaran asked Eolande.

She was white and shaking, but she murmured, 'A while longer. Elspeth wounded it . . . I can shield her for another attempt.'

'I doubt it'll give her the chance,' Cathbar said grimly.

The dragon was coming no closer. He stayed just above the tallest stones now, circling above them; moving only to direct his flame at them. The rain streamed around him, hissing off the ground till they stood surrounded by steam. No fire had spread within the stone circle, but the dragon himself seemed unaffected; his flame inexhaustible.

'He hates the stones,' Elspeth said suddenly, as another jet of fire streamed around them. 'Did you notice? He tried to keep from touching them, even before I hit him.'

The monster soared over them again, turning just past the circle's edge for another attack. He did avoid the stones, Edmund saw: as he wheeled, his tail lashed aside from the outer ring, with a crack of air. The circle was protecting them, as Eolande had promised. But for how long?

The dragon beat his wings to hover above them now, swaying his great reptilian head to look down with one burning eye, then the other. There was cunning in those eyes, Edmund thought – and it took all his strength not to duck as the head drew back. Instead, remembering his promise to Elspeth, he stepped in front of her father as the dragon struck.

The snake-like head whipped between them, spitting a lance of flame directly at Elspeth. Edmund and Trymman both flung themselves towards her, crying out with one voice as the fire burst through Eolande's shield, furrowing the ground and scarring the rock where Elspeth had been standing.

But Elspeth was no longer there. As the dragon attacked she had darted forward, around his head, to aim a single stroke at his neck. The creature shrieked again, and shot upwards. The scorching wind from his wings nearly knocked Edmund off his feet, but he stumbled to where Elspeth stood swaying; her clothes blackened, her hair on fire. Trymman had already reached her; he smothered the flames in her hair with his cloak, and the three of them staggered back to the shelter of the stone gateways.

Eolande was kneeling there, supported by Cluaran, who had his arms around her. She was white to the lips, but the shield seemed to be mended for now: the heat was less here, and no fires burned around them.

'She can't hold on much longer!' There was something close to panic in Cluaran's voice.

'Just a little more,' Eolande said faintly. 'They're coming.' She could hardly lift her head, but she raised her eyes to the northern sky.

A wisp of cloud was blowing towards them: a wavering line of white against the remaining blue. It seemed to pulse with a steady rhythm, like the wings of a bird, or . . .

'The ice dragon!' Edmund breathed. '*Jokul-dreki.*'

He could make out her shape, now that he knew what he was seeing: the crested head and the sweeping wings curved back in flight. Beside her, something else flew, darting in furious zigzags: a blue-black speck in comparison, though it must be huge to appear at all at such a distance.

'And Torment.' Eolande's voice was hardly more than a breath. 'I summoned him as well – to help us, this time.'

Elspeth stared at her, the horror in her face echoing Edmund's own. 'Torment – help us? He's Loki's creature!'

'No,' Eolande whispered. 'I rule him now.'

She cried out suddenly, as if in pain. The fire dragon had loosed another torrent of flame: it crackled all around them as a thousand tiny sparks breached the shield at once, and winked out a hand's-span from their heads. Searing heat took the breath from Edmund's throat. Eolande gasped and slumped against Cluaran, who turned his face to the sky above, his hands gesturing frantically. Rain poured down on all sides – but it turned to steam where the fire dragon hovered. Above them, the great jaws opened again.

There was a yell behind them, and the monster jolted in the air, his head whipping back. Trymman had produced a slingshot, and was bending over the rubble around a broken slab. 'Hurt my girl, you brute?' he shouted as he rummaged for another chunk of stone and let fly again.

With a roar, the dragon arched his body and flapped his wings to rise a dozen feet higher. Cathbar yelled soundlessly against the thunderclap, and ran for the pile of rubble to hurl a fist-sized lump of rock straight at the dragon's jaws. The monster writhed his head away, bringing his wings down again – but one yellow eye still glared into the circle, filled with calculation. Edmund looked desperately northwards, but the advancing dragons were still a league away. *Hurry! We can't keep Loki off with stones!*

The glacier dragon was rushing towards them. He could feel her distress, looking through the haze of her vision at the black trail of destruction she followed. Ahead of her was the group of rocks, ringed with fire; and above it, the creature that would burn her land. There was no need to urge her onwards: already she had left the smaller dragon far behind her. A north-wind caught her and sped her towards her goal. Edmund regained his eyes to see Cluaran standing behind him, pulling at the winds with his hands.

'Come to us, come quickly!' the minstrel whispered. As if in answer, the thunder sounded again, deeper and more rolling than before, and the wind of great wings blew about them – a snow-wind, cutting through the fierce heat.

The fire dragon had seen her. He wheeled high above them and shot a jet of flame that arched across the sky. *Jokul-dreki* met it with a breath: seemingly no more than the frosted cloud puffed out on a cold day, but when flame and cloud met there was a hissing and crackling as loud as the thunder, and the fire vanished in a smudge of black smoke which the glacier dragon shouldered aside in her flight. She was closer now; like a white cloud-bank, blotting out the northern horizon. The fire dragon bellowed in fury. This time the flame he spat was a flood that filled the air above them – and *Jokul-dreki* was there, as massive as the fire dragon himself, meeting the flood head-on.

It poured over her, hiding her from sight for a long instant. Then it cleared, and the ice dragon shook her wings with a great rush of chill air. A blizzard of tiny drops – water or hail – flew at her enemy.

In the stone circle below, cool air washed over them like a blessing. Elspeth had left the shelter of the archway to gaze up in awe as the two monsters circled each other. They rose in the air, each seeking advantage, and the thunder of their wings mixed with the roar of the battle. Dark clouds, shot with lightning, rolled around them until both huge figures were hidden from view.

'Is he weakening at all, can you see?' Edmund demanded, peering up beside his friend.

Elspeth shook her head doubtfully. 'I think . . . he may have wounded her . . .' He could hardly hear her, but following her gaze through the smoke he saw the edge of one enormous white wing, ripped and jagged. With a roar, the fire dragon pressed his advantage, dousing *Jokul-dreki* in a wave of flame that cast its heat down to the watchers below. Edmund felt his hair crisping. The white dragon faltered in the air.

And, out of nowhere, Torment was there.

He appeared like a flung spear, heading straight at the fire dragon's flank; tiny beside the blazing monster but sharp-edged as a stone. One eye was fractured and dark; one leg hung down, but as the blue-black dragon streaked over his head Edmund tasted nothing but rage, sharp as iron.

The fire dragon opened his jaws around another burst of flame – and Torment hurtled straight through his wing to cannon into his side. He shot away again, shrieking and covered in flame, but the fire dragon howled, a note that none of them had heard from him, and fell from the air. He almost hit the topmost stones before he pulled himself up, and by that time Torment had rounded: scorched, ragged, but with fury unabated.

The blue dragon launched himself again at the monster, and again; each time retreating in flames, and each time returning to do more damage. The fire-dragon hovered now, his head whipping from side to side as he tried to swat the little creature that dared to hurt him . . . And *Jokul-dreki*, rallying, drew back her enormous head for one more blast of ice.

White clouds billowed over the stone circle, dusting the highest slabs with frost. Both Torment and the fire dragon were lost inside, though in the depths the red flame still raged. *Jokul-dreki* breathed out once more, and within the cloud of ice the burning monster screamed. Lightning bolts shot from the cloud to earth themselves, spitting and cracking, all around the outer stones. Torment streaked out of it straight upwards, his scales crusted with white. And the cloud cleared to show the fire dragon still hovering, but strangely changed: red-black now, no longer blazing but gleaming like molten stone. He brought his wings down – and shattered, with a noise like worlds colliding.

Shards of black glass rained down around them, and Edmund yanked Elspeth back under a doorway that trembled in the din. And then there was nothing but wind and rain, and deafening echoes.

CHAPTER TWENTY-THREE

The fire dragon was gone – but Elspeth could not believe it was over.

Her ears still rang with the monster's destruction. His fires had gone out, and the heated stones around the circle sizzled in the last of the rain. The ground around them was scorched and scarred by the dragon's attacks and littered with the gleaming black fragments that had made up his body.

Eolande sat slumped against a column, while Cluaran bent over her. Cathbar was shaking Trymman's hand.

'Good work with the stones, man!' he said.

'It's Elspeth you should praise,' her father said, looking at her with pride. Elspeth shook her head.

I didn't kill the dragon, she wanted to say. *It was* Jokul-dreki, *and anyway . . .*

Something was wrong. The crystal sword pulsed faintly in her hand, and she could hear Ioneth's voice in her head: *Not dead . . . not yet . . .*

The remaining dragons were leaving. Torment flew slow

and heavily now; his wings tattered; his lame leg trailing. All the fury seemed to have drained out of him, and Elspeth felt an unwilling stab of pity for the creature as he flapped away.

Jokul-dreki hovered just above the circle's edge, her long neck turned so that one vast green eye looked down at Edmund. He stood beneath her, calling out a farewell.

'He's gone; your land is safe. You can sleep now: I'll never trouble you again.'

Elspeth wondered whether the ice dragon could understand him. But *Jokul-dreki* dipped her massive head as if in acknowledgement; then brought her frayed wings down with one final thunderclap to soar up and away from them.

'Well,' Cathbar said as the white shape vanished into the north, 'so Loki is dead. I never thought we'd do it.'

And there it was again: the sense of wrongness. The stone circle lay quiet now; the rain had stopped and the wind had died. Even the grey clouds that Cluaran had summoned were thinning above them. And yet Elspeth could not shake off a sense of threat.

'We haven't,' she said, and the sword thrummed more urgently in her hand. 'He's not dead. The dragon was only a part of him . . .' Ioneth cried out suddenly in her head, and Elspeth reeled around to face the circle's edge.

'He's here!'

Oh, well done.

It sounded in her head like a bell: the clear, beautiful, hateful voice. And Loki appeared, standing between two of the outer stones.

You always knew that I would come for you, didn't you? For you . . . and for Ioneth.

Flames played around his head and behind his eyes, casting an orange hue on his swirling black cloak. Behind her, Edmund and her father were shouting, but she hardly heard them. Loki's voice filled her head: *Come to me now . . .* She took a step towards him, and another.

She could hear Ioneth crying out; feel the tension in her arm. But the blade she held before her was pale now; hardly visible. Elspeth clenched her hand around what should be the hilt of the crystal sword, telling herself it was real. She had struck with it twice, unfelt and almost unseen, and it had wounded the fire dragon. Without giving herself time to think she darted forward, plunging the blade into the breast of the black cloak.

She felt no resistance; nothing at all. She pulled back for another blow – and found herself held, dragged forward towards the darkness. The cloak billowed out, filling her vision, and there was nothing behind it, nothing but emptiness, and the irresistible voice:

Come closer.

'Elspeth!'

Her father's voice, harsh with terror and anger, broke the spell. Rough hands pulled her backwards. She sprawled on the cindery ground, looking up in confusion: Edmund, his eyes wide with fear; her father and Cathbar each holding her firmly by a shoulder as if she might shake them off and run back to her destroyer. Even Eolande was on her feet, leaning on Cluaran's arm and looking anxiously down at her.

'He was pulling you outside the stones,' the Fay woman said. 'Drawing your mind to him . . . as he drew mine, once. But you're stronger than I was. Fight him!'

Elspeth struggled to her feet. The tall figure of Loki still stood at the edge of the stones, flame-ringed. There was a mocking smile on his face, and he extended a hand and beckoned to her.

Yes: strike at me, Elspeth! Come, fight me!

She took a step forward, and stopped. 'No,' she said, trying to keep her voice steady. 'I'll not go to you again. Come inside the circle!'

Loki's hand froze mid-gesture. The mocking smile widened, showing white teeth, and fire behind them.

'Why not?' he said, and this time his voice resounded through the stone circle, making the grey columns vibrate. 'What have I to fear?' He began to grow, the cloak whirling about him in a black mist shot with sparks.

Eolande laid a hand on Elspeth's arm. 'Are you ready?' she murmured.

No!

It was Ioneth's voice, clear and full of panic. *Don't let him come closer*, she begged. *I can't do it!*

But we must, Elspeth told her. The spiralling black cloud that was Loki had grown almost as tall as the stones now. *It's time – the only time we'll have.*

'Don't let her touch him!'

Cluaran was suddenly beside her, clutching at her hand. His voice was a breathless croak. 'You can't – please! You can see she's too weak.'

It was Eolande who pulled him back. 'She must,' the Fay woman said. 'They have to fight him now.'

'He'll swallow them both,' Cluaran moaned, but he let his hand fall.

Now. The word sang in Elspeth's head, and she stepped forward. The raven whirlwind towered above her as she raised her glowing hand.

I need more strength, Ioneth whispered – and her voice burst from Elspeth's mouth. 'Cluaran!'

Elspeth's head whipped round. Cluaran was staring at her, his face rigid with shock. Elspeth looked at him in confusion. 'She says . . .'

'Yes,' he said. 'Yes, of course.' He turned to Eolande. 'Mother – this is why I was brought here. Forgive me for leaving you.'

'There's nothing to forgive,' Eolande said. She embraced him, murmuring words that Elspeth could not hear; then held him by the shoulders, gazing into his face. 'Go to her, Cluaran,' she said. 'Go with my love.'

Elspeth had listened in growing dread. A vision filled her

head: a black-haired girl fading to nothing as the sword took her life, and the young man on his knees beside her, begging to take her place.

The face that Cluaran turned to her was suddenly that of a boy, transfigured with hope and fear. 'What do I do?' he asked her.

She opened her mouth, not knowing what to say, and the voice of Ioneth spoke through her.

'Take my hand.'

His clasp was warm and dry, though shaking a little in hers, and the faint light of the sword lay along his arm, seeming to merge with the skin. It grew brighter as she watched, spreading like glowing mist. The wavering light wrapped around Cluaran, and she began to lose sight of him. His eyes widened, and she knew it was not her face that he saw.

My love, Ioneth whispered inside her head.

The brilliance filled her eyes now. The hand clasping hers shuddered – and then she was gripping the hilt of a sword, solid and familiar as if she had held it all her life. A thrill of power shot up her arm, and the floating light merged into a single line of white fire.

The crystal sword had returned.

Elspeth began to shake. The blade in her right hand dazzled her, blazing as it had when it had first become a part of her, months ago. But Cluaran was gone – lost as though he had never been. Where he had stood before her there was nothing but the blackened ground. For a moment, she was shot through with guilt and horror.

'He's not gone; not truly.' Eolande was beside her. The Fay woman's face was running with tears, but her voice was urgent. 'You must use what he has given you. Quickly!'

A pillar of flame blazed between the stones, higher than the tallest of them, staining them with blood-red light. Trymman, Cathbar and Edmund darted around it, hurling rubble at it, retreating, then throwing again. The thing was man-shaped, Elspeth realised: a giant made of fire as the dragon had been, its feet burning the ground where it walked, its fingertips shooting flames. The hurled stones made ripples in its surface; each spot became pale and insubstantial for a moment, halting the giant's progress before the flame filled it again. But it moved inexorably forward, towards Elspeth. It turned white-blazing eyes on her and opened a mouth as black and cavernous as the dragon's jaws, spitting a torrent of fire.

Don't be afraid. Ioneth's voice spoke in her head, clearer and stronger than Elspeth had ever heard it. *You wounded the dragon when I was no more than a light.*

She wasn't afraid. The sword was firm in her hand, its strength pulsing through her. And the words she had heard were no longer from a single voice: there were two, intertwining like parts of a song, and both as familiar to her as her own thoughts. Then she was running forward, the sword blazing like lightning, to slash at the legs of the burning giant.

Flame poured around her, falling away harmlessly to each

side, and she knew that Eolande was shielding her for one last time. The giant screamed and buckled, shrinking in on itself. For a moment it dropped to its knees, toppling towards her blade. Then it was a whirlwind of flame, whipping back from her. Tendrils of thick black smoke snaked from it and wrapped around her, reaching for her throat.

Strike again! cried the voices together, and she brought the sword up in a sweeping stroke, severing the smoke-tendrils as if they were flesh. There was another shriek – and now a cloud swirled around her, impenetrably black, save for the brilliance of the sword in her hand. She carved a path through it – and came face-to-face with one of the stones.

Elspeth backed away, disoriented. The great slab towered above her, and she put out a hand to steady herself against its rough surface.

'Don't touch him!' shouted Eolande.

The face of the stone rippled. Elspeth brought the sword round to hack at it, and the whole column wavered before her and vanished. In its place was a small human figure: Edmund, his hands raised to fend her off and his eyes wide with terror.

'Help me!' Elspeth muttered, and closed her eyes as she struck. When she opened them there was nothing but mist in his place.

He's weakening! the joined voices urged her. *Drive him against the stones!*

But she could not. The sword blazed in her hand, the only solid thing as the world changed around her. The mist became a forest, its trees burning as she struck at them; a tidal wave, crashing down on her head; then a crowd of people with Edmund's face; her father's; her own . . . Elspeth could only stand her ground, keeping the sword steady as Cluaran and Ioneth guided her hand. Sometimes she thought she had hit him; more often her enemy simply faded to nothingness as she slashed or stabbed, and reappeared to taunt her in a new form. She heard her friends around her, crying out warning or encouragement, and she could not tell if it was their voices she heard or Loki's.

Then there was a piercing cry from Eolande, abruptly cut off. The things around Elspeth were shaped like wolves now, with lolling tongues of flame, ringing her ever more closely as she spun and hacked at them – but at the cry, they vanished. She was back in the stone circle, and Loki was facing her, man-sized and alone.

He smiled widely, but not at Elspeth.

'Ah, Eolande,' he breathed. 'I've worn through your charms again. You see, it does no good to turn on me.'

He turned back to Elspeth, his fiery mouth gaping wider. He stretched out his arms towards her, and from each hand a sword grew, blazing red. Elspeth could feel the heat on her face as he advanced, and hear Eolande weeping behind her.

'And now, little one,' Loki said to her, 'we'll fight.'

Edmund could bear it no longer. He had stayed at the edge of the fray with the others while Elspeth battled the shape-changer, standing close to Eolande while she kept up her charm of protection, and throwing the shattered stones where he could, for the small help they might give. Loki's shapes, all of them, kept away from the stones of the circle: when one of them brushed a slab, its outline flickered, became less solid. The flung stones had the same effect, but it was little enough, Edmund thought, against a power that could withstand the crystal sword.

And then Eolande screamed in pain, and the illusions vanished. For a moment Edmund thought his friend must have struck a killing blow – but Loki was on his feet, laughing, and Eolande crumpled to the ground.

'I can't protect her!' she sobbed. 'I can't . . . But the flames must not touch her!'

Loki held two flaming swords, brandishing them in the air as he walked towards Elspeth. She stood awaiting his approach, apparently calm, and Edmund could see that she was watching for her chance to strike. He clutched the stone tighter in his hand: if she should miss . . .

'No,' Loki breathed, and flung his arms in the air. Flame burst from the sword-tips and spread to both sides of him, forming a ring of fire around Elspeth. And supporting the ring, as the uprights held the hanging stones, were other Lokis; a dozen of them, all laughing with cave-like mouths, all advancing on Elspeth. A dozen silver chains winked red in the fiery light.

'Come, Elspeth.' The bell-like voice was ugly with savagery, coming from a dozen throats at once. 'What use is your sword now?'

And all at once Edmund knew what he must do.

He ducked between two of the fiery figures, ignoring shouts from Cathbar and Cluaran, and ran to stand by Elspeth. 'I won't distract you,' he said, as she turned an astonished face to him. 'Keep the sword up – pay me no heed. But if I point to one of them, strike him.'

Before Elspeth could protest, he closed his eyes, trying not to flinch as he sent his sight sweeping around the fiery circle.

The overpowering rage took hold of him, but he rode it like a shipwrecked man in the storm-waves, keeping his head above the current, forcing himself to look through one burning gaze, then the next . . .

They were advancing on Elspeth, their swords merging into a forest of flame, laughing as she turned from one glowing form to the next. He could feel their heat on his body, singeing his clothes and hair as he dragged himself to the next one in the circle.

It threw him off his feet. Blindly, holding on to the fiery vision so it could not escape, he reached up and grabbed Elspeth's hand.

'There!' he gasped. 'That one!'

His whole body shook as Loki felt him and tried to throw him off, but he clung on with all his force. She would only have this one chance. There was nothing in the world but fire and rage . . . and a tiny dark figure, a sliver of brilliant light in its hand, darting straight between the flaming arms. Too late, he felt the monster thrashing out, flailing at himself with his own fires, as the crystal sword pierced his heart. There was a whiteness too bright to see as the world exploded. Then the light winked out like a candle-flame, and Edmund's sight with it.

CHAPTER TWENTY-FOUR

It was four days later, and already the world was different.

The road east had been almost deserted as they took up their journey, but they saw no armed men, and by the second day carters and pedlars were venturing out again. Near Venta Bulgarum they had met with travellers who swore that the invading Danes were routed, driven off by the king's men. As Elspeth shook out her bed-roll in the peace of a summer morning, she wondered if Loki and all his works would soon be entirely forgotten.

No, she thought, watching Edmund as he sat with his face raised to the sunrise he could not see. *Not by everyone.*

She still could not understand how he could be so calm, how he could accept the loss of his sight without complaint or anger. She had begged Eolande to restore her friend's eyes as she and her sister had cured her hand, and when the Fay woman told her sadly that it was beyond her skill, Elspeth had nearly wept with frustration. But Edmund had shown no sign of distress.

Well, if he would not complain, it was not her place to rail. She had lost nothing . . . not in comparison with Edmund. She looked over at her father, washing his face in the brook, and the sight warmed her until she could almost forget the strange emptiness in her right hand. The sword was gone.

After she had stabbed Loki – after the ball of white fire which had filled the circle, filled the sky, and vanished without toppling a single stone – a great silence had fallen on her. She was nowhere, floating bodiless in the dark. *I must be dead*, she thought – but slowly her body had come back: heaviness, and blurred light, and a steady, irresistible throbbing as the threads unravelled from her arm. Strands of light had pulled free from her, streaming into the air. Ioneth's voice, and Cluaran's, were in her head again, so twined together it was almost a song; calling a greeting or a farewell. And then they had left her – and she was lying on the ground in the stone circle, a gauntlet of silver mesh slipping off her right hand.

Afterwards, she had not known how to speak to Eolande of her son's loss. The Fay woman had stayed with them only long enough to help dress their burns; then she had left them for her own people.

'There's nothing here for me now,' she said softly, and Elspeth took her hand, feeling her eyes pricking.

'They might come back, some day,' she said awkwardly. 'I heard their voices, Eolande. I know they're still together.'

'It was all he wanted,' Eolande said. She had been holding Cluaran's pack, and she pulled a small book from it now, bound in dark leather. 'This was written by my husband, Brokk: the story of the sword. My son added to it. I mean to finish it, so our people will know what he did for them – and what you and your friends have done.'

Before she left, she took both Elspeth and Edmund aside and slid a bracelet from her wrist, a finely wrought thing of twisted wood and metal.

'This is all I have to give you,' she said. 'But it was made to join the strengths of two peoples, and the charm on it is still strong. If you should ever be in need, place it near one of our doorways. I'll hear you.'

Elspeth looked at her doubtfully. 'But will your people allow that? I've seen what they think of our kind.'

'That must change,' Eolande said, and for a moment her eyes flashed with their old spirit. 'Twice now we've banded together. If we had not, none of us would be here.'

She took Edmund's hands and kissed him, and embraced Elspeth. 'I won't forget you,' she murmured.

Then she drew the doorway in the air, and stepped through while it faded behind her.

They left the stone circle the same day. Many of the great stones were soot-blackened, and the ground beneath them was scorched and scarred, but that would all fade. Only the gleaming obsidian fragments that had been the dragon's body would stay, scattered thickly around the central gateways, as signs that a battle had taken place here.

Cathbar picked one of them up and weighed it in his hand as they walked back towards the road. 'Something to show my children,' he said, and slipped it into his pack.

'You don't have children!' Elspeth said, startled. 'Do you?'

'Not yet,' the captain said. 'But I've time.' He smiled. 'There's time for a lot of things now: I think our warring days are over. Though it's as well to keep my hand in.' He patted a bow and quiver that hung over his shoulder, and Elspeth recognised them as Cluaran's. 'Eolande gave me these before she left,' the captain said. 'Told me to make good use of them – and I mean to.' His face was suddenly sombre. 'He was a good man.'

It took them two days to reach Venta Bulgarum, where Cathbar would return to his post. Elspeth could not repress a qualm as they approached the town gates: the last time she had been here, she and Edmund had stolen in like thieves, disguised and in fear of their lives. She moved a little closer to Edmund, and saw the strain on his face. His memories must be worse than hers: it was his uncle who had hunted them then. But as Cathbar strode up to the gate, calling a greeting to the men on guard, it was clear that they were welcome today. Both men started up with cries of joy and recognition, and competed to escort their captain and his honoured guests to the king's hall.

Beotrich came out in person to meet them, cutting short a meeting with his councillors. But Elspeth had no eyes for the king, for with him was a man she had never thought to meet again, dressed in the red of a Redesman, but otherwise unchanged from the day she had last seen him.

'Aagard!' she cried, running to embrace him.

'And so ends all my fretting!' the old man exclaimed. He held her at arm's length to look in her face. 'So many times I feared you could not succeed, and cursed myself for sending you. Forgive me for doubting you – and Edmund.' He turned to greet her friend, and his face darkened to see Edmund's blind eyes. 'I saw something of your battle from afar, but I hoped I had been mistaken about this. It was a heavy price to pay, Edmund: it grieves me that you have had to bear it.'

Much had happened in the last few days, he told them. Beotrich's men and the returned soldiers of Sussex had managed to repel the Danish invaders along their coasts, but there were further attacks from the east, where the fanatics had landed in the kingdom of Kent, spreading a religion of blood and fire. And then, two days ago, Wessex men returning from Kent had reported that the army facing them in a burned-out village had suddenly seemed to lose heart. They had stumbled as they ran, stopping and looking around them as if in confusion. The few who still attacked were easily defeated – but most of the men had simply turned and wandered away, some of them weeping.

'We made another discovery that same morning,' Aagard said, his voice grave. 'Orgrim was found dead in his cell.'

Edmund's shoulders jerked, and he made a small sound in his throat. Elspeth took his hand, but he recovered himself quickly and stood unmoving as Aagard went on.

'There was no violence, Edmund. He seemed peaceful, even; as if whatever held him to life had just left him. That was when I was certain Loki was gone.'

Beotrich was anxious to honour them both, and to put on the ceremony befitting a neighbouring king. Elspeth found herself, her father and Edmund brought before the King's Rede, while Cathbar held up the silver gauntlet to the cheers of the councillors. Elspeth's hand ached at the sight of the thing – but it was no longer anything to do with her, she thought, with a mixture of regret and relief, as Aagard took it and locked it in the chest where she had first found it. It would be hidden once more, kept in trust by the Rede and their descendants, until the day when it was needed again.

After the ceremony Beotrich asked them to stay and feast with him, but Edmund courteously declined, to Elspeth's relief. 'I must return home, to Noviomagus,' he said. 'My mother will want to see me.'

Aagard and Cathbar came with them to the city gates.

'Go well, all of you,' Cathbar said. He shook Trymman's hand, then took Elspeth by the shoulders. 'You did us proud back there,' he said. 'I'll look to hear more of you, Elspeth, in years to come.' He turned to Edmund. 'Next time I lay eyes on you, lad, no doubt I'll be bowing to a king. I'm glad I got to know you as a comrade first.' His voice was gruff now. 'And if either of you should want me, call on me. You're always welcome here.'

Both he and Aagard raised their hands in farewell, and stood at the gates to watch them walk away.

And now it was just the three of them, within sight of the town of Noviomagus, camping together for the last time. They sat around the remains of the previous night's fire, breakfasting on the last of their bread.

'What will you do now?' Edmund asked Elspeth. He sat close by her, turned to the fire as if gazing into its depths. Only the stillness of his face betrayed his blindness.

'We'll go back to sea, of course,' Elspeth said. 'We don't need a boat of our own. Any captain in Dubris will take my father as chief oarsman.' She looked with pride at her father as he banked the fire. She knew that he still grieved for the *Spearwa*, his ship, but he would never admit it. 'I started as nothing but a willing pair of arms, and I can do it again,' he had told her.

'And you?' Edmund asked. 'Will you row with him?' He did not say, *Will they give work to a woman?* but Elspeth heard the hesitation in his voice, and rounded on him.

'They'll give work to Trymman's daughter, and gladly!' She hoped she was right – but even if they would not, she would not be kept from the sea again. 'Or I'll dress as a boy,' she said. 'As I did when we came from Dumnonia.'

'That could work,' Edmund agreed, his voice thoughtful. 'Though you'd look more like a boy if you cut your hair again. It's grown past your shoulders now.'

'Well, yours is no better . . .' she retorted, and stopped. He had turned to face her. His eyes were as blank as before, the dark pupils staring sightlessly into hers, but he was grinning.

'How did you know?' she demanded.

There was a movement on an overhanging branch nearby: a sparrow, its head cocked so that its bright black eye looked directly at Elspeth. It fluttered its wings as she looked up, swooped down on a breadcrumb by her foot and darted away.

'I still have the power,' Edmund said, and his face shone with more than firelight. 'I won't use people's eyes, not without consent, for honour's sake. But I can borrow animals' sight, and birds'. It was so dim at first, I wasn't sure – but it's stronger each time.'

'Oh, Edmund!' Elspeth dropped the remains of her bread and threw her arms around him. 'He can still see!' she cried as her father came over to see what the noise was about. 'He's still Ripente!' And she punched the air, while Trymman looked down at the two of them in astonishment.

'But what about your vow?' Elspeth asked, as they scattered the fire and set off for the final time. 'Can you be king, and stay a Ripente?'

'Yes,' he said, and there was certainty in his voice. 'My father didn't think so, but how could he know? I promised him I'd become a king, and I will. But I'm not him, Elspeth.' He spoke calmly, without regret. 'I can't be a war-leader, a conqueror. I have other skills, and I must use them if I'm to rule well.'

'We don't need any more conquerors,' Elspeth said. He nodded, and they walked together in silence for a while. *You'll be a good king*, she thought; *a great one, even.* She tried to push away the heaviness that crept over her as the walls of Noviomagus loomed closer. *And our time together will be over.*

They were expected in Noviomagus. Trymman, who had been striding ahead, dropped back as they approached, and the three of them came to the town wall together. At the sight of them a guard ran inside, shouting, and before they reached the gate a woman was there to greet them.

She was slender and brown-haired, her skin almost as pale as Edmund's. She gave a cry, and ran to embrace Edmund. 'I had word from Aagard,' she said. 'I've longed so much to have you back – but oh, Edmund, your eyes . . .' She gave a sob, then drew back, controlling her face as Elspeth had seen Edmund do in the past.

'Welcome,' she said to Trymman and Elspeth. 'I am Branwen of Sussex. I owe you both more than I can say for your friendship to my son, and for bringing him back to me.'

Queen Branwen made less ceremony of them than Beotrich had, but her hospitality was as generous. The three travellers were given baths and fresh clothes, and a feast was thrown to celebrate Edmund's return. Only when they were fed and rested did she sit down with them and demand their story. Aagard had told her of her brother Aelfred and his fate, she said – his transformation to the sorcerer Orgrim, his treachery, and

his madness. Edmund passed lightly over that part of the tale, while his mother looked down to hide her tears at the news of her brother's death. But she gasped to hear of the dragons, and clutched Edmund's hand tightly as they described *Jokuldreki* rising from the glacier, and the fire bursting from the mountain. It was already beginning to sound unreal to Elspeth. Cluaran could have told the tale much better, she thought with a pang.

Branwen listened without questions until Edmund spoke of his meeting with his father in the land of the Danes. 'Teobald told me some of what happened,' she said softly. 'But you were there, the whole time?'

Both mother and son wept as he told her of Heored's murder. 'He told me to come straight back here, to be with you,' Edmund said. 'But I had to help to stop Loki. He'd killed so many, not just my father . . . I swore on that night that I'd pay any price if I could kill him.'

'And was it worth it?' Branwen asked softly. 'The loss of your sight, for vengeance?'

Edmund was silent for a moment. 'No,' he said at last, 'not for vengeance. But maybe for peace.'

'My mother will rule with me, for a time at least,' he said to Elspeth the next day, as they sat in the meadow outside the king's hall. 'She's reigned here as queen ever since my father went away, and the people love her. There's no one who can teach me more.'

Edmund seemed more content than she had ever known him, Elspeth thought, despite his blindness – or not-quite blindness. A hound-puppy, a gift from his mother, lay at his feet looking up alertly, and she knew he was watching her through its eyes.

She turned away: just for the moment she did not want to show her expression. Soon, now, she and her father must leave, to seek their fortune in the docks at Dubris. She did not know how to raise the subject. But Edmund turned to her as if reading her mind.

'I'd like you to stay here with us, you and your father,' he said. 'What do you think, Elspeth? Could you make this place your home?'

Elspeth looked around her at the peaceful scene: bushes in blossom, the white geese on the lake; the spacious hall behind them. For a moment she longed to say yes. But she shook her head.

'We can't. I'm sorry – I'll miss you sorely, Edmund. But my father belongs at sea. He can't be happy for long between four walls. And nor can I.'

Edmund nodded sadly. 'I thought you'd say so. But in that case I have something else to ask you.' He had turned to face her, and there was a new quality in his stillness, a suppressed excitement. 'Would you and your father serve me on your first voyage?'

'Of course,' she said, puzzled. 'But how?'

'Then I'll summon the shipwrights today!' he exclaimed.

'You'll need your own boat for this – a new *Spearwa*. And there'll be some land-journeys as well as the voyage.'

A new Spearwa. The words had taken Elspeth's voice away, and all she could do was stare. The dog looked at her with its limpid brown eyes.

'I'll be sending you back to Francia, and to the Danes – and to the Snowlands,' Edmund told her, and now the enthusiasm was clear in his voice. 'I want to send letters of friendship to the Frankish emperor and the Danish king, to start to build alliances. And you'll take supplies and gold to the Ice people, and to Fritha and her father. To help them rebuild after Loki, and to thank them.'

She was still speechless, gazing from him to the dog. A note of anxiety crept into Edmund's voice. 'What do you say, Elspeth? Will you be my messenger?'

'Yes!' she cried. 'Can you doubt it? We'll sail for you, as far as ever you want, and as often. Edmund – I don't know how to thank you.'

'No one could do this better than you,' he told her. 'And you'll come back afterwards, and tell me of all your travels?'

'Always,' she promised.

Tomorrow there would be work to be done. But for now they sat together in companionship, beneath the quiet sunshine. Edmund took her hand, and Elspeth smiled as they talked, gazing across the fields to the harbour, and the open sea.

And far to the north, off the rocky coast of Hibernia, something fell from the sky.

Torment had strained his ragged wings until he could fly no more. His enemy was destroyed, and the maddening voices had gone from his head. But his belly still burned with the creature's fire, and he was tired as he had never been.

There were cliffs ahead, grey and inviting, and he dived towards them, crashing into the water below. It cooled him, lapping over his scorched sides, and he folded his wings. He would rest here for a while, in the healing wetness. When he was whole again, he would fly . . .

The great rock seemed to have appeared from nowhere, the sailors said. It loomed out of the water, jagged and blue-grey, and its top, like a monstrous head, was visible even at high tide. The more superstitious of them shuddered and gave it a wide berth. But the children came to gaze at it from the clifftop, and some of their parents told them stories of battles far away, between monsters and heroes. It would become a landmark: a monument of the times when such things flew, and changed the world around them.

The Sleeping Dragon.